S0-AXS-747

TALLEY'S TRUTH

Books by Philip Ross

BLUE HERON
CHOICE OF EVILS
A GOOD DEATH
HOVEY'S DECEPTION
THE KREUZECK COORDINATES
TALLEY'S TRUTH

PHILIP ROSS
TALLEY'S
TRUTH

TOR

This is a work of fiction. All the characters and events portrayed in this book are fictional, and any resemblance to real people or incidents is purely coincidental.

TALLEY'S TRUTH

First printing: June 1987

A TOR Book

Published by Tom Doherty Associates, Inc.
49 West 24 Street
New York, N.Y. 10010

ISBN: 0-312-93015-1

Library of Congress Catalog Card Number: 86-51486

Printed in the United States of America

0 9 8 7 6 5 4 3 2 1

TALLEY'S TRUTH

CHAPTER 1

Pale-colored blurs flowed in two directions, intermingling, obscuring one another or combining, then continuing in their separate streams. They became fuzzy figures, their outlines drawing inward, hardening, and all at once they were—clearly—people passing along a path. As they were resolved, so was the black hairline cross. Moving slowly leftward, it found a young blond woman. She was wearing snug-fitting jeans and a tight white T-shirt. It followed her, drifting slowly right again, centered just above her breasts. Suddenly a dark, broken shape obscured her: a tree limb blocking the line of sight. The cross hairs swept left again, dropped, fixed on the cheek of a gray-haired man with a briefcase who was walking the other way.

". . . Eight and a half percent by the end of summer . . ." He could be heard very faintly.

The voice of his companion boomed loudly. ". . . If the Fed doesn't pull the rug . . ."

The circle rose. Into it came the figure of a man sitting on a bench. The magnification of the sight was sufficient for him to be identified absolutely even from the Smithsonian tower across to the north side of the Mall. He was in his midthirties, handsome as a hatchet. His dark suit declared with diplomatic understatement the elegance of his taste and the excellence of his tailor. The cross hairs centered on his mouth. He looked up, smiled, and when he spoke, his voice was clear but not too loud.

"So nice to see you, George," he said. "So glad you could come so quickly."

The other man, who had approached the bench from the direction of the Capitol, sat. The cross hairs moved to the middle of the space between their faces.

"Anton. What's up?"

"The game, I'm afraid." The younger man spoke with a meticulous enunciation that revealed English to be a foreign language for him. "They know about you."

"How? Tell me about it."

"The last two pieces you passed: they are false. They are clearly disinformation."

The newcomer stared at Anton for another moment, then slowly—as though merely enjoying the fine spring day, merely glancing with casual interest at his surroundings—scanned along the Mall toward the Washington Monument. He was firm-faced and tan, one of those men who—though he was dressed in jacket and tie—ought to be sitting in a canoe with a casting rod and an Indian guide; a man in his late fifties who seemed determined to make that age (and probably each succeeding one) the prime of his life.

"You can't see them," the younger man said. "If they're here. If they are somewhere over there"—he moved his head slightly indicating the Smithsonian and the Hirshhorn—"watching us, it does not matter, since they already know about us. However, they didn't follow me; they didn't follow you. Presumably, therefore, they are not watching, because they would have no way of knowing we are here—unless they learned somehow from you—would they?"

The American looked at the other levelly for a moment. "Everything I've given you before checked out, didn't it?"

"What could be checked on, yes. So we will assume they have become aware of your work for us only recently."

"They didn't 'become aware' because of me. You suppose maybe you've got a leak?"

"Doubtful. Possible, of course. In this business anything is possible, especially whatever seems most doubtful. But your identity has been very closely guarded. We will give thought to the question; but at this moment our primary concern is for you."

"That's decent of you."

"Grateful. We are quite grateful. We take pride in our reputation for helping those who help us. How may we help you?"

"Keep away from me. This was always one of the possibilities—that I'd be blown before I decided I'd got enough. I have my plans."

"May we know?"

"No. Only—I'll tell you this—most of my assets are already transferred or liquid. I've got myself complete ID. I can be on my way in an hour for a sunnier clime. So don't worry about me."

"I do. We do. You are welcome to go to Czechoslovakia on our next flight. You would probably be shipped under diplomatic seal as 'equipment being returned for servicing' and need no ID at all. And no one will come after you; and you can add to your assets, rather than depleting them."

"Well, thanks, Anton; but no thanks. I mean, you've been so generous I wouldn't want to suggest that if I were over there, then you could ask me about anything—even things I might not want to talk about—without having to pay me at all. Suggesting that would be ungrateful of me, so I'll just say I don't like dumplings and cold winters, okay?

"Now, what I'll probably do is: when I've set myself up in a new location, I'll probably contact your people, and see if we can't work out something from there that would be good for both of us."

Anton tipped his head in a way that seemed acceptance and disagreement at the same time. "Your going to Czechoslovakia—at least for a while—would be a way of giving credence to the material you've passed to us previously."

"Anton, you've had the choice from the beginning whether to think I'm legitimate and my material is square, or whether I'm part of some ploy and I've been feeding you. I don't know how you made your choice—or if you really made it; but the material stands or falls on its own, on how it checks out for you. So let's just keep it all friendly: I really appreciate your wanting to take care of me, but I can take care of myself. Okay?"

"I'm sure a man of your experience can take care of himself, George; but may I ask . . . how quickly do you plan to move? Will you return to your office now, for example, or . . . Perhaps we can be of assistance."

"Anton, I'm already on my way. I'll just check that I'm clean, stop at my apartment for my wherewithal, and I'm gone. And I'd really prefer to do it on my own. Thanks just the same."

Anton smiled, tipped his head. "Good luck, George."

The other man, winking, said, "See ya." He rose, and strode along the path toward Twelfth Street.

When George was out of sight among the strollers, Anton took a small radio from the breast pocket of his jacket. He pressed the thumb switch and spoke rapidly.

"What did he say?"

Rudi, the translator, sitting at the console, looked up at McCluskie. "He told two of them to follow George. He said he was going back to the car. He said they were going to pick George up."

"Snatch him?"

"I think that's what he meant."

"Warn the team on him!" McCluskie spoke over Rudi's head to the man beyond him, who also was standing. McCluskie stood upright, the top of his hair half an inch below the van's roof. Deming, just that much taller, hunched and tipped his head. He grabbed a microphone from the panel, began speaking quickly.

McCluskie went on, "No contact. Keep back, unless they try to grab him right off the street. Just let us know where everybody is."

As Deming relayed the orders, a fourth man, sitting next to Rudi at the console, asked, "Should I shut down, Steve?"

"Yeah," McCluskie answered without looking at him. The technician punched buttons, and the tape reels stopped turning.

Deming finished, spoke to McCluskie again. "Well, I guess they've decided the game is hardball."

"May be."

"We'll have to go for George right away, then, instead of intercepting him trying to skip town the way we planned."

"Yeah. As soon as we can set it up. But . . . you know . . . we can use this. The best thing for us would be to catch him with them."

"The longer we wait, Steve, the more chance there is he'll

shake us all. George knows the thing he has to do now is head for the hills. He'll give it all he's got. He's not going to let it be easy for anybody to take him.''

George Murtaugh went north on Twelfth Street, walking fast to suck along anyone who might be following. Then, where the IRS building arcades over the sidewalk, he stepped to his left and paused, looking around the street side of one of the big pillars. The Czech across on the ICC building side had no place to hide and no excuse for not going on, so he kept the pace, evidently hoping he'd be noticed less that way than if he halted suddenly. When he got to the Metro entrance across the street from Murtaugh, he did stop, and took a map from his pocket as though deciding whether to take that line.

Murtaugh crossed, and came up beside him.

''Take any train to Metro Center, change to the Red Line for Shady Grove. You get off at Dupont Circle and go back to your embassy. I go on to Woodley Park. You tell Anton I appreciate his sending you guys to watch out for me''—Murtaugh tipped his head to show he had also spotted the man who'd been behind him on the other side—''but if I see any of you around my place, I'll take it badly. Okay?''

''That didn't take him long.''

McCluskie nodded. ''Pleasure to see the man work. Almost a shame he ever came in from the field.''

McCluskie and Deming had switched from the van to a sedan. McCluskie sat in the back, Deming beside the driver. They were parked illegally on Twelfth beside the museum, back far enough that Murtaugh wouldn't have noticed them, but Deming could watch him with binoculars. They had seen Murtaugh's action, and had it reported to them also by the man up ahead at Pennsylvania.

''We go straight to his place now?'' Deming asked.

''Yeah. He may shift around on the Metro just to be sure there isn't anybody behind him he hasn't seen. But he's going to his apartment for his stash. He has to have it.''

''But he knows now they're watching him. He'll figure they'll be there ahead of him. He may even figure a snatch.''

"Yeah. Probably will. I'll be interested to see how he handles it. We'll go for him ourselves there; but we'll hold back just enough to let them make a move so maybe we can hook them all."

Deming stared through the windshield for a moment, toward the Metro entrance down which Murtaugh had disappeared. "How do you think they'll try to take him?"

"If they could close in on him on the street near a car, they might just try a fast hustle. Otherwise . . . I don't know . . . probably a needle and a splash and the drunken friend routine. What's the matter?"

"You don't think . . . if they can't grab him, they might just take him out?"

"Why should they?"

"So if we get him he can't tell us what he gave them."

"They don't know we're on them right now, or they wouldn't be trying this. So they can figure if they lose him this time they have as good a chance of picking him up again as we would. They want him. The picture looks the same for them as for us: he doesn't do either of us any good dead."

"Let's hope that's how it looks to them."

Murtaugh pulled only one switch on the way home. When the Metro train stopped at Dupont Circle, one station before his own, he waited until the two-tone warning sounded, then dashed through the doors just as they started to close. He went up to the street and took a cab the rest of the way. He expected the Czechs to be at his apartment when he got there; he just wanted to be certain none were behind as well.

"Alpha, this is Foxtrot. Buddy-boy just came into the alley behind the apartment."

McCluskie leaned forward between the front seats. Deming handed him the mike.

"Roger, Foxtrot. Has your Red Dog seen him?"

"Affirmative. He's reporting."

Deming, holding an earphone against the side of his head, nodded. "Rudi's hearing him, Steve."

The voice from the radio continued, ''Buddy-boy is going in through a service entrance.''

''Roger, Foxtrot. Thank you.''

''Anton's advising the ones inside,'' Deming reported.

McCluskie's car faced south on Connecticut, a block below where Murtaugh's apartment building sprawled along the avenue and around the corner. Anton's car stood on the same side, just north of the corner, so that he and the men with him could see the side street and anyone going to the entrance there. The Czechs' other car stood in a tenant's space in the parking area behind the building, near the side street, facing outward. Two of the men from that team were already inside the building. The third had remained in the car. He had been the one to spot Murtaugh. The monitoring van was completely out of sight around another block.

''He faked them out on the first move,'' Deming said appreciatively. ''They should have figured, though, that he'd have himself a key to the back door.''

''Yeah. Good old George. But they'll take him now, since they're already—''

McCluskie broke off as Deming raised a hand and pressed the phone to his ear. ''Rudi says Anton's telling them to go up and stake out George's apartment, in the corridor. In case he uses the stairs, or there's more than one way up.''

''Yeah. Like I was saying. Good old Anton. Okay, best guess is that they'll bring him right back out that service door to their car there.'' McCluskie pressed the button on the mike. ''Alpha to Echo and Foxtrot . . .'' He gave instructions to the alley and side-street teams.

Deming reported again. ''Anton's man says they're in place. They used the elevator—it was at the lobby—so they're sure they're ahead of George. Have you been up to his place?''

''No.''

''The corridor turns a corner at one end, and there's a room where you drop your garbage down a chute at the other. They'll have him between them.''

''Well, then, they won't have any problem. He won't try to fight them.'' McCluskie used the mike again. ''Alpha to Delta. Estimate three to five minutes. Put out your man. Charlie, on your toes.''

Even though the air-conditioning cooled the car, even though he seemed calm, McCluskie had to take a handkerchief from his pocket and wipe his forehead. Deming had his thumb to his mouth. He waggled his jaw, running his lower teeth back and forth across the nail. The driver drummed his fingers silently along the top of the steering wheel.

Traffic moved steadily but lightly along the avenue, the volume about equal in both directions. A few people had stopped for an early lunch under an awning at the Italian restaurant across the street. A young black man with a blue scarf tied tightly around his head sat on a box against a storefront. He laughed aloud and spoke to passersby. Evidently what he said wasn't offensive, at least not enough to draw more than an admonishing glance from the black policeman who strolled up toward the corner. A bearded man in running togs loped past, going the other way, apparently headed for the parcours track in the park below the bridge.

McCluskie began humming. He stopped. He sighed. "Maybe somebody's tied up the elevator," he said.

A gray limousine, as long as two ordinary cars, glided past.

"He wouldn't try to fight, would he?" Deming said.

"He wouldn't fight. Not two of them, up alone there in the corridor." After another moment McCluskie started humming again. Then he said, "Could you turn that air conditioner up a little?"

Just as Deming reached for the knob, a voice crashed in from the radio. "Alpha, he's— This is Foxtrot. Buddy-boy is coming down the fire escape!"

"Jesus H. Christ! What is that fucker doing?"

"Making it hard. I told you, Steve—"

But McCluskie was already talking into the mike. "Foxtrot, say again: what is the situation?"

"Buddy-boy is coming down the fire escape from the roof. He's passing the fourth floor. Now he's—"

"Has Red Dog seen him?"

"Negative. I don't think he has. I think his car roof blocks his line of sight. At least to the roof level. Maybe he can see the third— Buddy-boy is going in through a window on the third floor."

"His apartment," Deming offered. "He's on the third floor. It must be."

"Jesus H. Christ," McCluskie said again. "Went up past them: he'll get in and out, they'll never know it."

"Good old George," Deming said ruefully. "Nobody can accuse him of not making a real try."

"That son of a bitch."

"We could just go in and take him."

"I still want to try . . . No. He has to come out. They've got him staked. We'll wait."

Murtaugh came through his kitchen window and stood, balanced. He didn't think they could have picked or broken the special locks he had put on the front door, at least not in the time they would have had, but he waited, listening, feeling for any presence with the nerves in his skin.

Then he went quickly to the dining end of the main room, took out the lowest of the drawers built into one wall. He lifted what appeared to be a solid bottom under where the drawer had been and took out the flat carry-on bag. Putting it on the floor, he snapped it open. He didn't check the bundles of bills, or the plastic bags that held a change of underwear and a razor and toothbrush. Quickly he tossed his billfold into the drawer and put the new one from the case into his back pocket. He put the passport in his jacket. After pumping in a round and checking the safety, he shoved the pistol barrel down inside his waistband. Small and flat, the pistol looked like a toy—both because of its size and because it was made almost entirely of plastic.

Murtaugh replaced the false bottom and then the drawer. He stood, buttoned his jacket, looked once around the room, and went back to the kitchen.

"Alpha, this is Foxtrot. He's coming out again. He's going back up to the roof."

"Roger, Foxtrot."

"Faked them out," Deming said.

"Son of a bitch," McCluskie seconded, half angrily, half admiringly. "Well, they'll get him when he comes out the back way again."

Although the building on the near side of the corner blocked the line of sight to the rear of the apartment, all three men sat twisted, watching.

"I'll bet Anton's pretty strung out by now," McCluskie said, as though thinking about his opponent's tension relieved his own. "He doesn't dare contact his men, in case George is coming by right then."

A minute passed.

"He ought to be coming out any time now."

"You know, Steve, there's only one of them back there now. George must have made him when he went in. He could figure to slip him or take him—only one."

"As soon as he comes out, we'll move."

Another minute.

"It's taking too long," McCluskie said.

"He's figured something else."

"What?"

"The building's in two units. It's got two entrances. He could go across the roof to the other tower, come down that elevator."

"That would put him out right across from where Anton's parked."

"He came in the back way. Maybe he hasn't figured Anton there."

"Sure he would. If he's figured everything else— Jesus Christ, there he is!"

"Where?"

"Up the block!" McCluskie called into the mike, "All units! Buddy-boy is on Connecticut, going north." To Deming again he said, "He went across the roof to the next building!"

"He's crossing the street."

McCluskie repeated. "Buddy-boy is crossing to the west side. Charlie and Delta—"

"Anton's seen him. They're coming out."

"Charlie and Delta—"

"Hold it, Steve! He's flagging a cab!"

"Hold, hold, hold!"

"Here he comes!"

McCluskie jabbed his driver's shoulder. "Get the number."

"They're coming after him."

"Alpha to Bravo. Contact Diamond Cab. Get the destination of number . . ." The driver gave McCluskie the cab number, and McCluskie repeated it. "Fall in behind," he said to the driver.

As the car pulled out from the curb, McCluskie continued giving instructions. "Charlie, come on. Try to move up ahead of them. Delta, pick up your man, follow us until we have a destination. Echo and Foxtrot—"

"Bravo to Alpha!" the voice from the communications van broke in. "National Airport. I say again, National Airport."

"All units: Alpha to all units: destination is National Airport. Charlie and Alpha will continue in visual contact with subject. Bravo, Delta, Echo, and Foxtrot take the parkway."

"Back to catching him trying to leave town," Deming said.

"Yeah. But it'll be better now, with them there, too."

The taxi driver stopped to pay so that he could pull in front of the terminal. Murtaugh shoved a bill at him. "Here. Keep it."

"Hey!" the cabbie shouted, "You can't—"

But Murtaugh was already out and heading for the nearest break in the railing along the driveway. He went through the first set of doors in that wing of the terminal, walked directly to the video display of departures. The first was to Atlanta, leaving in forty minutes. It wasn't boarding yet.

He scanned behind him, then went on toward the gates and around to his left into the adjoining section of the terminal. He looked at the monitor there. The first flight of any airline in that section didn't leave for fifty-five minutes. He paused, apparently considering whether to go on around the terminal checking every airline, then went back to the first section, got in line. It took nearly seven minutes for him to get to the desk and buy a ticket. By that time the Czechs had caught up with him.

He didn't break away. He may have guessed that they had sent just one man into every section first, so there'd be no point in trying to shake the one who'd spotted him. That man went out at once to report. Then he and another came back and stood to the left by the doors. Then Anton came in and stood to the right. By the time Murtaugh finished buying his ticket, two more had come from the adjoining section and were blocking the way into it. Murtaugh went toward the ramp anyway. The security gate for that ramp hadn't been opened. A dozen people stood near it. Murtaugh joined them.

Anton glanced at the men near him, then began walking toward the gate. The men moved up the other side of the area. As they cleared the lines of people at the ticket desks, they spread to the sides of the room.

Murtaugh must have known he had to do something. If he did nothing, they would quietly close on him, jab him—right there, in the middle of a group of bystanders, in plain sight, in public—catch him as he fell, and carry him out before anyone understood what was happening; certainly before anyone was able to do anything about it.

A black policeman came strolling along the corridor to Murtaugh's right. He paused where he could look into the two terminal sections, and stood with his thumbs hooked into his belt, idly surveying them. Murtaugh moved casually over and stood beside him.

All the Czechs held position. Anton and Murtaugh looked at one another, and Anton smiled. A man in uniform opened the gate to Murtaugh's flight. The people in front of it began moving together. If Murtaugh stayed by the cop, he'd miss the plane. If he moved, they'd get him. They could distract the cop, even needle him, too. Murtaugh looked around at the positions of the Czechs, then at the people crowding toward the gate, evidently judging whether he could move fast enough to bury himself among them before the Czechs reached him.

And then McCluskie and his men appeared.

They came up in the same pattern as the Czechs had: McCluskie and Deming through one section, two other men through the adjoining, another pair down along the corridor by the gates.

Seeing Murtaugh react, Anton scanned, caught the pairs of men advancing, understood. Raising his hands to waist level, he made a quick cutting motion with both palms. Then he froze, and his men did likewise.

Murtaugh, though, went into action. He snatched out the pistol from under his jacket, holding it close to his stomach, screening it with his carry-on. Twisting quickly left, then right, he flashed the bag just enough so that the CIA men could see his weapon. They all halted.

McCluskie gestured much as Anton had done. The terminal

was filled with people. There must be no gunplay. There was no need for it—Murtaugh couldn't move far. For five seconds they all waited.

Then, suddenly dropping his bag, Murtaugh stepped forward and grabbed the arm of a young woman as she was passing, swinging her in front of himself, his pistol up against the back of her head. She screamed and struggled for a moment, but he pressed the muzzle under her ear, kept her off-balance.

Like waves from a rock hurled into a pool, people all around began falling back. Three of the CIA men started as though to whip out pistols, then froze.

The policeman did the same. He had started to crouch, his hand had touched the butt of his pistol, his forefinger had unsnapped the safety strap. Then he stopped as though turned to stone.

With one arm around the woman's waist, Murtaugh moved half backward, half sideways away from the gate. The shock wave swept down the terminal. People fell away toward the reservation desks and the entrance. When all who could escape quickly had done so, everyone in the room was still. Only Murtaugh and the girl moved, and—behind them, along the wall opposite the ticket desks—the display of baggage from an incoming flight carried on a track. The track emerged from the wall halfway down the length of the room and made a projecting loop, came along the wall, looped again, and went back behind the wall. At the near end a doorway opened into the baggage area behind the wall.

Murtaugh moved slowly, carefully, checking the men who had surrounded him. Those who had come up through that section of the terminal had backed off across the room to leave his escape route clear. The only place Murtaugh didn't check was directly behind him.

Incoming passengers had been taking their luggage. Someone had put down one bag at the edge of the moving track while waiting for another piece. Backing, Murtaugh stumbled against it. He lost his balance, tottered. His grip around the woman's waist loosened. She broke free and threw herself away from him.

Instantly the policeman drew his pistol. He thrust it out and forward, his left hand coming over to meet it. "Drop it!" he shouted.

Righting himself, but still off-balance, Murtaugh flung out his arm and fired, then spun toward the doorway to the baggage area. The policeman fired, and a bullet smashed into the metal-sheathed wall behind the track, in a line with where Murtaugh had been.

"Don't shoot!" McCluskie shouted. Three CIA men had snatched out pistols. Holding them pointed upward beside their heads, they had started to move when McCluskie's voice halted them.

But the policeman was already in motion. In three bounds he was through the doorway. "Stop or I'll—"

"Don't shoot!"

One shot sounded from inside the room, and—framed in the doorway—the policeman brought down his pistol and fired three times.

For a second he held the stance, ready to shoot again. Then he stepped to the side, back through the doorway, looking down the baggage track.

The wide strips of black plastic that curtained the opening where the track came out from the wall were pushed outward. A duffel bag emerged. The strips fell back, then were shoved forward again. George Murtaugh, on his knees, facedown, lay crumpled over three bags. The back of his head was wet and red, and rivulets ran down the side of his face and dripped onto the track in front of him. The track carried him on display, and no one moved until it had turned to go back behind the wall again.

CHAPTER 2

They certainly never suggested that Talley would be in any danger. The job was only supposed to take a couple days. It wasn't supposed to be much trouble to him at all. That was what they told him. They may even have believed it, then.

Talley's horoscope didn't warn him. His aunt had given him one of those page-a-day calendar and horoscope pads. He didn't believe in astrology; he had kept it to confirm his disbelief. All the page for June ninth told him was that he should garden to his heart's delight, and that a little romantic music and candlelight would go a long way that night under a New Moon of Love.

Talley had been at work in his study when Walter Simson called. Jane was showering. As soon as she had fulfilled her final professorial responsibility by going to the commencement ceremonies, they had moved up to his house in New Hampshire for the summer. She had been singing as she bathed. Her singing broke his concentration on the appraisal he was writing for one of his clients about the probable effect on the sugar market of the upheaval in the Philippines. He was annoyed at the interruption. He was more annoyed at her thoughtlessness, particularly so since she was sharp if he disturbed her when she was working. But her singing delighted him—her happiness, her presence, filled him with joy. He had been teetering between one emotion and the other when the phone rang.

After he finished talking to Simson, he took off his glasses and rubbed his forehead and sat for several moments. Jane was now in the bedroom. He would have to tell her, and she would be angry, he knew. He thought about waiting. Maybe later in the day after . . . maybe that night, after they had gone to bed, perhaps after making love . . . But he didn't think he could get through the day without her knowing something was wrong, and even if he could, then she'd be angrier because he'd been pretending.

She had dressed—jeans, a cotton shirt—and was combing her hair. Its color had begun to shift to a lighter brown, some strands almost to blond, from her being in the sun all day working with Talley in their garden, walking with him in the meadows and up to the mountaintops, sitting outside with her stacks of books. For a moment he paused in the doorway, watching, fascinated as he always was by her simple, routine movements; always as though seeing them for the first time. She stood with one hip out to the side, her body—trim and firm—curved into a slender S. As on that first day in her office two years before, he felt lust and also pure aesthetic pleasure from her gracefulness.

She hadn't put her glasses on yet; surprisingly she looked older without them. They hid the little lines that were beginning to form. Seeing them brought a surge of tenderness, a sense that they were growing old together (although they both were only into their forties), that they had been together for more than only those two years.

"Walter Simson just called," he made himself say.

She hesitated in midstroke, then went on brushing, but looked at him in the mirror, squinting her big wide-set eyes a little. "Oh?"

"Yeah. Good news and bad news. The good news is—"

"Tell me the bad news."

"They want me to do a couple days' work on the Czerny thing again."

"What? Why?"

"I don't know why. I'm not supposed . . . Screw it. You already know about it all. Walt just said that they believed there was a need to go over some of the Hovey-Czerny material, to assure themselves . . . Well, he wouldn't tell me, of course; but obviously for some reason they've changed their minds. They think that maybe there was—is, I don't know—a high-level penetration in the agency, after all."

Jane had turned to face him. "But I still don't understand. Why *you*? Why do they keep calling you back, after you walked out—"

"They don't *keep* calling me, Jane. For God's sake, it'd be the second time I've done anything for the agency in seventeen years."

"After the last time, I still think you'd be the last person . . ."

"Yeah. Well, none of us is very happy about the idea; but I can see it makes sense. I did the work before. I might be able to spot inconsistencies, see the significance of something new—realize when something *is* new. I'll be able—"

"You will?"

"What?"

"You will. You said, 'I will.' You mean you've already agreed."

"I have to."

Jane turned away abruptly and began pulling at her hair from underneath with the brush.

"I have to, Jane. After the way I took Larry Hovey away from them, brought him here knowing he might be killed, I think I owe—"

"You took Larry away to save my life, Tom. You did it because you knew the CIA wouldn't try to save me. You know how I feel about them. I don't think that you owe . . ." She caught herself, put the brush down on the dresser. She came to him and touched his arm. "Tom . . . I don't see how doing this . . ." Then she put her arms around him, her head against his shoulder. "You feel you have to."

Talley drew her to him. "Yes."

"Is there any way I can help you?"

"I don't think so. Anyway, I'm not really doing much. It'll be about two days' work."

"Will you have to talk to Larry?" Jane asked softly. She had been living with Lawrence Hovey at the time the Czechs imprisoned him as a spy. Talley had met her then, while investigating the case. Although Jane and Hovey had been on the point of breaking up before his arrest, she and Talley would always feel they had betrayed her lover.

"No. They don't need anything from him."

"Good."'

"But let me tell you the good part. There really is a good part."

Jane pulled away again. "Oh? What is it?" She made her voice pleasantly inquisitive, but looked skeptical.

"We're going to get a trip to Vienna. Both of us, together."

"How?"

"I have to talk to that Frenchman again—D'Avignon, the stage designer. The guy we think probably set up Czerny for the Czechs. He's in Vienna now. I said I would go only if you could come, too: if they gave us both a paid vacation—transportation and a big per diem for me for ten days. Now we won't have to wait until I finish paying for rebuilding the house. We can go now."

"Now? When?"

"The end of the week. Right away."

Jane turned, but still looked at him doubtfully.

"Come on, Jane. We've been talking for a year about going there together. Just because it's the CIA . . ."

She smiled suddenly. "You're right. I'm sorry I was being a pill." She came to him again, hugged him. "You're so clever to make them pay for a trip for us. I'm sure we'll have a wonderful time. And since the CIA is paying, I'll enjoy it even more."

Although Anton had been sitting in the little room for nearly four hours since the last time they'd tried to question him, he looked as elegant and assured as ever. He needed to shave, and his eyes showed that he hadn't really slept during the times he'd put his head back and dozed, and his face looked gray in the fluorescent light from the ceiling fixture; but his manner was confident. He was sitting comfortably erect when McCluskie entered, his forearms out in front of himself on the table, and though he raised his head, he didn't pull himself any straighter.

McCluskie took the other wooden chair, across the table. "Hello, Anton," he said. "I'm Steve McCluskie." His tone was pleasant enough, but he didn't offer his hand, since both of them knew they weren't going to be friends.

McCluskie was wearing his really good, London-tailored

genuine Scottish wool glen-plaid jacket. He sat back, a little away from the table, as comfortably as a stocky man might in that kind of chair, put one ankle on a knee. Over the edge of the table, Anton could just see the instep of the gleaming cordovan brogue. And whenever McCluskie made one of his small gestures, Anton caught the flash of a discreet but obviously solid-silver cuff link.

"I hear the springtime is beautiful in Prague," McCluskie said.

"Very lovely. Very much like Washington."

"Summers muggy, too, though, I hear."

"They can be. The countryside is pleasant, like here."

"What's it like in autumn?"

"Sometimes it is very pleasant. Sometimes it is rainy. It is difficult to say about autumn."

"And the winter?"

"You could look it up in an encyclopedia, Mr. McCluskie. If the weather in Prague is of interest to you. In an almanac, perhaps. You could find records and tables."

"Yeah, but I haven't got an almanac now. And we've got to talk about *something*. It'll be another two hours before we have to let you go, and we have to talk about something. Obviously we can't just let a foreign agent—who's subverted and was trying to kidnap one of our men—we can't just let you go before we have to. We have to question you. I know you're not going to tell us anything we want to know, but the forms must be observed.

"So how are the winters in Prague? Long and cold, I hear."

"Longer and colder than Washington, yes."

"Not much nightlife, I guess. From what I hear. Culture—state theater, Lanterna Magica, concerts, opera. If you like that. No discos like Clyde's, though. No F. Scott's or Samantha's."

"I have friends. I was born in Prague, you know."

"Yeah. But still, it'll be a while before you get a meal in a place like Le Lion d'Or again."

"I have been planning to diet anyway."

"Good. Then you won't miss it. I should follow your example, I guess, but I can't seem to kick the habit. But I'd think you would miss those winter weekends in Tortola."

"Yes. Probably so."

"That makes me think about George. Going to a 'sunnier clime,' he said. Any idea where he had in mind?"

"No."

"You get to know George at all?"

"Not really."

"I thought you might have, a little bit. I mean, you know, there's always a little conversation. And then, naturally, you'd want to draw him out enough to get a sense of him. See what was making him work. What had turned him. Whether he was reliable. Whether it was put up, to feed you. You know. I'd think you'd get to know him a little, personally."

"George was a professional. He didn't reveal anything of himself that he didn't want to."

"But you believed the stuff he was giving you anyway."

"We were interested."

"He was a good man. No horseshit, or covering his ass all the time. I guess that's what got him. I mean, he was good, and he knew he was good, and he really didn't deserve the treatment he got after the Czerny-Hovey thing."

"I'm sure he didn't."

"Yeah. Well, so you're going home again. Be nice to be home again, I imagine. And not to have to worry about being shipped off again anytime soon."

"Yes."

"At least not to anyplace in the West, where you must have to spend half your salary to keep up appearances. Or do you get something extra for your clothes here? I mean, obviously it's part of your job to look good. Do you get an allowance?"

"The expenses connected with my work are not a problem."

"Yeah. I would have thought so. Well, at least you won't have to worry about justifying your expense account for a while. I mean, we're not going to just expel you. We're going to take the position that what you did is so out of line with the usual rules of the game that you are going to be absolutely non grata as a full-time embassy staffer with anybody who wants to do business with us. So I guess your assignments are either going to be at home or somewhere in the bloc, for a long time to come."

"I would have been due for rotation soon, in any case."

"Yeah. I imagine so. That's the trouble with our business.

You just get to know a place—really know your way around, get accustomed to the life-style—and they ship you off to Ouagadougou or someplace, and you have to develop a taste for fried snake."

McCluskie shrugged slightly, as though shifting himself under a burden they both bore. Then he looked off toward the wall somewhere above and to the left of Anton's head. Anton had put one hand over the other on the table. It was a position, McCluskie had observed, that allowed one to appear—and to be—at ease while having the sense of holding a good grip on oneself.

McCluskie spoke again, apparently from a free association of ideas. "I wonder what George was going to have to develop a taste for. Probably passion-fruit daiquiris served up to him by golden-skinned teenagers with bare boobs. If there is an unspoiled tropical paradise anywhere anymore, George would have been the one who knew where it is. Too bad you didn't get that out of him.

"How long did you say it was that you'd known George?"

Anton smiled ever so slightly, sharing the joke. "I don't believe I said."

"That's right, you didn't." McCluskie shook his forefinger once as though admonishing himself for absentmindedness. He folded his arms across his chest, rocked his head for a moment.

Suddenly he asked, "What's going to happen to your Porsche? Will they send it back for you? Will you be able to have it over there? I mean, if there's any chance of your making a sacrifice sale . . ."

"Unfortunately, it is leased."

"Ah. Part of the image for your job here. Sure. Geez, foreign assignments! I mean, I have a leased car, too—a Dodge Aries. A Dodge Aries, for chrissake—what kind of a car is that for somebody in the secret agent business? I suppose if I could get myself assigned to Berlin or something . . . Or defect. I mean, you put in twenty years with the company, you get a leased Dodge Aries; but somebody who's a trainee telephone operator defects with the Moscow phone book, *he* gets a Porsche to keep. Do you suppose the Czech Intelligence Service would give me a Porsche if I defected and went back with you?"

"I don't know, Mr. McCluskie. If you like, I'll ask. Are you thinking of defecting?"

"Well, I hadn't really been thinking about it. But, you know, they say every man has his price."

"Yes. I have heard them say that. Of course, not every man is worth what he thinks of as his price."

"Right. Right. But something like the location of George's island, or whatever it was: something like that—boy, I'll bet people would pay a lot for something like that."

"I'm sure you are right. Well, Mr. McCluskie, if you should find where George was going, or anything like that, and you would consider sharing it with us, please let us know."

"Thanks a lot, Anton. I appreciate it." McCluskie nodded briskly, with apparent sincerity. He smiled, shrugged.

"Well," he said, "we're certainly going to miss you, Anton. You've been a real ornament in the local scene. Real class. Real ability. Best of luck to you. I'm sure you're going to do well no matter where they send you. You've got what it takes. Ouagadougou, East Berlin, Moscow, maybe, Ulan Bator—in no time at all you'll be lapping up that tea and rancid yak butter just like a native—here in Washington, San Francisco, or, say, Philadelphia (nice town, Philadelphia), it doesn't matter, you'd still do very well for yourself."

Anton smiled again. "Thank you, Mr. McCluskie. That is very kind of you."

"I mean it." McCluskie paused, then slapped the table lightly, rose. "Well," he said, "see y'around."

Anton raised one forefinger indolently. "Later."

All of the windows along one side had been opened. Sunlight and warm air sweetly scented by the chestnut trees in the courtyard below permeated the conference room. They seemed not to have forced their way through the thick casements to conquer the room's usual atmosphere, but simply to be there, making the wintry severity of unadorned walls, long, plain table, straight-backed chairs irrelevant.

Even Colonel Suk looked gentle and benign. That appearance was one he could present easily when he chose to. When he let his white hair grow out from its normal close cropping to match the luxuriance of the snowy mustache he always wore full; when he put on a costume of soft tweeds instead of a uniform; when he curved the deep lines around his mouth to look like they had been carved by habitual smiling, not sternness; when he made his eyes seem to sparkle rather than gleam: then everyone took him for old Uncle Jozef. But at that moment he was not putting on a face. He simply sat, looking out at the blue sky and the tower of Hradčany Castle that he could see over the wing of the building across the courtyard, and the spring day alone transformed him.

He had imagined his own mind: seen it as a dark, fiercely roiling cloud full of chains of lightning. By concentrating, he had made the flashing cease. The presentation he would make had been prepared. There was no need to think it through again. The dynamics that would move the meeting had been understood. The director would want to demonstrate and take credit for the expertise of Czech intelligence, but disassociate himself from any errors—past or future—of some subordinate. The officers from the army general staff would be eager equally for assurance that they were being given priceless and reliable information, or for proof that the members of another service were incompetent. The Russian observers (one army, one KGB) would assume the latter to be the case.

Colonel Suk pictured his mind as a thunderhead, made its turbulence slow, then stop as though frozen in a photograph. Then he made the contours fade together, the color lighten, the storm cloud become a featureless fog. Finally, with no further conscious manipulation, he let the spring air and sunlight tint and penetrate and dissipate it.

As was his custom, he had arrived at the conference room five minutes before the appointed time. As usual, the director was two minutes late. The other men, including Anton Korda (now in uniform), who came in and took seats during the time between, were impressed enough by Suk's rank, his reputation, or his look of ascetic meditation not to disturb him.

When the director finally did enter, the junior officers rose. Colonel Suk turned from the window, shifting position enough so that it might have been thought that he was getting up, too. But the director was already bustling in, waving one hand, saying, "Please, comrades, please." He took his chair at the end of the table opposite Suk. His secretary sat in her place just at his left shoulder, opened her tablet, and poised her pencil.

Colonel Suk sat quietly, one gnarled hand over the other on the table in front of him, looking pleasant and attentive while the director made introductions and welcoming remarks. He modulated his expression to one of admiring interest as the director began recapitulating, as though it had been his own, the operation that Suk had conceived and carried through in every detail.

"The matter that brings us together actually began two years ago with the entrapment of Janos Czerny. The Czerny-Hovey affair itself has seemed to have been almost totally successful—more so than we truly expected it would be when we planned it.

"First, we put an end to Janos Czerny's activities. *We* had known for some time, of course, that he was the conduit by which materials relating to so-called human rights issues that were damaging to the state, and to others in the community of socialist nations, were reaching the West. But it was believed by higher authorities that to take action against him would have been counterproductive, given his standing as the world's foremost director of cinema and theater." The director's hands moved apart ever so slightly in a gesture of deference to a wisdom beyond his poor ability to comprehend. "I assigned Colonel Suk to this problem, and he suggested the scheme that seemed to solve it."

The director nodded toward Suk, who inclined his own head in apparently grateful appreciation of being acknowledged. Suk did fully appreciate the gesture, as well as the words "assigned" and "suggested" and all the "seems." If the operation continued to be regarded as successful, the director could claim it; if it resulted ultimately in disaster, the fault would be Suk's.

The director took up the story again. "By providing Czerny with *military* secrets and then apprehending him, we were able both to stop him and to discredit him.

"Secondly, by recruiting the American professor Lawrence Hovey to receive the material from Czerny; and then by convincing him that he had been recruited and betrayed by the CIA, and persuading him to so testify at his trial, we scored very nicely against the CIA—in terms of public opinion in both East and West, and in terms of discouraging other potential traitors like Czerny.

"Finally, for a time we were able to plant within the American intelligence community the paralyzing suspicion that someone on the upper level of the CIA might be acting for us. We ourselves sent to the CIA a copy of the material used to entrap Czerny. We made use of a network of traitors the KGB had penetrated. It began in the USSR and ended in Vienna in the person of Maxim Alexandrovitch. The material seemed to come from Czerny. With it went a warning—also, of course, supposedly from him—that he feared he was being betrayed by a mole in the CIA. We know they investigated that possibility, and eventually, it would seem, concluded that it was false.

"However, the CIA then seems to have adopted two mutually contradictory courses of action—a procedure all of us who work within bureaucracies may recognize." The director's rueful smile suggested that he, like his colleagues, had suffered because of the failing, and so could never be guilty of perpetrating it.

"On the one hand, they assured themselves and their colleagues in the other intelligence branches that the suspicion of a penetration was totally fabricated by us. On the other hand, they penalized two of their own officers: passing them over for promotions and, in fact, moving them into less sensitive positions.

"One of these men, claiming to be enraged by being chosen as scapegoat, made contact with us. He said that if he was to be regarded as a traitor and therefore, as he saw it, impoverished, he might as well *be* a traitor and make himself wealthy.

"Naturally we assumed that this was a trap for us: a device to entrap our own agents or to feed us disinformation. However, there is so much precedent—in every intelligence service—for disgruntled agents offering themselves to the other side that, exercising the greatest caution, we did explore the contact.

"So taking great care, and with great skepticism, we began receiving material from this man. His workname was Eyebright, but now there is no further need to conceal his identity. He was named George Murtaugh. He was killed in the Washington airport two days ago.

"The material has been various. In a way that would be deeply suspicious if it were not so typical, Murtaugh seemed to have been removed from a position of decision-making responsibility, but left—in a more or less clerical capacity—with routine access to highly sensitive information.

"The material that he has given us has included the identification of a net working from Budějovice, the name of a double agent in our embassy in London, and an appraisal of our maneuvers last autumn in the Bohemian Highlands. There have been other things as well. Every one of them has checked—has been accurate. Every one would seem to be of value to us. But none has really been devastating to the other side. For example, we had already penetrated the Budějovice net. One piece of his material, however, is priceless if it is true. Isn't that right, Major Šrámek? Major Chirkov?"

Šrámek, the Czech officer, nodded, making himself an accessory. The Russian was wiser. "Yes, *if* it is true."

The director acknowledged his countryman with one nod, and the Russian with two. He continued, telling them what they all knew, so that it would appear in the record of the meeting. "The material we were given is the order of battle and battle plan for a strike, in the event of a European war, into Czechoslovakia from Bavaria through the Bohemian Forest. As the entire world knows, NATO planning had called for their forces to fall back from, and to delay, an essentially irresistible advance by Warsaw Pact forces out of the DDR. This new plan, though, is in line with the Americans' new deep-penetration battle doctrine."

Showing his command of strategic matters, the director continued, "Now, it is obvious that our knowing of such a plan—being able to anticipate such a counteroffensive, absorbing and destroying NATO's limited strength—could be decisive for us. It is equally obvious, though, that diverting some of our forces to meet such an attack that never comes could weaken our main thrust fatally.

"Ever since this material reached us, all of us have been busy assessing its veracity. The KGB busiest of all, no doubt, Comrade Radin"—the director smiled toward the other Russian—"though I am unaware of your having discovered anything more definitive than have we." He smiled again to show no offense was meant, then went on. "The killing of our source now requires us to take stock of our efforts and to see what tentative conclusions we can reach.

"So has Murtaugh provided us with information of incalculable value, or has he sold us a Trojan Horse? Colonel Suk?"

The director had not become director—over the heads of

older, more experienced men like Colonel Suk—simply through his friendships. He possessed a keen intelligence and skill, both of which (Suk appreciated) he had at that moment demonstrated.

"Thank you, Comrade Director." Suk's deep voice was not pitched so low as to make hearing him difficult, but he did speak softly enough so that the other men had to attend. "We have been trying to answer that question by seeking information from other sources that might corroborate or disprove what he has given. The hints we have so far are positive. But if the plan is planted, then so would be the hints.

"But the level of complication increases. We recently received material from Eyebright—Murtaugh—that we *know* to be false. Whatever his authenticity when he approached us, it became certain three weeks ago that he was feeding us. Or that he was being used to feed us.

"In order to test Murtaugh, we informed him that the CIA had identified him. His attempting to flee, and his death, would indicate that he, personally, was authentic. That he was not knowingly feeding us false material supports the possibility that some of what he gave us is true.

"Our problem is this: when did his feeding us disinformation really begin?

"Can we learn anything to help answer that by observing what the CIA does? One thing they have done is to reopen their investigation of the Czerny-Hovey affair. They have requested another interview with M. D'Avignon, our assistant in trapping Czerny. It will be crucial for us to learn whether this investigation is genuine.

"So the death of Eyebright was a setback for us. Had we been able to bring him here, we would certainly have learned a great deal. But now the following seem to be in order: First, we must regard the battle plan with skepticism. However, it is too valuable to be discarded—and discarding it may be exactly what they are trying to make us do. Secondly, we must continue to collect information to corroborate or disprove the plan. We all will do this, but the KGB will perhaps be able to do more because of its greater resources. Thirdly, we will watch this Czerny-Hovey reinvestigation. Is it a charade? Because the original operation was ours, we should continue to have responsibility for it.

"Finally, while believing that this reinvestigation may be a ruse, we must also accept the possibility that it is sincere. If it is, then our interest requires that we reverse what we did before: whereas we tried to convince the CIA that Czerny was betrayed by a mole, now we must make it clear that he was not. We must make the CIA believe Murtaugh became our agent less than five months ago, so that if the battle plan is authentic, they will not know that he gave it to us.

"Those are the steps that I propose at this time."

Suk's presentation was finished. He moved his hands for the first time: turning them and interlacing his fingers. He had looked from under his bushy eyebrows at one and then another of the men around the table while he spoke, without playing to them as the director had. His posture now seemed to indicate that he would respond to comments, but did not invite them.

"Thank you, Colonel," the director said. "Are there any questions?"

The KGB man nodded toward the director first, but he looked directly at Suk as he asked, "What you have given us is an outline of possible courses of action. Some details, please?"

"They involve matters that are not . . . of interest . . . to everyone here, comrade. Perhaps we could meet in my office to discuss them."

The Russian nodded. Turning again to the director, he said, "Obviously this battle plan—this is not a matter of concern solely, or even primarily, to you, to Czechoslovakia. I will review the details of Colonel Suk's plans with him, and we will expect to be kept informed. For the present, though, the actions that Colonel Suk has outlined seem the only ones available."

"Thank you, Comrade Radin. So, Colonel, we all agree that the matter is now in your capable hands." With a turned-up palm the director slid responsibility down the length of the polished tabletop.

Suk did not immediately open his hands to take it. "Comrade Director?"

"Colonel?"

"Because of the importance of this matter, I suggest authorization for extraordinary measures in the event they become necessary. We had authorized the abduction of Eyebright if he refused to come to Czechoslovakia voluntarily; but that was a special case. He was known by the CIA to be working for us; our claim that he had defected could have been believed, so they would not have been compelled to retaliate. However, discovering the truth about Eyebright, about the battle plan, about the Czerny-Hovey reinvestigation; disinforming the CIA . . . Achieving these may require actions that risk retaliation. But does this matter not justify them?"

The director had not become director without knowing how to escape a trap. He hesitated only an instant. "You end with a question, Colonel; but you began with a statement. Of course the matter is of utmost importance. That's why we are grateful to have you to deal with it. We are not going to look over your shoulder at every moment. The matter is in your hands. Deal with it, and we will look at the result."

The director smiled, and Suk nodded gravely, and all of the men got up and began leaving. In the ebullience of his farewells the director showed his pleasure with the way the meeting had gone. He had, he felt, maintained his position of authority while avoiding any dangerous responsibility. Although Colonel Suk revealed no emotion, he was elated, too. He not only had retained responsibility, which gave purpose to his life, but had also easily maneuvered the director into removing all prior restraint on how he could discharge it.

As Jake Kaczmarczyk always proclaimed, the BigOx line of walk- and ride-behind tractors was the best equipment of its kind in the entire world. Sure, Jake would admit, some of those new Japanese models were good value for the money, and they were cheaper; but for real quality and reliability, BigOx set the standard. And for support. What are you going to do if your Kubota breaks down? he would ask. Send it back to Tokyo? What are you going to do if you can't read those directions that sound as though they were translated into Czech from Japanese by the Minister of Agriculture himself? Do you see any guys even shorter than I am, with funny eyes, visiting your farm so that they can troubleshoot and help adapt the equipment for individual applications? he would ask. BigOx made top-quality machines, and Jake was a top-quality representative, so the little American in the baggy suit was allowed to work and travel freely and talk with everyone he met, even though the Czech Intelligence Service was certain he was a spy.

Sometimes the CIS came down out of nowhere and stopped

him and searched his van. Sometimes they followed him and thought he didn't see them. Sometimes they went into his room and searched his bags—with or without letting him know it. Often, a couple of them would come into a restaurant like the one where he was having lunch with Milos Nagy, the field man for a brewery in Budějovice, and sit at the next table and breathe hard; or they would question people he'd talked to; but they never put any real pressure on anyone or tried to isolate him.

"When I go, will you have to go, too?" Milos asked.

The restaurant in Želnava (just east of the Moldau, not far from which lay the West German border and the Bohemian Forest) was full of midday eaters, none of whom looked out of place. The noise level was high. Jake had (as usual) lifted a slice from the bread basket, peered underneath, and said, "Hello? Hello?" but the men had no fear of being overheard.

"I don't know, Milos. It just depends how the CIS wants to play it. Unless they take you, they won't actually have anything more on me than they do now. On the one side, they can cancel my visa anytime they want, right now. On the other side, I don't think they've got anything they could take me on and make a serious trial out of. And I don't think they'll ever just snatch me without bringing charges, because then we'd do the same to one of their non-diplo people in the States.

"Unless this turns out to be just the last straw—which I doubt—I suspect I'll just roll along behind the BigOx like always."

"Unless they take me," Milos warned. "I'll tell them, Jake. I couldn't hold out. You know, I told you from the beginning I'd tell them."

"I know, Milos. We agreed. That's why I'm going to work so hard to make sure that they don't take you."

"You say 'soon.' When is soon? Tomorrow? Next week?"

"Soon, Milos. Not tomorrow. Probably next week. All I know is I'm supposed to tell you: things are moving, so 'soon.' Whatever this is, is coming to a head.

"What else do I know? What do I ever know about anything? All I know is what you know: Fat Ferenc is a fink. Having you recruit him blew you. Our Lieutenant Hrady has got to be CIS, since Ferenc got him for us. So all the hot poop the lieutenant has passed us about defenses for this district is just cold bullshit. Why, then, do our fearless leaders want it? Why do they want you to put your balls on the block to get it? Why does Gorbachev wear tassels on his loafers?

"All I can tell you is to be ready to move anytime soon, and keep thinking about yourself as the Prince of Pilsen in Zinzinnati, U.S. of A."

CHAPTER 3

As the waiter passed, Talley asked, "Check, please?"

"In German, that's '*Zahlen*, *bitte*,' " Jane told him. "Z-A-H-L-E-N."

"Zzallen," Talley repeated.

Zahlen. The 'Z' is pronounced like T-S."

"T-sallen."

"*Zahlen*."

"He didn't seem to have any problem with 'check, please.' "

"I thought you might like not to sound like a tourist."

"I am a tourist. We are tourists."

"You know what I mean. I don't know why you're resisting learning any German."

"I'm not good with languages."

"How can you say that, Tom? For God's sake, you speak Japanese! You say you understand Vietnamese, and Thai—"

"Just a few words."

"The point is, you can learn foreign languages when you want to."

"Then I guess we have to conclude I don't want to learn German, okay?"

For an instant Jane matched his glare. Then she looked down. "I'm sorry. I'm being critical again." She stared at the table, then up at Talley. After a moment he smiled and touched her hand.

The violin player came by them, dropping a handful of

excess notes out of the abundance of his arpeggios. He wore tight black trousers, and a full-sleeved white shirt, and a wine-colored vest with embroidery down the front, and had a fringed sash around his waist. He was probably supposed to be a hot-blooded gypsy, but the more wildly he played the more dull and unfocused were his eyes, the more set and claylike his face. Nonetheless, his playing had delighted Talley and Jane.

So far, nearly everything about the trip had delighted them. The plane had been half full. They'd been pampered, and had been comfortable enough to nap during the flight so that they were not exhausted on arriving in Vienna. The Hotel Ring, where Jane had stayed before, was small and unpretentious but excellent. It fronted on a tiny stone-paved plaza, adjoining another building that shielded it from the noisy street to its left. At the top of the plaza, to the right of the hotel's entrance, a wide rise of steps led to a higher level, the rear of a church, a narrow street that ended there.

They had agreed to postpone visits to palaces and churches and museums until after Talley's business had been completed on the morrow. In the afternoon they had merely strolled, absorbing the sense of history in the old buildings, the landmarks—the Hoher Markt, the Am Hof, the shops along the Graben and the Kärntnerstrasse. They had indulged themselves with rich, whipped-cream-heaped coffee and the ultimately sinful Sacher torte; had gone back to their hotel to nap and make love, and had strolled again in the twilit evening until they reached ravenous hunger and the Restaurant Budva simultaneously. And, until that moment after their dinner, they hadn't bickered at all.

It was late evening. They had eaten heavily of goulash and drunk half a liter of dark red wine each. Jane probably wouldn't put on weight anyway. Of course, Talley would; but he had almost resigned himself to the idea that trying not to be pudgy was to fight his destiny. Despite drowsiness, their excitement at truly being in Vienna at last spurred them to wander back toward their hotel through the old Jewish quarter behind the Hoher Markt.

There, a kind of music, bizarrely rhythmical, full of strange sounds, wailings and chantings, pulsed through open, deep-set doorways and echoed along the narrow streets. That district, only a few blocks square (in which none of the blocks, it seemed, was square), was now the meeting place for students from the nearby universities. Cafés with names like Kaktus and Krokodil catered to them.

Talley stared at the young people going in and out. The fashion in clothing contradicted the human figure. In bulky sweaters or oversized jackets with padded shoulders, and baggy-seated trousers, the young men and women looked like children playing grown-ups in their portly grandpapas' old suits; except that the sleeves and trouser legs were too short and tight for them. Both sexes wore their hair cut close up the back, then sprouting fully or spikily on top.

Many students in Jane's classes had adopted the style two years before. But somehow—perhaps because here the garments' shapes were more extreme than those Jane's students wore, perhaps because more vivid color splotched the young women's faces, perhaps because all the population had that look, and because of the music and garish lights and shadows—Talley felt that they had penetrated the very center, the sacred precinct from which a new theosophy was spreading.

The lighting came from lamps mounted high on the buildings. Its color was amber-white, like sunlight after noon on a sultry summer day. Jane was disappointed.

"They must be lighting the streets to try to counter terrorists—the synagogue is just down there. Oh, it's too bad! The last time I was here there were colored lanterns and floodlights outside the bars. Right over there, there was a green one on the wall that silhouetted people sitting at tables out in the street, and there was a yellow streak . . . It was like Toulouse-Lautrec. No, it was more extreme. It was pure Expressionism. Now it's not nearly as much fun."

Having had no preconception, Talley had been happy, almost gawking, feeling like one of the Polos entering Samarkand. But he responded to the change in Jane's mood. "Well, do you want to go back to the hotel, then?"

"Not if you're enjoying yourself."

"Oh, I don't care. I guess I've seen it. Whatever you want."

"We can walk back slowly. There are some interesting shops and galleries. They'll be closed now, but we can look in the windows."

They crossed Marc Auriel Strasse and started down a

darker side street in the direction of their hotel. When they'd gone halfway along it, Talley turned back for a moment, only interested in absorbing the look of the city.

He and Jane had not been the only tourists in the Jewish quarter. Other people, foreign more by age than nationality, had strolled there, too, looking at the young natives. Among them, Talley had seen without making special note a man dressed in coat and tie like himself. The man had also crossed Marc Auriel.

Talley would never have given him a moment's thought had he not been followed, pursued, almost murdered in that very city two years before. He took Jane's hand, folded her arm up under his. "Let's go this way," he said, steering her abruptly around a corner to their left.

"What's the matter?"

"Nothing. Let's just see what's down this street."

There were no shops, nothing of interest, in that section of the street. Talley steered Jane right again at the next corner. No one stood or walked in the long block ahead of them. There were only solid walls and closed shops—darkened windows, doors shut and locked, here and there an iron gate, a crisscross of high-tensile mesh, a gridded portcullis, a wire-lace curtain, a grating of filigree steel.

Talley tried to hurry Jane without her knowing it.

"Are we in a hurry?"

"No. No, this just isn't very interesting."

"I think it is. Look at that doorway. Look at the carving."

"Yeah. It's great. But you can't see it very well now. We'll come back tomorrow. Come on, let's see what's around the next corner."

Soft lights did glow in one shop's windows.

"Oh, look! It's a gallery." Jane swung toward it, pulling away to the length of her arm.

Clutch her hand? Drag her—protesting—down the street? He couldn't. He swung over to the window with her, stood beside her, looking past her the way they'd come.

"They're old prints! Old views of the city!" she exclaimed.

The man had come around the corner, too. He paused, took interest in whatever he saw in the darkness of an unilluminated storefront.

Jane said, "We should come back tomorrow and look at

them. It'll make seeing places the way they are now more interesting."

"Right," Talley said. "That's a good idea." The man had paused, maintaining the distance between them: the threat was real, it was there, but not at the moment drawing closer. "Maybe they'll have an old guidebook. Can you see? Do they seem to have books?" What would Jane do if she knew? Run in fear? Never. She would more likely march down the street and confront the man.

"I don't think they have books," she said, peering in, her face almost against the glass. "But that's a wonderful idea. I know where the old-book stores are."

Talley might once have done that himself: confronted the man. At least, if really apprehensive, he might simply have strolled to a brightly lighted, heavily populated street, thinking there he'd be safe, thinking, 'What can he do with all these people around?' Now he knew better. He knew now that a man can walk up to another in a crowded place and shoot him before anyone understands what's happening.

"Let's do that," he said. Then, with a gentle, unhurried pressure on her arm, he said, "Let's go on and see what's around the next corner."

As they rounded the corner, Talley looked back. The man was passing the lighted window, but keeping to the darker side of the street.

Scanning ahead, Talley tried to see how they might slip away. One of the buildings at the end of the street housed a disco on its ground floor. The building to the left was dark; black with age, somber, without a sign of habitation; its arched entrance-porch gate closed. Suddenly Talley realized the building was a church. The map of the city he had pored over when planning the trip with Jane flashed into his mind. The little church must be the very one whose back was just above their hotel!

All at once, half a dozen people burst from the disco, one young man writhing and dancing in the street. They fell into rank, side by side, some with their arms linked, and laughing, shouting to one another, swept toward Talley and Jane. Politely two of them broke, dropped behind for a moment while they passed, then took arms with their companions again.

Screened for an instant, knowing the follower would be

blocked when he came around the corner, Talley said, "Let's go this way!" and pulled Jane toward the street going left beside the church. "I think I know where we are. I want to see."

"Tom—!"

"Come on!"

"I wanted to see—"

"Look at this church! I think it's the one behind our hotel. Come on, let's see!"

Talley's sense of direction was true. Straight ahead was the stairway down to the little plaza and the hotel entrance. As he and Jane approached the top of the stairs, they could see the entrance; and they could see the two men standing, waiting in front of it. He stopped, halting Jane, too.

She, naturally, still thought the plan was to return to the hotel. She pulled at his arm.

"Wait!" he said.

"What's the matter?"

"Nothing. I just wanted to look around."

"Tom, what is going on with you?"

"Nothing's going— I just wanted to see . . ."

Talley tried to sound calm, tried to appear calm. Two men ahead, one behind; the one behind would be upon them in another moment.

At the rear of the church the street turned to the right and went along the other side between it and what seemed to be a four-story block of row houses. Just at the turn, wrought-iron railings framed what must be another stairway down. At a little distance lighted windows in upper stories flanked a view of other buildings much farther away. The stairway must lead down to the streets that paralleled the Danube Canal; the distant buildings were across it.

Talley considered dashing down that way. But the follower would surely come around the church in time to see them—they wouldn't be able to escape him in that direction. Better, he thought, to double back: go along the other side of the church.

"I just wanted to look . . . Let's see what's back here!"

"Tom—!"

Ignoring her protest, Talley pulled Jane past the rear of the little church and into the street on the other side. Four cars were parked against the curb of the two-foot-wide sidewalk, leaving just room for another compact to squeeze past without scraping paint. But beyond those four, the street began to narrow. Reflection from the sky, and light from some window high above them, fell faintly into the space. They could see the stone paving, could see that it seemed to bend around toward the church's front. They could just make out each other's face.

A few steps farther on, the street became a footway only.

Although all the masonry muffled sound, Talley could hear hurried footsteps reaching the back of the church from the other side. They paused.

Talley held his finger up before his lips. "Shhhhh!" Jane, clearly growing angry, started to speak, but he shushed her again. Then the person who had come to the head of the two sets of steps went down the one toward the hotel.

"Isn't this great?" Talley whispered. "What a location for a spy thriller. Come on, let's go on around and make our escape from the enemy agents."

Jane didn't seem convinced that they were having fun, but she let Talley hold her hand and lead her farther into the passageway that was becoming barely a cleft between the buildings.

Playing the scene with the inspiration of desperation, Talley paused. "Listen! Are the KGB men coming after us?" Of course, he knew, they weren't. The follower would have joined his colleagues. They would have established that Talley and Jane hadn't come down the stairs. They might wait there outside the hotel. They might come back up to search. They might divide their forces and do both. Maybe they'd just give it up and go away. It wouldn't matter. Once he and Jane were around the church, they could lose themselves in the maze of streets, find a café with a phone. He'd make an excuse, call the number he'd been given for Steve McCluskie, and let the CIA take care of the matter without Jane's ever having to know about it.

Forced to walk single file now, Talley with his hand stretched out behind to hold Jane's, they came around the tight bend at the depth of the stone crevasse and faced the sharp, sealed apex where the walls joined.

"Ooops," said Jane.

"Shhhhh!" said Talley.

No doorway, no hidden gate, no jutting buttress unseen at first in shadow, no crevice where the walls didn't truly meet as they seemed to do, no fissure just large enough for people to slip into. Talley scanned the surfaces around him. Looking upward, he saw pale amber light glowing on the stonework, and realized the wall that joined the church and building ended there: there, two or three times his height above them.

"This looks like a job for Spiderman," Jane said.

"Shhhhh!"

Deep at that dead end, sounds were twisted. The omnipresent roar of motorcars, the rumble of trams on the thoroughfares, all the constant heavy noises, must have been too thick to bend and reach the chasm's bottom. Instead, in the cryptlike quiet, those sounds that were normally masked, the soft, thin, hushed ones that could skinny their way into the vise of the passage, were suddenly clear. From out on the street he knew they could not reach, a girl's giggle crested the wall and cascaded down. The many swift clicks and slidings of shoes scraping grit on the steps reached them clearly; as did the one man's voice, perhaps precisely because it was tense and hushed.

"They must have come this way! I was right behind them!"

Jane started to say, "Tom, this really isn't being much—"

"Shut up! For chrissake, shut up!"

He had jerked her hand down. He was clamping it, holding it rigidly, almost shaking it with his own tension. She stared at him, wide-eyed, open-mouthed.

"What's that? An alley?" another voice asked. "Did you look in there?"

"No. I thought they were going back to the hotel. I didn't even notice . . ."

"Let's see."

The footsteps moved into the mouth of the alley. Talley started to take a step, to pull Jane behind him, to flatten both of them tight against the bend of the church's wall. Maybe they wouldn't be seen. It was so dark. The alley turned. He and Jane hadn't seen that it ended there. Maybe the man wouldn't see them. If they flattened themselves . . . if they didn't breathe . . .

"Who's there?" Jane demanded loudly.

Jane stepped out of her dress. "I don't blame you for being afraid," she said. Keeping the skirt from more than an instant's contact with the floor, she lifted the dress and inserted a hanger—

right shoulder, left shoulder, briskly—and hung it in the wardrobe. "After what happened to you last time, it was perfectly natural."

Talley sat on the bed, watching her.

She did not look at him. "I'm not angry at all about that," she said.

Both hands went behind her back. She unhooked her bra, slipped it off. One hand flipping over the other, she folded cup into cup, folded straps over cups. She put it into her small laundry bag in the dresser drawer.

Talley had gotten no further than loosening his necktie.

"What I'm angry about is your not telling me." She slipped her panty hose down, sat on the other side of the bed, her back toward Talley, to take them off.

"I'm sorry," Talley said.

"Being sorry is not the point," she said. "What did you think you were doing? Protecting me? Did you think that if there really was a danger I'd really be safer being ignorant about it?" She folded the panty hose lengthwise, carefully rolled them from the top down. "Or did you think that if I knew, I'd be so terrified I'd go all to pieces?" She got up, went to the bureau, put them into the bag, closed the drawer without quite slamming it.

"Well?" she asked.

"No," Talley answered.

" 'No,' which?"

"No . . . neither," he said. "I just thought if I was making it up, then there wasn't any reason to scare you."

"But you thought you weren't making it up. You were really frightened."

Setting his jaw, Talley looked away from her.

"So?" she demanded. She waited. "So, then, after you became convinced, why didn't you tell me then?"

"Because I knew you'd do just what you did: confront him."

"If we had confronted him right away, we'd have discovered he was an American right then, instead of getting ourselves so worked up that . . . You were so busy playing secret agent that you didn't even realize they were speaking English until after I spoke to them."

"If they hadn't been Americans . . . McCluskie didn't tell

me he was going to have us guarded. How could I have known? I was afraid if we confronted him and forced his hand, maybe he'd pull out a gun and . . ."

"You couldn't have said, 'Jane, we're being followed, and I think we should try to get away, and not confront him, because if we force his hand, he might shoot us'? You couldn't have trusted me to do what you said on the basis of my being an adult and a person of good sense, and someone who trusted you?"

"I'm sorry."

"I accept that you're sorry. I've told you that's not the point. The point is that I don't like being treated like I'm silly, brainless, and emotionally unstable, and I have to be protected and led around, and taken care of like an incompetent."

Talley suddenly twisted to stare at her directly. "And—goddammit!—I don't like being talked to like I was a child! I made a mistake. I'm sorry. I made a bad decision. Under pressure I was so caught up thinking about what the hell to do that I didn't think about you the way I should have. Right. I accept it. But I don't accept that you should tell me about it in that tone, like I was a bad little boy, and I have to stand in the corner until I've learned my lesson . . . write on the blackboard one hundred times—"

He spun away from her, and up from the bed. Striding across the room, he tore off his jacket, flung it down onto a chair. He pulled at his necktie. "You can't just tell me about it. You can't just"—he tossed the tie and began jerking at his shirt buttons—"tell me how it is from your point of view, and hear how it is from my point of view, and maybe we can understand—" He yanked the shirt out from his trousers, stripped it off, and threw it to the floor behind him. "You have to correct me. You have to *reprimand* me!" For another moment he stood shaking with anger, glaring at her. Then all at once he pulled his T-shirt over his head and hurled it down, too. "I am not one of your students!" Abruptly he crossed to the bed, wheeled and sat, began pulling off his shoes, which he slammed down one after the other.

Watching him, but not speaking, Jane went to her side of the bed. She folded down the blankets, turned away, took off her underpants, got into the bed, pulled the covers up to her chin.

Talley jerked off his socks, flipped them away. He stood, stepped out of his trousers, which he threw across the room at the chair, took off his underpants, got into bed.

For several moments they lay side by side, not touching. When, finally, Jane spoke again, she made her voice soft and light. "I'm sorry, Tom. I didn't mean to seem to be reprimanding you. But I was hurt and angry, and I wanted you to know it. I thought you should."

After a short silence, he said—his own voice still rough—"Yeah. I want to tell you, love, you communicated effectively."

"Thank you. You're not just saying that to make me feel good?"

"Nope. Just giving credit where it's due, kid."

"Oh, you make me so proud of myself I just don't know what to say. You did very well at communicating, yourself, just then."

"Gee, thanks. You don't think it was overdone?"

"Not at all. The timing with your shoes was exquisite."

"You really think so? I didn't plan it, or anything."

"Just your natural genius."

"Golly, thanks."

"Don't mention it." After another moment, Jane said quietly, "You do know, Tom, I hate my ball-breaker act, too."

"Yeah."

"Maybe even as much as you do. And that's a lot, isn't it?"

"Yeah."

"Thank you for putting up with it as much as you've had to. That takes a lot of strength on your part. And thank you for not letting me get away with it, either. I need your help."

Talley took her hand. After a moment, he said, "I'm sorry I didn't tell you when I saw the guy following us. I just was so caught up in my own thinking that I couldn't tell you about it."

"Yes, I understand. That's always a problem. When something is really important, you go into yourself, and there isn't any 'us' anymore."

Talley nodded. "Maybe you're right—that's one of the problems." He touched her hand to his cheek. "*I* think the big problem is that I'm not perfect; and you can't accept that. Everybody is supposed to be perfect, and if they're not, you"—he smiled, to take the sharpness out of it—"scold them and tell them to wipe their noses and pull up their socks."

Jane squeezed his hand. "It takes one to know one. When people don't match your ideas of what they should be, you just withdraw from them."

Again they were silent.

"Shall I turn out the light?" Jane asked.

"Sure."

They lay in darkness.

"Do you think we're going to make it?" she asked.

"I don't know. I hope so."

Jane turned her head so that her cheek touched his shoulder. "I hope so, too."

Talley put his hand on her arm.

"I'm frightened," she said. "I mean, not just about us, but about what you're doing."

"There isn't any danger. I was just being ridiculous tonight—because of last time."

"Then why were we followed? I don't really believe it—that they were protecting you even though they were already one hundred percent certain. There's got to be something more to it."

"That's just the way they are. Don't worry about it. McCluskie and I will talk to D'Avignon tomorrow; he won't tell us anything new; and it'll be all over."

"You promise?"

"I promise."

After another moment Talley said, "You were very brave, calling out to those guys in the alley."

"I didn't know there was anything to be afraid of."

"You'd have done it anyway. That's one of the things, you know, that I love you for: you don't let people push you around. I really admire that."

"Thank you. I love you, Tom."

"I love you, Jane."

CHAPTER 4

From a dirt track on the side of the long hill to the east, Jake watched Milos Nagy's car come down the secondary road from Český Krumlov toward Zahrádka. Milos pulled off at the crossroads where he'd been told to wait. Jake continued to watch until he was certain Milos had not been followed. Then he drove down himself.

He knew Milos would have trouble as soon as he saw him sitting, still gripping the steering wheel as though the car were hurtling down a mountain road, brakeless.

"What d'ya say, Milos? Great day, isn't it?" Jake stretched his own arms forward, palms up, presenting the blue sky, morning sunshine, the green fields, like a treasure on a huge tray.

"What's gone wrong?"

"Nothing. Not a thing in the world. As a matter of fact, everything is one hundred percent positively absolutely hunky-dory perfect, and about to get even better. That's why I called you."

"This is it?"

"This is it. Take a good last look, Milos old buddy; because when you see the sun come up next time it's going to be in the land of beer in cans, and your cousins are going to be dancing a dumka in their polyester pantsuits."

Milos bit at his lower lip. "What do I do?" he asked.

"You just keep going. No good-byes, no contact with

anybody. Go over to Kaplice. You call Fat Ferenc from there. I've already got word to Karl; by the time you get to Kaplice he should be clear. You call Ferenc.

"This is what you tell him: you tell him the net is being dissolved. You tell him the word has come down that the net may have been compromised. This is not positive yet, but there's a possibility there may have been a leak on a high level. If that's true—which isn't certain—the CIS has probably known about the net for some time. But now something unexpected has happened, and there's no reason for the CIS to keep letting you play so as not to reveal their source. This is a precautionary move. Tell Ferenc he should pass the word on to Lieutenant Hrady, and they should use their own judgment about whether they want to try to get out. You don't tell him anything about your own plans. If he wants to know, just say you are waiting for instructions.

"Then you get right on the E14 and go on down to Dolní Dvořiště and cross there. You should be there by ten-thirty. I'll—"

"How—? I thought . . ."

"Plan B. This is better. The other was just for an emergency bail-out, in case something blew up and I couldn't reach you. Here." Jake brought out the packet. "Surprise, Milos. You've been promoted. You're replacing Harry Dubcek, handling export for the brewery for all of Upper Austria! Congratulations! He's been promoted, too—you don't know to what: some kind of supervision. Everybody's made out. Here's your new company ID. Here's your travel permit. Austrian visa. Letter confirming your appointment this afternoon with the distributor in Linz. Hotel reservation confirmation." Jake handed over the documents one by one. "The name and background cover is the one you've already learned."

"But . . . what if Harry . . . ?"

"That's why I asked you for his schedule, Milos. We think of everything. He's not due for his trip to Linz till next week, so he's not going to show up just when you do. You're going early because of the promotion—so you can meet people right away."

"If they call the brewery office . . ."

"Why should they? Your trip's authorized. You're on an official mission for a state-owned enterprise. You're going over there to grab some of those good, hard, lousy, decadent, capitalist schillings. Anybody gives you a hard time at the border, you tell them their heads will roll!"

Milos looked at Jake with an expression of profound incredulity, then at the documents in his hands.

"Top quality, Milos. If I could only persuade the guys who made them to turn out money, we could buy Europe and retire. Believe it."

Milos looked up again. Jake nodded vigorously, and Milos mimicked him as if learning by rote how to pronounce words in Swahili.

Although that morning's sun shone brightly on Vienna, too, Talley walked like the cartoon character under his personal thunderstorm. He saw that the bright straw-colored light brought alive the carving and trim on the buildings he passed; knew that he should have been delighted by the merry pink and blue and ocher facades around the Am Hof. Last night's quarrel with Jane, it seemed, had been gotten over. They had gone to sleep in each other's arms, held each other again on waking, been cheery at breakfast. Jane, at least, had gotten over it. She had been unreserved in kissing him good-bye when they parted, she to visit the old-book stores, he to meet McCluskie and D'Avignon. His kiss had been full of love, too, but also hid apprehension.

Jane had been right, he knew. She almost always was. He did, he'd suddenly recognized, live and love by idealizations. He'd fooled himself all his life. Because he never talked in terms of absolutes, formulating rules and precepts; because he didn't believe that there were ultimate truths that he could think about and know, Talley realized, he'd deceived himself that he was easygoing, pragmatic, a realist.

But he'd blown up and quit the CIA over Vietnam when they violated what he'd believed to be their honorable purpose by suppressing The Truth because of "politics." He'd quit teaching after two years because colleges weren't the ivory towers he thought they should be.

And Jane . . . He'd fallen in love with her because she seemed to be everything he'd always wanted: the sharpness of her mind, the breadth of her interests, the love of nature they shared, and her deadpan, put-on humor. She'd seemed to be his ideal. And she wasn't, of course. There was her analyzing everything to death, her impulsiveness, and her sometimes downright bitchiness. She was, without argument, a wonderful and loving person; but she wasn't perfect, and he didn't know if he could really live with that.

The weather was fine, the day glorious. Vienna was beautiful, charming, interesting, delightful. He was there with his lover for a week's paid holiday. Sunlight filled the streets, the old city smiled with spring, and Talley walked to the Kärntnerstrasse under his own cumulonimbus, soaked to the skin.

He was supposed to meet McCluskie there, at one of the benches under the trees in the middle of what once had been a busy street and now was a pedestrian mall. McCluskie was there, but Talley didn't recognize him until he was called by name.

"My God! I didn't recognize you. You just come from a funeral?" McCluskie was wearing a midnight three-button three-piece suit.

McCluskie smiled. "No. Wrong image. Wait." He took a pair of glasses from his pocket, put them on. The heavy frame made a solid black bar of his already dark eyebrows. "There. Now," he said. He had stopped smiling. He set his lips tightly.

"I can back up every deduction," Talley said.

"Right. You got it."

"I'm sorry . . ." Talley glanced down at his own corduroy jacket and checked shirt, his tielessness. ". . . I didn't think that I needed to . . ."

"Right. Right. You look great, Tom. Just exactly. If you'd worn a tie, I'd have said, 'Take it off.' This is so we can do 'friendly cop, tough cop.' "

"I don't think that's a good thing to do, Steve. Have you met this guy?"

"No."

"Well, he doesn't think much of the agency; or Americans at all, for that matter, I think. I don't think he's going to respond well to being pushed."

"Fine. Then I'll just kind of glower in the background, and you can show your obvious distaste for me."

"I'll work on it."

"Right. Right, Tom. And I won't have to hide how I feel about you, either. That's something people just don't understand about this business: you don't have to hide things and fake and lie all the time. You just come right up front with things, and use them.

"I mean, if you'd pretended you felt bad, and you wanted maybe to do something to make up for the shit you pulled on us with Hovey, well, all you'd have gotten would have been a quick trip over here, in and out, tourist. You make no secret that you think you're really doing us a great big favor, you get a first-class junket with your ladyfriend. Honesty is the best policy."

McCluskie had spoken earnestly but, seemingly, lightly and with good humor. The manner prevented Talley from revealing his own anger. He spoke levelly. "Why didn't you tell me you were going to have us followed, then?"

"Because I didn't think you needed to know. You wouldn't have liked it if you thought there was a reason; and you wouldn't have liked it if you thought there was no reason. But I didn't tell you you *weren't* going to be followed."

"How about telling me again that there is really no danger involved in this."

"There is really no danger involved in this. That's the absolute truth, to the best of my knowledge."

Monsieur D'Avignon seemed to have done well by becoming a stage director as well as a designer. When Talley talked with him two years before, D'Avignon gave him the only chair in a cubicle that belonged mostly to a drafting table. Now he invited his guests into the spacious sitting room of his suite at the Imperial, gesturing to indicate the sofas and armchairs grouped before the marble chimneypiece. His former "work space" had been in a building of raw concrete, exposed pipe, and plastic: the style Talley thought of as "power-plant chic." The Imperial's style was style defined: rococo. Pale blue damask covered the walls. The furniture's frames were ivory and gold, its upholstery biscuit satin and primrose brocade. Before, D'Avignon had effaced himself in black slacks and turtlenecked pullover; now he wore fully pleated camel-colored trousers, an oversized, eggshell cashmere sweater, and a silken scarf. His beard was as sparse, but more carefully trimmed.

"It's very good of you to see us," Talley said, after they were seated, after he had introduced McCluskie, after no one had offered to shake anyone's hand. McCluskie had asked,

"How do you do?" saying all the words carefully and looking as though D'Avignon's reply would be recorded for computer analysis and used as evidence against him.

D'Avignon smiled briefly, thinly. "No, Mr. Talley, it is not good of me. I am discussing with the Metropolitan Opera my doing, three years from now, a *Forza del Destino*. I should like for there to be not a problem concerning my working in America. Shall we say that it is good *for* me to see you?"

"We appreciate it, in any case. As you must have surmised, we're looking again into some questions concerning the arrest of Janos Czerny two years ago."

"Yes."

"I wonder if you would just retell what Czerny asked you to do—getting the message out for him: what he asked you, the words he used—as exactly as you can recall them—when it was, the circumstances, the whole thing."

"Very well. I arrived in Prague on eleven January that year. It had been arranged since the previous summer that I would come at that time to discuss the *Hamlet* that Janos would direct in Paris the following spring. Janos and I worked together throughout the succeeding several days—five days, I believe—meeting for an hour or two each morning and again in the late afternoon. Janos must have been called to the Ministry of Culture . . . let me see . . . the day after I arrived. Yes. He was quite agitated that afternoon and throughout the next day. Then it was on the third day that he asked me to bring the message to your Mr. Henderson. I remember, we were standing at the drawing table in the design studio with which I had been provided—at the State Theater—talking about the atmosphere he wanted for the first scene (on the ramparts, when the ghost appears), when he . . ."

Talley listened to the story to its end, his face expressing polite attentiveness. Only when D'Avignon had finished did he show any puzzlement. "Thank you, Mr. D'Avignon. I wonder . . . Of course, this is pretty much what you told me before; but . . . I remember . . . last time you said that Czerny asked you about getting the message out while the two of you were walking by the river. I remember, because it made a very vivid image in my mind. And I think you had previously told the first people who talked with you that he had asked you only at the end, just right before you were leaving Prague."

D'Avignon's face registered no shock, no chagrin, no dismay or discomfiture of any kind. The only thing it revealed was that he was keeping it under absolute control.

"Did I?" he asked. "I wonder, now, which is correct? Does it matter?"

McCluskie spoke for the first time since they'd sat down. "Everything matters," he said in a voice like a good lock turning.

"How? Surely, whether I remember Janos speaking to me on one occasion or another is not an important difference."

"It's a difference. You're telling us two stories. That's important in itself. And the substance is: it's one thing to have gotten that information on Czerny just when you were on your way out of Czechoslovakia, and it's another thing to have it and be carrying it around for—what was it?—two days, right there."

D'Avignon's composure did break. His eyes flared, his jaw set. "You mean that in those two days I might have found ample time to inform the Czech police. Mr. McCluskie, had I wished to inform on Janos—on my dear friend and colleague—I could undoubtedly have found some way to do so even after I had returned to Paris. I resent this. I resent this insinuation intensely."

Talley knew he was supposed to step in and say, "Now, come on, Steve," and take D'Avignon's side. He kept quiet. He didn't want to play the game.

McCluskie had tipped his head slightly forward, so that he looked out from under the bar of the glasses frame. "That's too fucking bad, buddy. This Czerny thing is important to us, and we're going to get to the bottom of it, and we don't give a flying fuck how you feel about it. Now, you don't like my insinuations, you prove there's no basis for them. You give us a straight story and a consistent story."

For an instant, D'Avignon looked as though he might explode in wrath. Then he took a breath, gripped the arms of his chair, turned his head slowly to look at—or through—the chimneypiece.

"And you Americans have such surprise, such pain, when everyone does not love you," he said finally. "So I have told you two versions of my story, and I do not—at this moment—know, myself, which is correct. I shall have to try to remember more clearly. Perhaps I can find something in my journals—no,

I would not have written Janos's request explicitly—some allusion or association that will fix the event in time.

"I shall call you. In the near future." He stood.

Talley and McCluskie rose, too. McCluskie continued to stare at D'Avignon for a moment, then nodded abruptly as though acceding to a temporary stay of execution.

D'Avignon followed them to the door, but let them open it for themselves. Talley said, "Thank you" and "Good-bye," which D'Avignon did not acknowledge. He did say, though, "May I hope, then, that you will withhold a bad report of me for a few hours at least? I have a luncheon engagement, and would prefer not to fear that the waiter is putting poison in my soup."

"What do you think?" McCluskie asked when they were on the street again.

"I think—!" Talley started to respond angrily. He stopped himself, began again. "I don't know what the hell to think. I mean, what was that, Steve? What the hell were you doing? Tough cop, all right, sometimes maybe it's useful, necessary. But there was no need . . ."

"It got results, didn't it?"

"So would putting him on the rack, I guess. We could have gotten the same result just by—"

"Look, Tom, you've got your way, I've got my way. And I'm the honcho here, right? So just bite your tongue and bear it.

"Now, we're going to have to bring you in again. I mean, I'm sorry to cut in on your vacation and all; but you're going to have to come back in and hear what he thinks up to tell us. What are you doing this afternoon?"

"Jane and I are going to Schönbrunn Palace."

"What time'll you be back?"

"Three or four."

"That should be okay. Just check in at your hotel for a message. Okay?"

"Sure, Steve. Okay."

McCluskie removed the glasses, put them into his breast pocket. As though that external change made all the difference, his face brightened and he smiled. "Good, Tom. And thanks a lot. I really appreciate your help. I'll see you later. And have a great time!"

Talley saw Jane from half a block away. She had gotten to the café on the Ring ahead of him. She was sitting at a table out on the sidewalk, reading, her back to him. Sunlight made her hair gleam. Her head was tipped at an angle, the same way it was the first time he'd seen her. A pang shot through him: of love, of loss. He reached the table. She looked up and smiled. He kissed the top of her head.

"Hello, love," she said. Then, indicating her book, "This is wonderful! *The Charm of Vienna*, 1897. You just open the cover and you hear a waltz."

"You found it! You are a demon researcher!"

The waiter came. They ordered.

No one was sitting at the tables nearest them. At the first silence after they finished commenting on what she'd read, Talley told her—in outline—about the interview with D'Avignon. "I don't know what it means—if anything. And, you know, I really can't— That's about all I think I can tell you."

She smiled. "Thank you for telling me what you think you can."

Talley smiled in return, but he couldn't hold it.

She began, "What are you—" then stopped herself and looked out toward the street.

"Thank you for not asking me what I'm thinking now," he said. "I don't know what I'm thinking now. I mean, I don't know what I think about it."

"About us," she said.

"Yes. I just don't know . . ."

"Could you . . . ah . . . like they say . . . ah, like, share the process?"

He chuckled. "I don't think so. I don't think I can . . . that I want to put it into words yet. I'll try to, as soon as I can."

"All right," she said, her smile a little too fixed, her eyes too bright. "I'll try not to push you."

Watching from a café parking lot at the south edge of Suchdol, Jake Kaczmarczyk saw Milos Nagy drive past on his way to the border. Milos didn't see him. Jake hadn't intended that he should. He had parked on the far side of the café, so that he wouldn't be noticed by someone coming down unless the person looked back. Jake needn't have bothered. Milos's head never turned. He was looking either straight down the road or straight into his mirror to watch behind.

Jake finished his semmel in two more bites and pulled onto the highway. There would be little or nothing he could do if Milos ran into trouble. He wouldn't put himself close enough to Milos to make anybody associate them: Jake knew they knew about him, so being too close could be the kiss of death. And—the other way—if there were trouble, he certainly didn't want Milos trying to jump into his arms just ahead of the wolves. But Jake figured that if he hung back a little, sheep-dogging, then he might possibly see a way to do some good in a pinch. Anyway—help or not—he just wanted to see, to know what was going on.

The big thing he could do, Jake told himself, was to buy Milos a drink on the other side. There wasn't going to be any trouble. There was no reason for there to be any trouble. There was no reason for his own ass to itch just because Milos was squirming around on his.

As usual for that time of a fine early summer day, traffic was moderate. It crawled through Dolní Dvořiště, but only because of the normal congestion in the town—not as though it was backing up from the border station a couple kilometers beyond. That said to Jake the guards there weren't having one of their black-ass days when they made everybody open up their engine blocks so they could check the cylinders for contraband. They wouldn't be just waving people along to get them through, of course. They never did that: light traffic, heavy traffic: it made no never-mind to them. Everybody got whatever going-over they felt like giving. In all his crossings—and at one time or another he'd done every one from Weissbach to Bratislava—he'd never figured a pattern. Obviously, sometimes they were looking specifically for somebody or something. But for the rest: they might stamp the visa without hardly looking up, or peel the soles off the people's shoes. They might do either to everybody in the line, or mix them up according to—they must have a computer grinding out random numbers.

He came up to where the traffic was stopped. They held

the cars and trucks in a couple lanes back away from the booth and barrier, waved them up for the check one at a time. Jake was in the automobile lane, three cars back; but because his van was higher, he had a good view.

The border guards seemed to be just normally, a-good-sunshiny-day pissed off. Two or three minutes for each vehicle. The usual "We're letting you through this time, asshole, but don't think you're putting anything over on us" look; the "Chickenshit is too good a name for you" tone of voice. Ordinary officers of the people, doing their job the way they're supposed to.

When the line moved forward, Milos stalled his car. He didn't flood it, thank God; got it started right away, so nobody noticed. It happened often to people when there was a lineup. Then Milos kept racing his engine, and the next time he jumped the car and almost hit the one in front and killed it again. Milos was still two cars from the front of the line, and although a guard looked back, Jake didn't think he noted Milos particularly.

Jake took a deep breath and let it out slowly, and hoped Milos would do the same.

Milos moved up to the booth. Looking over the cars ahead, Jake could see him through his back window. Milos was clutching the wheel, staring at the guards ahead like he was a mouse and they were snakes.

"Easy, Milos. Take it easy. You're going to go through like a greased weasel through a ten-inch pipe."

"Shut off your engine." Jake couldn't hear the order, but that was what they always said if you didn't have sense enough to do it right away yourself. "Papers."

Milos handed the papers through the car window. The guard studied them. He asked a question.

"They always ask something, Milos. It's routine. They just want to hear your voice."

Without looking at the papers again, the guard asked something else.

"What's he asking? About your neighborhood? About what route you take to get to work? They always do something like that."

The guard was staring at Milos.

"They just want to see if you're nervous. Of course you're

nervous. Everybody's nervous. They just want to see if you're *especially* nervous.''

There was a pause. ''You can count it, Milos: five seconds. They just look at you without saying anything for five seconds. There must be a regulation.''

Jake could see Milos's profile. He wished he couldn't.

The guard looked down at the papers. He asked another question. When Milos answered, he asked something more without looking up.

''You're okay, buddy. He's doing the routine straight through. Now he pretends what you said made him suspicious, so he's checking your papers more carefully. You're okay so far, or he wouldn't have gone on to that. Just don't say too much. He's not reacting, because he wants to see if you'll say too much to try to reach him.''

Milos's fear must have been more the freezing than the dissolving kind. He answered briefly. The guard nodded. Finally the guard looked up and spoke again. Milos's face went even flatter with horror. As the guard stood back, Milos slowly opened the door and stepped out. He looked like a stack of marbles.

Jake's own insides had turned into Ping-Pong balls.

Then the guard spoke and gestured.

''You're home free! If he wants you to open the trunk, then he hasn't got anything on you, yourself, at all!''

Keeping one hand touching the car as he went, Milos moved back and opened the trunk. The guard glanced inside. Then he turned and went into the booth, taking Milos's papers with him.

''Now you wait. Maybe one minute, maybe three. They look you up on their list. You're okay, Milos. You name's not on their list.''

Jake could see Milos staring at the guard who had spoken with him. Milos's mouth worked as though he were trying to swallow and couldn't. A second guard stood inside the booth. He had a submachine gun slung over his shoulder.

Touching the car again, Milos walked up beside the driver's door. He kept his eyes on the guards the whole time.

The guard who had taken the papers stood turning the stapled pages of a book of mimeographed sheets. Milos watched him, then glanced away toward the red and white bar blocking the lane. He turned back to the guards. The first one stared up at Milos, down to his booklet, up again, down again. Milos looked once more at the bar, then lifted his head slightly as though seeing across the sunlit stretch of highway to the one on the Austrian side of the border half a kilometer away. He glanced from side to side, at the fences, the watchtowers.

The guard with the submachine gun had been looking back along the lines of cars. The other spoke to him, and he turned and then stared at Milos.

Milos stared back, wide-eyed. His right hand was pressed against the side of his car, the left—held rigidly, purposelessly at his waist—quivered.

"Milos, you're golden! You're home free! You fucking asshole, you're blowing it!"

Milos licked his lips.

The guard with the submachine gun came out of the booth. He spoke. Milos stared at him stupidly.

The guard inside the booth raised the barrier.

Milos stared at it in disbelief. Then, realizing all at once that he was being permitted to leave, he flung open the car door, scrambled in, turned the key in the starter. The engine caught. Milos threw the gearshift, the car jerked forward and stalled once again.

The guard outside stared at him. He held up one hand, then pointed back and to the right with the other, toward a low building.

Milos restarted the car.

"You're still okay. You're fucking up, you're so nervous they're suspicious, but you're still okay. They're going to make you pull over while they question you some more. If they were sure, they'd have taken you right now. You can still make it if you just hang on to yourself."

The guard stepped forward pointing again. The man inside the booth began to lower the barrier.

Milos stared up, watching its descent. Perhaps he thought the bar was the border, that once beyond it he was safe. Perhaps he calculated the distance and the odds and made his choice. Perhaps he merely panicked. Just before the gate reached the level of his car's roof he suddenly floored the accelerator and shot tires-screaming forward.

At once the man inside the booth hit the siren button, the

guard outside swung his weapon around, and the sentries on either side out beyond the booths whirled.

Milos may have made it up to twenty kph. Still, the guards had time to aim carefully. A few holes appeared in the car's body. Most of the bullets first disintegrated the rear and side windows, then poured in through the openings. Swerving right, the car crashed into the bank at the side of the road. After the shooting stopped, the siren went on shrieking for another five seconds. Then it moaned down, and for a moment everything seemed preternaturally quiet.

CHAPTER 5

When Talley and Jane returned to their hotel after seeing Schönbrunn, there was a message at the desk for him to call McCluskie. He did so from the lobby booth, while Jane went up to their room. She was sitting on the bed, in her robe, when he came up.

"We're supposed to see D'Avignon in a couple hours. He called McCluskie. He's going to be working at the theater—there isn't any performance tonight—and we're to meet him there after his rehearsal this afternoon.

"I don't know . . . Maybe you'd better plan on having dinner by yourself. Unless you want to wait . . . But I don't really know how long . . ."

"All right. I'm not hungry now. I'll see."

Talley took off his jacket, hung it in the wardrobe. He sat in the chair on his side of the bed, removed his shoes.

Jane made her voice light, pleasant. "Are you ready to talk yet? I think we ought to try to talk, Tom. I don't think either of us had much fun this afternoon. I think we should try, together."

Talley looked at her, smiled, his heart full. "Thanks for making that sound like you weren't criticizing me."

"You're welcome. I wasn't criticizing. Thank you for noticing."

They looked at each other steadily for a moment. "Thank you for thanking me for thanking you," Talley said.

"Oh, the pleasure was mine," Jane said.

"Oh, no. The pleasure was *mine*."

"It was mine! Mine, mine, mine!"

They grinned at each other for another moment. Talley was still sitting forward, from putting down his shoes. He sighed. "I . . . I keep thinking about how it was."

Jane watched him. Her arms were folded, her hands concealed under them.

"I mean, when we met. The first summer," he said.

"It was something very special," Jane said quietly.

"Yeah. It was. And longer—after that, through the whole . . . well, at least through most of the first year."

"Until we got to know each other better."

They were silent for a moment.

"Your disgusting, filthy, perverted, bestial habits," Jane said.

"Well, at least *I* hadn't been hiding that I have a wooden leg!"

They were quiet again for a while.

Talley sat back. "It's still special, still wonderful, sometimes. Yesterday. Last night . . . at least through dinner."

Jane nodded, not looking at him. "That's the way it is. At least, that's the way it always has been for me. It starts out so well. And then you find—each of you finds—little things about one another . . . Little things that annoy you. And the annoyances grow."

"It isn't the annoyances. You don't annoy me; I mean . . . Of course there are little things; but they're trivial in themselves. It's that . . ."

"It's that our two hearts don't always beat as one," she said. "It's that there are discrepancies: we're not always perfectly in tune, which means that one of us—at least one of us—isn't perfect. Or isn't the perfect one for the other, anyway."

"I guess so. I know— I'm not fourteen years old; I know there's no such thing as a perfect romance. I know you have to be tolerant, and you have to negotiate and work things out. But I just . . ."

Jane smiled sadly. "But you don't believe it. You think it shouldn't be that way."

"Do you?"

"Probably not, Tom. What do you think we should do? What are you going to do?"

"I don't know."

McCluskie came to the hotel to pick Talley up to go to their meeting with D'Avignon. McCluskie still wore his federal prosecutor's costume. He sat in the back of the car. Two other men sat in front, so Talley got in with him.

"Pleasant afternoon?" McCluskie asked.

"Yeah. Very nice. It's really a magnificent palace."

"Good. Glad you had a good time. I hope this won't take too long, so you can have a good evening, too."

Talley heard no sarcasm in that, even though he was listening carefully.

The driver had been introduced as "Scott." He was an American, but he seemed to have assimilated the driving style of the Viennese cabbies: waiting with good-humored patience when the early evening traffic stopped them, then flooring the pedal whenever it opened.

"I don't see why it should take long," Talley replied. "I really don't see what the point of seeing D'Avignon again is at all. I've been thinking about it all afternoon, and the more I think, the less point I see.

"What's going to happen, Steve? He's going to have thought about it; maybe he's found something in his journal; and he's going to tell us he was mistaken this morning, or he was mistaken when he talked to me before. But, anyway, he's got it clear in his mind now: it was so and so.

"And so what? It doesn't really prove anything either way. We still believe he was the Czech's man, or not. I still think he was, and I don't need this."

McCluskie shook his head. "You're not doing yourself justice, Tom. Sure, who cares what bullshit he tells us about when Czerny put him onto his mission? But I know you. You don't just read facts on paper. You read people, too. You're good at it.

"So what we're doing is keeping the pressure on him and giving him a chance to crack a little and slip. That's why I'm going to keep doing my Perry Mason routine: I don't know if I can scare him, but I sure as hell was making him mad—and that can be just as good. We just keep bearing on him, eventually something'll give.''

They got out of the car at the corner and walked around to the stage door. Although the avenues had been busy, the side street was empty, shadowed, and still. McCluskie had his fake glasses on by then. When they reached the maroon-painted metal door, he jabbed the bell button in the wall as though accusing it of not wanting to ring. After trying his patience for a few moments the door opened.

From some file of stereotypes, Talley had picked an image of the stage-door porter as a kindly old fellow in a fedora. He was surprised by the stocky, dark-haired young man who looked out at them.

''*Ja, bitte?*'' the man asked. He wore dark running shoes, dark trousers, and a tight black turtleneck with the sleeves pushed up away from very big hands. Talley switched pictures and brought up the one of the young actor working at odd jobs around the theater until his big break comes.

McCluskie spoke loudly and clearly so that the man might not excuse himself for any failure to understand by claiming ignorance of English. ''We are here to see Mr. D'Avignon.''

''Please,'' the doorman said, and stepped back to let them enter.

They came into a narrow hallway, with a tiny, windowed porter's office on one side.

''Herr D'Avignon, he have to go outside for a few minutes only. He ask that please you to wait for him. Upstairs. Please.'' The young man gestured.

''How long is this going to be?'' McCluskie demanded.

The man shrugged. ''For a few moments only. Please.'' He followed them until they reached a circular metal stairway. ''Please,'' he said again. ''You go upstairs.''

Their footsteps ringing on the treads, Talley and McCluskie found themselves coming up directly onto one wing of the stage. To their left high black curtains screened what must have been the stage itself. All along the brick wall to their right was a double line of ropes rising from the floor into darkness high above, like the strings of some gigantic musical instrument. Talley stared at them.

''Ever been backstage in a big theater?'' McCluskie asked.

''No.''

"Impressive, isn't it? That's the flying system."

Talley looked questioningly.

"They hang things from overhead. Move the scenery up and down. You see: those curtains are hung on pipes. They call them battens. The battens are hung from cables; and the cables go up, way up there—look, can you see? There's a steel gridwork way up there over the whole stage, over us here. Must be seventy, a hundred feet. The cables go over pulleys, and come over here to the wall; and then they're attached to what they call an arbor. Look there. It's that kind of framework thing. You put iron weights in it to balance whatever's hung from the battens. As long as the weight of whatever's hung from the batten and the iron weights on the arbor are equal, one man can move a load—maybe three hundred, five hundred pounds—almost with one hand."

McCluskie pointed high over the stage again. "See? There's scenery hung up there, now. They would have gotten it out of the way for D'Avignon to rehearse this afternoon."

Talley looked upward, and could make out shapes, some broad and bulky but otherwise undefinable, some catching enough light from below to reveal them as large ladderlike constructions, apparently of metal bars.

A single low-wattage light bulb at the front of the stage lit the wall behind the ropes softly. Those nearest it were silhouetted, sharp black lines. Toward the rear, the light faded on the wall but could be seen on the lighter colored ropes standing out before it.

Talley walked over to them. The ropes all passed behind a horizontal bar and, he saw, through clamps attached along it.

"Don't touch those handles," McCluskie warned. "Like I said, everything is supposed to be in balance; but if it's not exactly right, then when you release the clamp, it moves."

"I wasn't going to play with it," Talley said. "How do you know so much about this?"

"I was in some plays when I was in college. Just—you know—an extracurricular activity. I took a couple courses. We had a 'general studies' requirement. You know." For the first time that Talley had ever seen, McCluskie seemed almost embarrassed. As though unsure of Talley's reaction, he glanced away from him, to the side.

Light from the stage streaked the floor faintly through

some break between the curtains. "Let's go out on stage," he said.

"You are a continual amazement to me, Steve," Talley said.

McCluskie checked for an instant, but detected no irony in Talley's tone. "Yeah," he said. "Well, I enjoyed it. I learned a lot."

They moved toward the front. The curtains were hung in parallel panels, providing entrances onto the stage but blocking the lines of sight into the wings from the audience. The center of the stage, within the screen of curtains, was bare except for a small table and a folding chair set at either side of it. They were placed in the center of a circle, an island, of light from a spotlight directly overhead. The men stood at its edge for a moment, looking around the playing space and out at the void of the darkened auditorium.

McCluskie stared at it, at the first few rows of seats, which Talley could make out clearly; at the line of the balcony that he could barely distinguish; toward where the back corners of the orchestra must be.

McCluskie raised a hand toward the auditorium and declaimed. "For brave Macbeth—well he deserves that name—disdaining fortune, with his brandisht steel, which smoked with bloody execution . . ." He turned back to Talley. "I played the Bloody Sergeant in Macbeth. And one of the murderers. And then fought in both armies at the end—we just changed a kind of a plume thing on our helmets: changed a red one for a green one."

Talley asked, "Is that where you learned how to change yourself—to dress up and play different characters?"

"Yeah, I guess. Maybe. I did take the one acting course. For the requirement." Again McCluskie checked, apparently decided Talley's interest was sincere. "One of the things I learned was that . . . You know, what most people think an actor does is pretend; that what he learns is how to do things with his voice and his body so that he can *act* like he's somebody else. But what an actor really does—at least in the American style of acting—is to try to learn *not* to act. What an actor's really trying to do is to find the truth about a character, a situation; to feel the truth and to play that."

"Ummm," Talley said. He moved to the nearer chair, and

sat. "Yeah, I understand. I've read some things in magazines, in the theater section of the Sunday *Times*. I know the theory. But what I wonder, are you sure you're feeling the truth in the character or the situation, or have you just learned to believe that what you feel *is* the truth?"

For a moment McCluskie stood in silence, then he shrugged. "I don't know, Tom." Hands in his pockets, he walked slowly past Talley and around several paces behind the other chair. "I just know I did learn, and it does seem better to me, to try to feel a truth in a situation instead of faking something. Anyway, it was interesting."

Shielding his eyes with one palm, he looked up at the row of lighting instruments clamped to the pipe directly above the table, from which the single light shone down.

"The other course I took was an introduction to scenery design and stagecraft. That was interesting, too. Learned something about stage lighting. Look, you can see some of the instruments they use, on the batten right above you."

Talley looked up, and then back at McCluskie, wondering why the man was telling him all this. Perhaps he simply relished the opportunity to speak to another person unguardedly.

"And how to make rocks out of chicken wire and cloth. And how effects are created—not just special effects, but how you can control the audience's attention, make them see what you want them to. For example, you can make them look where you want by controlling the light: people's attention will always be drawn to the brightest part of the stage. Or the way you organize the space on stage. The design teacher would have the stage bare, and then he'd put one chair on it . . ." McCluskie stepped forward to the second chair, lifted it from behind and set it down again. ". . . Then he'd have someone come onto the stage, and naturally they would go—"

He stopped suddenly and looked toward the side of the stage where the ropes were. In the silence Talley heard a soft metallic clink.

"Out!" McCluskie screamed, grabbing Talley's shoulder, yanking him, toppling him over backward, flinging himself staggering backward even as the batten loaded with lighting instruments crashed down on the table, and the single light flashed and was smashed out.

Instinctively Talley had tucked his chin to his chest as he

fell, so his head didn't hit the floor. His shoulders were slammed painfully down on the chair back as it hit, but despite the shock he rolled onto his left side and up to his knees. He could see nothing.

"What—!" He started to shout.

"Quiet!"

Invisible to one another, Talley and McCluskie crouched, staring at the blackness to their right, trying to make their eyes accommodate so they might see a figure with a pistol coming between the curtains, trying to hear the step of a cushion-soled shoe.

Talley was unable to see anything, but after a moment he heard another clink, and then a whirring rushing. He jerked his head up. Just enough light reached into the high loft to reveal a shape, a shadow dropping. He crouched lower, knowing that another batten was falling, unable to tell exactly where it would hit. The cables raced in their pulleys; whatever descended forced a wave of air before it. Something crashed to the floor to his left.

But the whirring continued. The man offstage must have heard Talley's shout. Realizing his first strike had not killed, he was releasing clamps and pulling ropes one after another to bring other battens loaded with scenery and lights hurtling down to the stage. Only the first one must have been unbalanced so that it would crash instantly. The others had to be pulled to start them; then they ran free, accelerating as they fell.

Another piece hit the floor and broke with the crack of a great tree struck by lightning. Another batten of lighting instruments thundered down and shattered. Talley and McCluskie huddled like men below an avalanche, hands up over their heads, instinctively yet hopelessly warding the boulders dropping upon them.

Another crash. But the storm was moving away. Another, then silence.

Talley, still on his knees, came upright. McCluskie straightened from his crouch. They waited with no sense of time.

From the floor below, they heard a door slam.

McCluskie took a breath. "Let's get out of here."

"How about we get a drink?"

Talley nodded. Strollers filled the sidewalk. Some were

shadows; some, figures sketched but not filled in. Some images flashed vividly: a girl with her head back and a laugh like water rippling; a thin man wearing an Austrian jacket—green lapels and bone buttons—and an air of owning the city; a round face with eyes peering through thick glasses, not believing what they saw. Talley, numb, followed McCluskie as though through a dream.

As they walked, he was aware that the steady rush, the hummings, rumblings, and roars, the gleaming shapes sweeping past, were traffic on the street. But the knowledge somehow followed and was separate from the sensation. In the same way, he knew that the two men who approached, spoke with McCluskie, and then moved away but shadowed them, were McCluskie's men. Not until they had reached the Kärntnerstrasse, and found an outside table at one of the awninged cafés, and McCluskie had ordered cognac for both of them, did Talley finally focus.

"What the fuck is going on!"

Fully aware again, he didn't shout. Hands on the edge of the little round table, he bent on McCluskie an outrage all the fiercer for being whispered. "You told me there wasn't any danger! You fucking, lying, son of a bitch!"

Clasping one hand in the other in his lap, McCluskie nodded slowly. "Well, I guess I sure didn't know what I was talking about, did I?"

"You bastard! You fucking bastard!"

McCluskie leaned toward Talley, evidently without effort despite the stream of Talley's anger.

"Look, Tom, I just about got killed myself in there. Now, you can think what you want to about my appraisal of risks, but you calm down a minute, you think about it, you'll see—my ass was on the line right there beside yours. And I value mine just as much as you do yours. So don't accuse me of lying to you. Wrong, yes; lying, no. Now you just—"

The waiter appeared with their drinks. McCluskie sat back to let him place them on the table. Then Talley did likewise. McCluskie paid. The waiter left.

McCluskie gestured with his chin toward Talley's glass. "Long life."

Talley glared, picked up the drink. He had to put it down at once; his hand was shaking.

"Take a deep breath," McCluskie said. He raised his own glass. It quivered.

"You're not so fucking calm yourself, Ace."

"Adrenaline. That's why I need a drink." McCluskie leaned forward to take in half the liquor. He scowled, swallowed, let out a breath, then looked back at Talley. "No, I'm not. But I've got myself under control, and I'm going to be all right. You going to be able to get yourself under control, or do you want me to call for the medics to take you home on a stretcher?"

Talley looked for an instant as though he were about to explode again. Then he picked up his drink and sipped. "Okay. I've got myself under control. As a matter of fact, I have myself under control most of the time. But just remember, double-oh-buddy, this is not my line of work. I am not used to people trying to kill me. And I'm especially upset when I've been told it's not going to happen. I've got a right to be upset about that without being considered a basket case."

"I think you're absolutely right, Tom." McCluskie drained his glass, caught the eye of the waiter, and signaled for another round. "I think you're absolutely right. I'm sorry. What can I say after I've said I'm sorry? But you want to cuss me out some more, you go ahead and do it."

"I don't think I could do justice to the way I feel on the spur of the moment. I'll write you a memo." Talley finished his brandy.

"Do it."

The waiter came, the men sipped their new drinks before speaking again.

"Well," McCluskie said, "I guess we don't have any more doubts about D'Avignon."

"No." Talley looked at McCluskie as he spoke, then stared down at his glass. Holding the stem, he revolved it slowly on the table. "No, I guess we don't. Not after a setup like that."

McCluskie drank. "You're thinking . . . ?" he said over the rim.

"That we don't have any doubts. I mean, if we'd had any doubts before about D'Avignon working for the Czechs, we sure don't now. They've made sure of that."

"So?"

"So why the hell would they do that? We were nearly

killed there. We might have been killed, but we weren't. I don't think that guy really cared whether he killed us or not—if he had cared, he could have done it with two shots while we were going up those stairs. What he did was make a big, spectacular attempt that we had to be set up for, which means D'Avignon had to be the one who set us up.

"Look, Steve: D'Avignon was one of the two main keys to the whole Czerny-Hovey thing. The other was the material that Alexandrovitch passed, which supposedly proved that Czerny thought he might be betrayed by someone in the agency. But D'Avignon was the important one. If we had *known*, never had any doubt, that he had given the Czechs the recognition signals that he also carried out to us, then we'd never have looked any farther. We'd have discounted the Alexandrovitch line as a plant right from the beginning. We'd never have suspected anybody in the agency.

"Well, we weren't sure about D'Avignon. We did suspect a mole. Everybody got really shook up, which is what the Czechs intended. But we settled it. We investigated; you snatched Larry Hovey out of Czechoslovakia; what he told us convinced us there was no mole. The game was over. Why should they, now, make a big production and prove we were right? Why?"

McCluskie shrugged. "The obvious guess, Tom, is that they're trying to get in another inning on their original game. We started it. We reopened the investigation. If we did that, we must have doubts about our conclusion. We must think maybe there was a mole."

Talley nodded. "That guy, Murtaugh—I read the newspapers, Steve, like everybody else—you think Murtaugh may have been the leak about Czerny?"

"You read the newspapers, Tom. You draw what inferences you want."

"Okay. But it still doesn't make sense for them to prove to us that D'Avignon was their man."

"Doesn't it? Like you say, if we believe he was the bad guy, then we don't look for one under our own bed."

"No. Look: let's say Murtaugh was their man. Then to hide that they make us think it was D'Avignon—who's really innocent. But one thing we know for sure now: whatever this game is, D'Avignon was a full-fledged player. They haven't pretended, framed him, to throw us off; they've *proved* he was their man.''

''Maybe both things are true, Tom. That was always a possibility: that there was somebody inside the agency giving them some of the stuff, and that they got the rest outside. In which case, there is a point to showing us D'Avignon—makes it look like it was all outside.''

''But Murtaugh is already blown. He's dead. There's nothing to hide anymore!''

McCluskie shook his head. He sighed deeply. ''I don't know, Tom.'' After a moment he sighed again. ''What do any of us know? This whole business—what we do—it's like looking through a keyhole into a room to see what somebody is building. Or maybe they're taking it apart. And we never see all of it, and we have to use mirrors to look in, and sometimes the parts we see are already reflected by mirrors inside the room.''

Talley pondered that, staring straight ahead. ''Mmmm.'' He nodded gravely. He sipped his cognac. He looked at McCluskie, nodded again. ''That's nice, Steve. That's really very profound, very literary. The agency give some Samuel Beckett scholar a nice grant to write that up for you? I mean, come on. Who do you think you're talking to? There's something going on here that you haven't told me about. Okay, I don't have a need to know. I don't even have a *want* to know. But if you're not going to tell me, just *tell* me you're not going to tell me. Don't give me this bullshit about intelligence being a branch of epistemological philosophy.''

McCluskie chuckled. ''Oh, Tom: nobody fools you, do they? Well, I'll tell you: the one thing I can tell you—and this is absolutely straight—is that this investigation is a very serious matter. You don't have to know why, but it is. We want to do anything—and everything—that anybody can think we could be doing to find out when Murtaugh began working for the Czechs.

''So where are we? Never mind this D'Avignon business. Never mind trying to figure out for yourself what it all means. Just tell me one thing: what else can we do?''

Talley stared at him for a moment. ''Are you really asking me? It's obvious, Steve; has been from the beginning. The other main key to the whole thing was the duplicate material that Czerny supposedly sent through Maxim Alexandrovitch. We concluded he didn't really do that; that it was part of the CIS ploy. I still think that's true; but there's one man who knows for sure: Czerny himself."

"Try to talk to Czerny?"

"You asked me."

"How could we do that?"

"How the hell should I know? Don't play games with me, Steve. I read the newspapers, you read the newspapers. Even if you don't know from any other source, you can read: Czerny's not in prison now. They let him out to make movies. I don't know whether that does you any good; but if it does—if there's any way you can get to him—then that's what you should do. If you're serious about this."

"I told you we're serious."

"I'd think you would be. Personally. Aside from whatever this whole business—whatever it is—has got to do with the fate of McDonald's hamburgers, I'd think you'd want to know why they tried to kill us tonight. I sure as hell would like to know."

McCluskie shrugged. "I guess I'm easier about living with mysteries." He sipped his drink. "It's really too bad you left the agency, Tom. You're a valuable man. When you get onto a question, your persistence is fearsome."

"That's why I left. I was a little *too* persistent about getting out the truth. But you're right: when I get on to something, I want to *know*."

"You *really* want to know? About the Czerny thing?"

Talley started to say he certainly did, then caught himself. "What do you mean?"

"The agency wants to know about it. I've told you, I'll tell you again: this is very important. So—if we can—we'll probably try to get someone in there to talk to Czerny. But the problem is . . . Maybe we'll get somebody who's already there: some Czech who's working for us; we tell him to ask one question: 'Did you send duplicate material out of Russia?' He gets us 'yes' or 'no.' Of course, if the thing is more complicated—like, say, Czerny did send the duplicate, but without any thought on his part about a mole inside the agency, the Czechs intercepted it and added the warning—we won't get that.

"So, better we should get somebody from outside and brief him, so he can ask follow-ups and explore what Czerny tells him first. Of course, the person who already has the brief . . ."

"No! Jesus Christ! You want *me* to go in there?"

"No. I wouldn't ask that of you, Tom. You're a civilian. Maybe you'd just be willing to do the briefing. And debrief after he gets out. If you'd do that . . . After all, you are the one with the greatest depth on this."

"So I'm the one who really should go in."

"No. I said no. After tonight—you've already been put in jeopardy, and you shouldn't have been. It's not your job. You're not paid for it, you're not . . . psychologically prepared for it."

"What do you mean?"

"I mean, it's not your thing."

"You mean I haven't got the nerves for it. The guts."

"Why should you?"

"You bastard. Do you think I'm really so stupid that you can play me that way?"

"I'm not playing you, Tom. I want to find out the truth about this business; you say you want to find out the truth. You're the one who knows the most—what questions to ask—to get it. You're the man who ought to go, and if you were in the agency I wouldn't look for anyone else. But you're not in the agency; you're not the kind of man for this kind of work. So I'll get somebody else, and you'll brief him, and that'll have to do, and it probably will. At least, we'll all have to hope it'll do, because that's the best we can manage."

Talley turned his glass once more, then pushed it away, unfinished. "You are a bastard, Steve," he said. "A fucking, lying son of a bitch, just like I said. When I do have time to think about it, I'll tell you more about what you are. I want you to know I see you and see through you. You're not so slick that you can manipulate me and I don't know it. You have manipulated me, but I do know it; and I am making my own decision. I want you to know that and be thinking about it while I'm in there."

CHAPTER 6

Jane was sitting at the little table by the window. Books and brochures and the map of Vienna were spread before her.

"Hi," Talley said.

"Hi. You're later than you thought you'd be."

"It took longer than I expected. And then McCluskie and I stopped to have a drink and talk about it." He kissed her cheek.

"How did it go?" she asked.

Turning away, Talley went to hang his jacket in the wardrobe. "Okay."

"What's the matter?"

"Nothing. Did you get some supper?"

"Yes. I went up to that café on the Wipplingerstrasse. Have you eaten?"

"Yeah. I got something on the way back. What are you doing?"

"Looking at the guidebooks. I was thinking about what we might do tomorrow. Are you going to be free tomorrow?"

"Yeah. Sure. What did you have in mind?" He returned to look over her shoulder.

"I thought we could go to the art museum early, while we've got the energy for standing around."

"Good idea."

She looked up at him, concern in her face. "What's wrong, Tom?"

"Nothing's wrong. I told you."

Putting her hand on his arm, she said, "Well, you weren't telling me the truth. You're stiff as a board, you look awful."

Talley drew himself up. He went to the table by his side of the bed, began emptying his pockets onto it. "I'm sorry. I can't talk about it."

For a moment her hand remained extended as it had been to touch him. Then she lowered it to her lap. "I see. All right, if you can't talk about it, you can't talk about it. But that's not the same thing as saying nothing's wrong. That means you *won't* talk about it."

"Okay. I'm sorry. Yes, something's wrong; but I can't talk about it."

"Thank you. Can you tell me"—she seemed to be trying to keep anger from coming into her voice—"just generally, so that I can feel there is a relationship between us, did you find out what you wanted to?"

"I guess so. Yeah. We got an idea for a new approach."

"Oh?"

"I can't talk about it."

"Yes. Does it involve you?"

"Yes."

"I see. Then I suppose you won't be interested in what else I thought we might do tomorrow." She began brusquely reorganizing the maps and brochures on the table. "I suppose I should just make plans to suit myself."

"I'm not going to be involved tomorrow. It'll probably be a couple days . . ." He whirled to confront her. "Why do I have to defend myself? Why can't you just understand and— I had a really bad thing happen tonight! And now I've got to . . . And I can't talk about it. I don't *want* to talk about it! Why can't you see that? All the way coming back here, I just wanted to be with you and hold you. Why can't you *understand* how I feel, and let us just *be* together!" He spun back, strode to the bed, sat with his legs up and his arms crossed, glaring at the bare wall opposite where she was sitting.

"Oh, Tom, oh, dear love . . . ! I want to understand, and do what you want, but . . ." Jane rose. "I can't do that because I am not just a . . . a materialization of somebody inside your head. You have to tell me. I knew as soon as you walked into this room that something was wrong. And I do want to help you. But you have to tell me."

After a moment she went around to her side of the bed. Talley swung his stare toward the foot. Jane propped her pillow against the headboard and sat next to him, close but not touching.

After several moments more, Talley said, "They tried to kill us. In the theater."

"My God! Tom!" For an instant she stared at him in horror, then threw herself onto his chest, clutching his shoulders. "Oh, Tom! Who—why?"

"The Czechs, D'Avignon. I don't know why. That's . . ." He held her to him. She was crying. He held her for a minute or more. Then she sat up abruptly.

"We've got to leave here! You've got to get out of this!"

"I can't."

"Why can't you? You're not—you don't have to—"

"I do have to."

"How could they make you? They can't—" Jane stared at him in silence, then looked away. "How long is this going to go on?"

"A few days, a week at the outside. McCluskie has to get some information, and then I'll . . . be involved . . . for a couple days; and then it'll be all over."

"Will they guard you while you're waiting? Should we move?"

"No. What happened tonight . . . we don't know why they did it exactly, except that it was to make a point. The point's been made. There's no reason for them to try anything again. McCluskie'll probably have his men keep an eye on us, but there's no reason we can't go out and do whatever we want."

"You feel you must do this?"

He nodded.

"And you really are worried, aren't you?"

"Yes."

"All right." She took his hand, lay beside him with her head on his shoulder. "All right; then I'll try to be helpful."

"Hi, Tom. Thanks for calling me back so soon. I hope I didn't call too early for you."

"It's okay. We've been up for a while."

"Where are you calling from?"

"I'm in the booth in the lobby."

"Good. I thought you might like to know I just talked with D'Avignon. He called me."

"No shit. What'd he have to say."

"It was fantastic. What a performance, Tom. I wish you could have heard it. He was pissed off at *us*."

"You're kidding."

"No. Now here's his story: somebody called him, he says, and canceled our meeting yesterday evening. Said we couldn't make it then, we'd be in touch today. So at the end of his rehearsal he goes back to his hotel. As far as he knew, the theater was closed and locked up after that. They come in today, the place is a shambles. They're going to have to hire in people to try to repair the scenery, maybe cancel the performance tonight, and it's all our fault! He asks if we went there—he assumes we did. Obviously we have enemies. He doesn't address the questions of how they were supposed to know we were going to the theater, why they would try to get us there, how they got in. Clearly that's beyond him, and he's not interested. All that matters is that we're playing our power politics, carrying on our secret wars in other people's countries, and we don't care what destruction we bring down on the innocent bystanders. How about that?"

"No defense like a good offense."

"Yeah. He was terrific. I'd almost like to go see him again just to watch him do it in the flesh. But I'm not sure I could maintain my aesthetic distance. Anyway, we don't need to see him now, do we?"

"I don't see why we would."

"Yeah. For what it's worth, he checked his journal, and now he's sure that what he told you originally was correct. He was mistaken yesterday. He hopes this correction will satisfy us and that we won't have to meet with him again about it."

"What'd you say?"

"Oh, I said—really heavy—that we now knew everything about him we needed to know. Reduced him down to a heap of quivering jelly, I'm sure."

"What are you going to do about him?"

"I don't know. What they did—that was really kind of excessive. But I don't—"

"Excessive?" Talley broke in. "Kind of *excessive*? Jesus Christ, they damned near killed us!"

"I was there, too, remember? What do you want us to do about it—take him out? Drop a bomb on Prague? Sure, that would make me feel better, too. But if you go one-for-one for everything that happens in this business, pretty soon you won't have time for anything else. And who knows where it could end? I don't know. We'll be giving it some thought."

"Well, Steve, I guess we could go see his *Forza del Destino*, when he does it in New York, and throw eggs."

By midmorning, the rate of cars and tour buses coming to the Benedictine Abbey exceeded that of those leaving, but McCluskie found a place to park without difficulty. He hadn't been there before, so he paused to look up at the great green dome, the convoluted steeples at either side of the gate, the ornate grandeur of the massive palace.

The Austrians had the right idea, he thought: no having to suffer austerity in this life so you can get the goodies in the next. The way to appreciate what heaven's going to be, and make the congregation want to get there, is to have as much magnificence as you can right now.

He was glad that he and Jake Kaczmarczyk had agreed to meet at Melk. It was about halfway between Vienna and Linz; that was the only reason for choosing it. But why shouldn't a couple of spies meet outside a baroque palace, on a hilltop overlooking the Danube and green, rolling countryside, in the sunshine? Who made it a rule that they could only get together at two A.M. in grungy bars, and had to drink potato schnapps?

McCluskie recognized his feeling as a reaction to the danger of the night before. Why shouldn't he react? Why should he have been able to put it out of his mind and sleep like a baby? Who would believe he could, except a retread like Talley who had to be machoed along or he'd bolt from the whole operation?

McCluskie took a deep breath of the good air. When he got back to Vienna, he decided, he'd take the afternoon off and have a really nice lunch.

He started up the walk toward the abbey. Jake was already

sitting on the bench where he'd said he'd be. McCluskie sat beside him.

"Hello, Jake. How are you—otherwise?"

"I don't remember."

"What happened?"

"What do you know?"

"I read your report."

"That's what happened."

"I mean, why? Were they laying for him?"

"Why should they be, Steve? The papers were good, weren't they? The operation was secure, wasn't it? Why would they be laying for him?"

"I don't know, Jake. I don't think they should have been. That's why I asked you: you were there. Do you think they were?"

A double line of children, chattering and giggling but orderly, came up the walk herded by nuns. Jake watched them as he spoke.

"As far as I could tell, they were just giving him a routine hard time. It looked like he just panicked. He was already acting like he had an icicle up his ass when I met him, earlier. Maybe that's all it was."

"Then what's up your ass?"

"Maybe the same thing. It's been a long winter."

"You mean it's time for you to 'come in from the cold'? I thought you liked it."

"I did. Not like that."

The group had passed. McCluskie looked down at the river.

"Yeah. I know. Somebody tried to ice me last night. And the guy I was with."

"No shit. What happened?"

McCluskie told him briefly.

"Geez. Nobody's safe. D'ya tell 'em who you were?"

"I think they knew. So, Jake, you might as well stay where you are. You're just as well off." McCluskie shrugged.

A couple passed. The woman was attractive. Both men watched her from habit, without real interest.

"I'm sorry about your man," McCluskie said.

"Yeah. Me, too."

"Yeah. You don't get used to it, and not care anymore. If

you get to not caring anymore, then you should get out of the business."

"Yeah."

"Yeah. But you and I are pretty used to it, Jake; so what's so special this time?"

"I don't like this, Steve: I don't like this whole operation. I don't like recruiting a fink. I don't like—"

"Oh, Mildred, look at this view!"

Jake and McCluskie snapped to look. One white-haired woman walking ahead of a small group had paused to their right, and was pointing off to the panorama. The others came up to her, and they all gazed and exclaimed.

Jake turned back to McCluskie. He kept his voice low. "I don't like feeding questions to somebody who's got to be CIS! I mean, I don't know what this was; I'm not supposed to know—I don't want to know. But it sticks out to me like Aunt Lena's tits that this was set up to feed them; and it's about the thinnest operation I've ever seen! Milos was put out there, and he—and Karl and me—we've all been walking on our tippy-toes to keep from falling off the edge!" Suddenly he stretched his wide mouth as though he were smiling.

McCluskie nodded, smiling too as if enjoying the story. Pleasantly he said, "You're not supposed to know; you're not going to know, but I'll tell you this: if any of you had fallen, it wouldn't have mattered which way. This operation is not as thin as it may look to you, and we were ready to make it work coming or going."

"I'm glad to hear it—about the operation. Did you have a plan for picking us up again?"

Putting one hand on the bench back, McCluskie leaned toward the other man, still smiling. "Jake, you want to come in? You want to sell shoes? I know you're out there on the high wire most of the time. And you've got a right to expect we're holding the net, not shaking the pole. I know what you feel like—I had a close call last night, and it scared the shit out of me. So you want to quit, you tell me, I'll understand. Otherwise . . . we have the job, we do the job. Okay?"

He paused, then leaned back and surveyed the view again. "Now, I am really sorry about your man. But what I have to know is whether he fell, or was pushed, or jumped, or what."

"I think he jumped."

McCluskie continued looking pleased as the group of tourists made their way on toward the abbey. He was pleased. "Thanks, Jake. Okay now?"

"Okay."

"Good. Now, I've got to know something else." McCluskie took an envelope from the inside pocket of his jacket, removed papers from it, passed them to Jake. "Copy of an article from the *New York Times* on Janos Czerny. He's making a movie."

"Yeah, I heard. Nice way of doing time."

"The article says he is: that technically he's still a prisoner. The Czech government's line is something like 'although guilty of a heinous crime . . . nonetheless a great artist.' They're letting him work off his debt to society by doing what he does."

"Like I said, nice."

"Yeah. Nice for them, too: first they scored on him—and us—by convicting him; now they show how magnanimous and cultural they are. He's not running around loose, of course. The article says he can't be interviewed, and they lock him up at night, and keep security on him when he's out on location.

"Which brings us to our problem. The article says he's been planning an epic about the Napoleonic wars. Something about how the sturdy peasants resist the imperialistic war machine. According to the article—it's dated last February—he should be shooting about now. It gives the names of some of the locations.

"What I need to know is, where is he right now; and—this is the big one—can we get somebody in to see him?"

Jake seemed to be studying the light over the far hills. He nodded. "I'll find out. And out again, right?"

"Of course."

After visiting the art museum, Talley and Jane lunched in the café in the Volksgarten again. Jane fed the sparrows with scraps from her plate. The little birds came onto the table and took the offerings from her hand. Talley watched, smiling.

In the afternoon they took a trolley to the Prater and rode the Ferris wheel. Jane squeezed his hand as the car rose, and they gasped together with delight as they saw the city fall and spread before them.

They had dinner in a small, plain café just off the Am Hof.

The tables were bare wood, and candles burned from the necks of wine bottles. Most of the other patrons (there were few) seemed to be ordinary Austrians. Jane entertained him with scandalous gossip about the Hapsburgs.

The sun had shone, the air had been balmy, the city had been charming and gracious. For those reasons, in part, they had floated on a current of joy. The other reason was that they worked at it. Talley saw Jane's eyes sparkling too brightly, saw her smiling too easily for too long, knew the fine ring in her voice came from fragility, like crystal.

"Thanks," he said suddenly, as they stood breathing the cool night air again. "Thank you, dear love, for making these days so happy."

The next day they saw the cathedral and the Hofburg, and window-shopped. That evening they went out to Grinzing, where the wine is made. Oompah music drew them into one of the taverns. Every table seemed full, but they found places with a party of Dutch tourists. A waitress came, Jane spoke, a flask of wine appeared—a frosted-glass bulb shaped like a top, in a metal holder. Jane showed Talley how to hold a glass up under the point, pressing up against the stopper so the wine could flow out. Light, sweet but not cloying, slightly effervescent: Talley thought it was a very nice little wine. They filled their glasses again. They talked with the nice Netherlanders, who spoke English excellently and wittily. Another flask appeared. Everyone sang. Although the wine had no depth, Talley thought it was one of the pleasantest he had ever tasted. He and Jane exchanged addresses with their new friends. Another flask appeared. Some people danced. Jane danced with one of the handsome Hollanders. Talley engaged the man's strikingly beautiful wife in serious conversation. Another flask of wine appeared. Talley thought it might have been ambrosia, amazed that one could spend an entire evening imbibing with delight and not feel more than a cheery, sociable glow.

Someone said the time was almost midnight. The last trolley left at twenty after. They all had to say good-bye, and go. They all started to rise. Talley started, too, but he had no legs.

Of course he had legs. He looked down. There they were: he could see them. They had merely gone to sleep. He hit one with the heel of his fist, then the other.

"What's the matter, Tom?"

"My legs have gone to sleep."

"Can you get up?"

"Sure."

Talley was certain he could get up. He certainly didn't want anyone to think he couldn't get up. He certainly didn't want anyone to think he was drunk, for God's sake.

One hand on his chair back, one on the table, determination streaming from his will down into his recalcitrant limbs, Talley forced himself up.

He stood staring straight ahead. He had the sense, suddenly, that if he turned his head even slightly in either direction, the precariously balanced room would tip. He realized the band had stopped playing, but music continued in his head—a many-toned but high-pitched trilling.

He did turn his head, slowly, to look at Jane. He giggled.

Upright, not staggering, but clinging to Jane's arm and still occasionally giggling, he made his way down the hill to the trolley. He giggled once or twice on the ride back, and again when Jane was helping him undress. Jane giggled, too, then. The last thing he was aware of, after they were in bed and the light was out, was the two of them lying together giggling.

McCluskie might have brought his hotel room with him from the States, Talley thought sourly. The whole building might have been lifted over intact and plunked down just outside the old city. No, not intact: in prefabricated units, along with stamped-out sections of wall-to-wall acrylic carpet and standardized pieces of fake wood-grain furniture.

Talley thought about twentieth-century culture sourly, as he had thought sourly about hard rolls for breakfast, Viennese taxis, and—most of all—Austrian wine. The thought of Austrian wine was so sour that he tried not to think about it at all.

"Thanks for coming right over, Tom. Sorry if I woke you."

"It's okay."

"You all right?"

"I'm okay."

"You look a little sick."

"I'm okay. Just got to bed a little late last night. What have you got?"

McCluskie smoothed the diagnostic squint from around his eyes and sat in the other armchair, across a low table from Talley. From a manila envelope he took an American passport and other papers and cards.

"Robert H. Dobson. 'H' for Henry. Passport, credit cards, et cetera. All you have to know is your name and your father's mother's maiden name: Lendl. And the town where her family came from. I'll show you in a minute. Other than that, you're you: where you live, what you do. The only reason we're even changing your name is in case they might have you on a computer from two years ago.

"You're here in Vienna on holiday. You want to go across and visit the town where your grandmother's folks came from. Natural curiosity. You've rented a car."

McCluskie unfolded and spread a road map. "Here. Here we are, Vienna. You go north on the E7 to the border. Cross. No problem. They'll stare at you and act like you aren't fooling them, they know all about the secret compartment you've got built into your elbow; but they do that to everybody. It's just to see if you'll sweat. You will, and you should—if you didn't, they'd be suspicious. Then you go on—it's the same road, only it's numbered fifty-two there—toward Brno. Here's where you turn off.

"Now, you go along here about six kilometers, then there's an even smaller road that comes down the hill on your right. You go up that until you come to a bend where there's a pull-off. It's a sort of picnic area, scenic overlook, something. Anyway, you can park there. You wait. You're supposed to be there by 1700. You wait until 1800. Someone will come for you in that time.

"If they don't, or if you're late, or anything's wrong, here's the fallback: you see this town on beyond? You get there. You can get something to eat—there's some kind of guesthouse or something. Now, across this little river there's the town sports field. I understand it's not much—just a park with a soccer field and some bleachers. Anyway, you can drive over to it. You get there between 2130 and 2200. You park, just stroll around. Sit on a bench, whatever you want. You'll be spotted.

"Then what happens, they get you into the hotel where

Czerny's being put up. From what I'm told, that's the trickiest part—not because of security, but because with Czerny refighting the battle of Austerlitz they've got people six deep in every room in the district—not to mention the horses.

"But apparently, because there are so many people and so much chaos—so many people going in and out and seeing Czerny all the time, and him doing all the things he does—and he's not like under guard every second, they can get you five or ten minutes with him. That ought to be enough, shouldn't it?"

"It ought to be."

"Okay, so then they get you out and back to your car, and you go on and visit the family burial plot and come on back. Two days, one night. Okay?"

"Sounds easy."

"Ought to be. I mean, you're not breaking into CIS headquarters to steal the codebooks out of the safe."

"If it's really so easy, why don't you go yourself, Steve?"

"I probably could. On the other hand— I'm not deceiving you, Tom. I told you two nights ago—when you volunteered—that there was some danger: there always is. If that million-to-one chance comes up and something does go wrong . . . there are too many things that I know that they shouldn't know."

"Million to one?"

"Well . . . Pretty unlikely, anyway."

"That's a great comfort."

CHAPTER 7

North of Vienna the countryside stretched in long, wide, rolling hills patched broadly with fields of grain, vegetables, and grapes. Trying to picture some landscape he'd seen in America with which to compare it, Talley thought of Pennsylvania or Ohio; but the scale was bigger. And there were no farmhouses. He saw villages down in shallow valleys between the great swales, and realized he was in a land where people lived close together and went out from town each day to work their fields.

For most of the hour's drive, though, he had little real awareness of his surroundings. He was too caught up in the immediate past.

"You have to tell me, Tom," Jane had demanded. "You have to tell me things."

He'd told her he couldn't tell her.

"You have to."

He'd tried to explain—

"It's not just this one thing! You do this: you live in your private world, and sometimes you come out and visit me."

He had protested.

"I don't want to know your every thought. You have a right to privacy, but not when— You can't just say you're going to be gone for two days, and not tell me. I won't accept that, Tom. I won't!"

"All right! I'm going to Czechoslovakia. Okay?"

Of course, then she'd wanted to know why he was going, and he wouldn't tell her. And she'd demanded that he not go. And he'd said he had to, and that he would.

All the way from Vienna north to the border he'd played the scene over again, and thought of everything he should have said, and the things she shouldn't; and about why they argued at all, and that they shouldn't have to.

Then he came over a rise. Ahead rose a line of much higher hills—they might even have been called low mountains. Some sort of white castle or monastery stood on the crest of one, and a large red-roofed town spread across a slope in the middle distance. Talley realized with a start that he was coming up to the border.

He halted at the booth under a canopy built clear across the road, and showed his passport to the Austrian customs official, who waved him through without a word. As Talley drove on toward the Czech barrier, perhaps a quarter mile away, he saw that—just as he had expected from newspaper photos—the actual border was fenced, and there were guard towers at intervals along it.

From then on, Talley's attention stayed in the present.

There was no problem. Once his papers had been examined and he had answered two questions about his destination and length of stay, he had been directed on. He drove past the fences and guards and was again in a rural landscape. That town seemed to be like the Austrian towns he'd seen. People who looked much like the Austrians were going about similar activities. He saw no roadblocks, no patrols with German shepherds and Dobermans.

What he saw was an old man with a poodle in the basket of his bicycle; blue-painted trucks with yellow tarpaulins over their cargos; a farmer in a purple shirt on a red tractor pulling a wagonload of green, fresh-cut hay.

But also he was aware of the dark blue car soon after it began following him.

He was being—under the circumstances of his visit—particularly law-abiding, keeping his speed just below the limit. Other vehicles in the stream of light but steady traffic passed him—except for that car. It hung back, two hundred yards or so, uphill and down, obstructing truckers as he did.

Talley's chest tightened. A tingle seemed to have lodged

permanently along the length of his spine. He tried to think out a plan. Make a U, go back to Vienna? How would he explain at the border? Would they let him out?

No, he decided. He would give up his mission and just go on to see the "family graves," and return like the bona fide, up-and-up, nothing-hidden straight-arrow guy that everybody knew Robert H. Dobson was. Making that choice filled him with bitter disappointment and immense relief.

Then the blue car began moving up on him. It passed a truck. It passed two cars. Talley resisted the impulse to keep ahead. Why would Robert H. Dobson run from the Czech police? Why would anyone try to run from them, heading *into* Czechoslovakia?

The blue car moved up steadily. Its reflection came into his outside mirror. He fought the urge to stare at it. He countered the opposite impulse to pretend not to see it. He set himself to control his car if they forced him over. As the car drew beside him, he glanced casually, then looked forward again—just as anyone does when being overtaken.

The man in the passenger seat didn't glance at Talley at all. He seemed to be talking to the driver. He didn't look back as they went past. In two minutes the car was several hundred yards ahead. In five it had disappeared.

Talley shook his head, both to relieve the tension in his neck and in rueful amusement. Obviously he had been scaring himself, like a kid in bed hearing the wind as a mummy's hand rattling his window. A road sign informed him of the remaining distance to Brno. He was making good progress toward his turnoff.

He continued to glance in his mirror from time to time as a matter of normal driving practice. Because he was telling himself so persistently that the Czech police had not been following him, would not follow him, he at first didn't notice and then refused to believe that the white car that appeared and then stayed behind was indeed following him.

It stayed farther back than the blue one had done; often it was out of his view.

"Oh, come on," Talley said, laughing at himself. "Rattle-rattle: give me my golden arm!"

Watching that white car, focused on the mirror, Talley hadn't seen the truck ahead of him slow. Only his peripheral vision caught the black mass rushing toward him. He hit his brake too late to stop: if the truck had halted completely, he'd have smashed into it. He was only inches away when his deceleration and the truck's renewed acceleration kept them apart.

Talley made himself take deep breaths, and as soon as the shoulder was wide enough he pulled over.

He had his road map up and seemed to be studying it when the white car came up and swept past. This time the passenger, a man with a dark mustache, did look at him; but didn't look back after the car had passed.

Again, the "following" car went out of sight; again Talley felt he had been a fool.

It was as well that he had stopped, though. His first turnoff was coming up. If he had continued to watch behind, to imagine himself being tailed, he might have missed it.

Parked at last at the overlook, Talley cut the engine. Ten before five. He was early. He got out to stretch his legs and look around.

The narrow road he had taken up the hill appeared to have been paved recently. Talley guessed it might have been simply a dirt track a year or two ago. It rose sharply, making several curves, from the secondary road below. Perhaps at the time of its paving, a pull-off had been created at the outside bend of a near-hairpin turn halfway up. The view was striking: the bucolic countryside, green and rolling, with farms and here and there a hamlet nestled in it. To the north and east the hills grew, and a blue shape beyond must have been a mountain range. Talley couldn't judge how far away the mountains were, nor how high: late afternoon haze lay over the land, softening and blending.

He looked around. A path led from the road up into a belt of trees. Over the treetops he could see the pale tan wall of a building, pointed windows, the edge of a tile roof, a steeple: a small church on the crown of the hill.

He turned to look over the panorama again. It surprised him. While he had not imagined anything specific, somehow he had not expected a land behind the iron curtain to appear so velvety. He couldn't see any people, but could more easily imagine they would be dressed in embroidered scarlet jackets and lacy shirts, dancing, than marching in gray uniformed lockstep.

Looking more carefully, he did see people in the distance: a tractor pulled some piece of equipment across a field, and people must have been raking around its edges. A little tree-bordered river meandered toward him from the northwest. Checking his map, he could see that it swung around the hill he was on and flowed past the town where his fallback rendezvous point was. Beyond it and the field where the people were working, a road crossed diagonally from the middle distance, visible in a long stretch between a hill to Talley's left (which blocked the line of sight toward the highway to Brno) and the rise to his right. A dark car was coming fast along the road.

He sat on the fender and studied the map. Yes, a cross showed the position of the church on the hilltop above. The road he was on ran around it, wound back and forth, then went to the town. That diagonal road from the northwest went through the town, and the one he had taken from the highway did, too, after skirting this hill. The map showed a thin line connecting them before they intersected. He stepped forward, peered over the edge of the road to check. Yes, he could just see it. He had identified his position correctly.

He heard a car coming on the road below, from his left. He leaned farther to see, then jerked back. It was the white car!

A white car, he told himself.

As soon as it had passed, he looked over again. The car was going on toward the town. Then it slowed. It halted at the junction with the connecting road. The dark car had turned onto that road from the other end. As Talley watched, that dark car—he became sure its color was blue—reached the white one.

For a moment they stood there, side by side. Then the white one proceeded toward the town, and the other came back toward Talley.

Both cars *had* been following him. He had slipped them by turning off after the white had passed him. When that had been realized, both had turned back. Now one would go into the village while the other checked this road. They would have him between them.

"Okay, take it easy, think about it," he told himself. "I'm Robert H. Dobson, I'm on my way to visit the family graves, I just stopped here to enjoy the view." Sure, he could try to brazen it out. But he knew it wouldn't work. Obviously they weren't following an innocent tourist named Dobson. Somehow, they knew who he was. They would arrest him, and hold him, and possibly torture him until he told them anything they wanted to know.

What was the alternative? Try to get away, on foot, a stranger in that country—a fugitive? No. He had been given a fallback rendezvous. He did have a chance if he could get to it.

He whirled and ran toward the path into the trees.

The footpath zigzagged sharply up through the trees. Firs, their blue-black branches spreading widely and thickly, screened the hillside. They must have been planted to hold the earth from erosion—the wood had begun where the slope steepened as it rose toward the hairpin turn, and Talley could see blue sky between trunks in the other direction. The grove would conceal him while he went through it, but offered neither a real hiding place nor cover for escape in any direction but up.

By the low-gear whine, he could hear the car when it turned onto the little road and began coming up. He thought of himself in low gear: putting power into his legs to drive him upward, not trying for speed. Planting his garden, and the early spring hikes he and Jane had taken in New Hampshire, had gotten his legs in shape. The path—only a rut through the turf—ran behind the thick tree trunks, offering solid footholds on gnarly roots. Talley placed his feet carefully, concentrating on breathing steadily, on hearing the car approach and judging its position: on all the moment-by-moment tasks of getting away; on not allowing "getting away" to turn into panicked flight.

He was glad he'd chosen to wear lightweight hiking boots for his everyday shoes on the trip. He kept his corduroy jacket on, although he was burning with heat and soaked with sweat, because he could move better with it on than if he carried it. He did not let his mind spin over what he would do when he reached the top of the hill, since he had no information to give it traction.

He came out of the trees, up another six yards of grassy hillside, and then the slope leveled. His heart sank.

The church had been placed at the top of a little knob, but only the side he had climbed was at a sharply different height from the land adjacent. Only that side was treed. The church on its knob finialed a long fold of land running north and south. To Talley's left, the little road—having accomplished its strenuous ascent of the steep end—wound through grassy fields along the gentle side slope and down to the town in the distance.

He could see the town. He could see the road. He could see over all the fields for two or three miles. He could see no place to hide.

In the flat amber light of late afternoon every feature of that smooth countryside showed clearly. Three separate groups of buildings, undoubtedly farms, stood along the roadside. How could he hide in one, if he could reach it? What could he say, in English, that would make the people there want to protect him? And he couldn't reach them. If he started walking toward them, his figure—brightly sidelighted, long-shadowed—would stand out against the vivid counterpane of fields as sharply as did those of four men working in one half a mile away, or of the person even farther distant who must be riding a motor scooter: its buzz carried clearly across the stillness.

Talley went to the front of the church. To his surprise, the wood-paneled door was open. Since the church was the only place to hide, it would be the first place they'd look for him. Since it was the only place to hide, he went in.

Inside as out, the stucco covering the building's walls had aged to a creamy gray and tan. That neutral color, and the dark wood of pointed ceiling and rows of pews, might have given the room a restfulness. To Talley, the simplicity seemed severe despite the painted altarpiece, the cheery yellow and pink and red flowers in a bowl below it. The calm seemed one of tension, waiting.

The church's windows were set above head-height, but a bench ran along the wall below them. He stepped up, looked down, saw over the trees to his car. The blue car had been pulled in beside it, and two men were looking into his. One went back behind the wheel of their own. Talley imagined him reporting by radio. The other man looked up at the hillside and then at the church.

Talley froze. With his face at the bottom corner of the window, back from the glass, he probably couldn't be seen. The man didn't give any sign of seeing him.

The man in the car stepped out and spoke over the roof. The other seemed to answer, then shook his head resignedly, shrugged, and crossed the road toward the path. The driver got into the car again. It backed, turned, and started up the road.

Obviously they were going to check the woods and come upon the church from both approaches.

Talley got down from the bench and began—without hope—to consider where he might hide.

Behind a pew? Talley walked down the side aisle looking along each row just as the policeman would do. The next most obvious place would be behind the altar. But as he approached the rear of the church he could see that the altar had no behind: it was a simple shelf projecting from the wall. He went up the three steps onto the dais and looked into the vesting rooms—cubicles, really—at either side. Each contained a straight-backed chair. One had a small table. Both had pegs projecting from the walls and a small cabinet built in; but neither had any closet or cranny that even a man stretched as thin by tension as Talley could squeeze himself into.

Finally, there was the pulpit. Eight feet above the congregation, projecting from one side of the arch, canopied with a wooden roof, it had a solid railing that would conceal the priest up to his waist as he stood in it to deliver his homily. It would conceal a sitting man completely.

Talley stood for a moment, considering. The pulpit might not be the *final* obvious place after all. To someone looking from the doorway, its prominence might be inescapable.

The drone and putt of the motor scooter was drawing closer. And then Talley realized he could hear another engine as well—the car approaching the crest of the hill. He went quickly up the little winding stair into the pulpit.

Once seated there, his knees up against his chin, he realized that the carving on the pulpit's face pierced the panel. With an eye against it, he could look through.

The church faced west. Outside, light filled the air. Antithesis of the pews' solid block of furrowed darkness, the light yet seemed a substance, too. The glimpse of grass that Talley could see shimmered slightly, as though seen through currents of energy.

Talley heard the car stop on the road down below the rear of the church. The driver would walk up the curving path around the side to the entrance. The motor scooter bumblebeed by, and then began whining and popping as it started down the way the car had come.

The light spilled into the church. It could not animate the

cloistered air, but did give a shine, a glow of life, to the smooth stone floor that some pious soul must sweep and scrub daily to eradicate every sinlike stain or grain of sand. But the work was blemished. Pointed at by a finger from the low sun's rays lay a clot, a little clump of dirt. Talley might never have noticed it at a different time. Looking down and toward the doorway, though, into that all-revealing light, he did see. Tiny, it might have seemed insignificant. The relentless light magnified it by casting its shadow black inches beyond it.

He considered the object. It was, of course, a clod of mud, a stone, something carried in on his boot.

He felt along the edges of his boots, brushing fingertips over the cleated soles. They were clean. The path had not been damp. He couldn't have left a trail of muddy tracks.

Maybe it had been there before he came. Some other visitor might have brought it in.

It wouldn't matter who had brought it. It showed a hunter that someone had gone into the church. It wouldn't matter if they got the wrong man.

He tried to tell himself they wouldn't see it. But he knew they'd be looking for exactly that sort of sign. When they saw it, they'd know he was there. They'd search the room thoroughly. His only hope—foolish and forlorn, but better than despair—had been that they'd just walk through and out again.

He had to remove the thing.

How could he? The man must be coming up the path from his car. There wouldn't be time to get down from the pulpit, run the length of the church, grab up that thing, run back, climb up again. He'd be caught down there in plain sight. He'd probably only make it as far as the entrance, be right there at the front to greet the man when he arrived, presenting himself, saving the guy the trouble of looking inside.

But if he didn't get that boulder out of sight, there'd be no point in hiding at all. It said, "I'm in here. Come find me." And the man would. He'd come straight down the aisle, up the steps, look at Talley hunkered there, and say, "Peek-a-boo, I see you."

For one more split second, Talley felt out his choices. Then he sprang. He almost tumbled, racing down the winding steps. He leaped from the dais and sprinted down the aisle. He had never moved so fast in his life. Every muscle in his body tensed and strained, stretching and snapping, propelling him.

He reached the end of the aisle, stooping, scooping, spinning, slipping, never stopping, racing back again.

In one bound he was up on the dais. Grabbing the handrail, he took the steps to the pulpit three at a time. He fell to his knees against the railing. His chest heaved. He couldn't hold his eye steady to look through the carving. But he did see that no one had come into the doorway.

He looked at the object in his hand. It was a tiny, immature fir cone. It might never have been seen, but if it had been, it would have proven that someone had come into the church after passing through the wood.

A voice called from outside, near the front of the church. Another answered from farther away, at the side. Talley believed he understood: the man who had driven up and reached the church first wouldn't come in alone, without cover.

Except for the sound of the motor scooter receding far down the hill, all was quiet for a minute. Then, presumably as the second man came up the last slope, the two began talking again. Talley could comprehend nothing, of course; but he inferred that a brief report was given and a next move planned.

Talley sensed annoyance in the voice of the man approaching. That might have been only because he was completing a stiff climb; but the discussion went on long enough that Talley guessed that the men disagreed.

Whatever difference they might have had about what to do, they were as one in doing it. Talley had expected to see sinister figures silhouetted in the doorway, long shadows advancing into the church. All at once the light was slashed by a black shape, and then another; and Talley realized the men were inside. He could see them, one on either side of the doorway, separated as far as their leaps could take them, crouching, each holding a pistol out in front of himself with both hands.

One man moved forward and to the aisle on the pulpit side. He came along the wall, prowling half sideways, looking carefully along each row of pews as it opened to him. The other man sidestepped to the rear corner on the opposite side. Talley could see him checking over the entire bank of seats, into the arch toward the altar, and now and then up at the pulpit. Talley exerted every bit of physical control he had to steady his breathing lest it rock him and that movement show somehow through the tiny piercings of the carving.

The moving man reached the front of the church. He said something that could only mean, "No one here."

The other man responded with what had to be a directive.

The first man's tone had not been deferential; the second's, though firm, was not of unquestionable authority. Talley sensed the men were equals.

Passing almost directly below Talley, the man stepped up onto the dais. He glanced into one of the vesting rooms, then the other. "No one here," he said again, more definitely.

"Look in the pulpit," said the man in the rear. Talley couldn't understand the words, but he knew.

The man looked up. Talley could see his face. Talley had pulled off his glasses in order to get his eye close to the tiny hole. Could the man see his eye? It suddenly went dry, but he didn't blink.

"No one there."

"Look."

Expostulation. The man had just climbed the hillside. He did not want to climb to the pulpit. It wasn't necessary. No one was there. He was sure no one was there. Talley hoped that was what he was saying. Talley hoped he was saying he knew absolutely, with all his senses—five, the sixth, two dozen more—beyond any possible, conceivable doubt, that that pulpit was empty. Talley hoped he was saying they were wasting time; that their quarry must have gone down the hillside or been met and carried away; that they should be spreading the alarm, having traffic stopped, getting the bloodhounds on the trail. The man took two sentences to say that, or whatever it was. He turned and went down the steps from the dais and back along the aisle.

Talley didn't begin breathing again until the men had dragged their shadows out the door behind them. When he couldn't hear their voices anymore, he let himself slump against the railing. Not until he heard both car doors slam, heard the engine start, heard them turn around and head back down the hill, did he lift himself onto his pins-and-needles legs and finally stagger down the steps.

He lay full-length along the first pew, calming himself, trying to think what to do now. He looked at his watch. It was barely past five-thirty. He was still within the time period for his contact. If he could get back down to the overlook unobserved, he might . . .

But he knew that was a wishfully ridiculous idea. The police wouldn't just go off and leave his car unwatched. A wave of horror swept him. Whoever was supposed to meet him would come there, see his car, approach, and be trapped.

He sprang up, crossed to the windows, stepped up onto the bench. Crouching, he raised his head carefully, coming up in a place beside a window, then peering around and down.

His car stood as he had left it at the overlook. The blue car was nowhere to be seen. Had one of the men been dropped off to watch from the woods? Or had they gone on down? Maybe the stakeout was being set up at a greater distance.

He couldn't go down there without being seen. He couldn't head off the contact, without knowing who it was, where he'd be coming from. He tried to think logically. The overlook could be approached only from one direction or the other on the road, or from the church's hillside. Of those, the most sensible one was the hillside, because the contact could come down under cover to check—

The motor scooter.

Someone—perhaps his contact, more likely a lookout who had every reason to ride down that road at that time—had already checked, seen the blue car at the church, Talley's car abandoned below, and gone on his way. Talley didn't have to worry about the contact being caught. There would be no contact in that place.

Worse—assuming (for the sake of argument) that he could possibly make his way undetected to the fallback location—there might be no one waiting.

Talley got down from the bench slowly. He tried to tell himself his legs and back were stiff from exertion, not the chill of hopelessness. He walked toward the door, stopping before the light would touch him. After checking, he went up to the threshold and looked again.

The light over the landscape seemed thicker, mellower; shadows stretched longer. Other than that, all looked as it had: unthreatening, peaceful. He wanted to sink down, sit on the entry steps in the sun, his back against the warm wall, be lulled, doze. But the church could provide him no sanctuary, he knew. Although left open, unattended, for the spiritual succor of any souls in need through the day, it surely would be locked at evening. The sun would be below the hilltops in less than an hour. He would have to go.

He couldn't go in that much light, though. Although the two policemen had missed him, others surely would be back. If they didn't come on foot combing the countryside, one helicopter passing over would spot him out on the road.

He went along the wall to the side of the church opposite the hill where he'd come up. Peering around the corner, he could see the graveyard. Most of the markers were modest headstones. A few of the departed, though, must have been thought (or thought themselves) worthy of more prominent monuments.

Crouching, Talley scuttled across the lawn, down a path, and behind one of them. Lying next to it pretty well concealed him, at least from anyone at a distance. He'd wait, he decided, for about an hour after sunset. Twilight would linger, but that figure-revealing highlight and shadow would be gone. And workers would be in from the fields. It would be suppertime, so fewer people would be abroad to see him.

He still had his map, stuck into a jacket pocket when he'd run for the trees. It traced the roads, showed the locations of unpronounceable towns and villages. He wasn't lost; he could find his way—across a land as foreign to him as Borneo, unable to speak or understand one word of the language of any people he met, any of whom could be headhunters.

CHAPTER 8

When Jake finally recognized the man eating alone at the corner table, it was too late. Jake had glanced through the archway into the dining room and spotted him while crossing the lobby to the telephone booth.

The hotel had a telephone booth that could be used without having to ask the girl at the desk, one of the amenities of the chain of establishments that had recently been built in apparent imitation of American Holiday Inns. A traveler brought there blindfolded might not at first have known what country he was in. An experienced one, though, would have noticed the cracks jagging across the textured ceiling, the edges of the plastic sheathing lifting and chipping, showing that the shoddy concrete-work underneath had started to sag. Someone as experienced as Jake would then be sure that however secure and private the booth seemed, any conversation might be monitored. A call going out of the country most probably would be; one to the BigOx headquarters in Linz certainly.

The monitoring didn't trouble Jake. He called in almost every day on legitimate BigOx business. On those infrequent occasions when he had a message for the CIA, no one listening would know the difference: only a few code words would be compressed within straightforward sentences, or encrypted and buried in lists of parts or model numbers.

What did trouble Jake was simply the facts he had to report: Talley had missed his rdv, his whereabouts were unknown, and the CIS was on to him. That message had passed from the man on the motor scooter through two other couriers to reach Jake, and had taken over an hour to do so; but he was as close to the action as he dared to get.

More worrisome was the question of why this had happened. The CIS had not had the rdv point staked out, which they would have done if the operation had been blown on the Czech end—by one of Jake's people. They must have known who Talley was, and followed him—which said there could be a break on the other end: the originating end: the agency end. The happiest possibility along that line would be that something was wrong with Talley's papers, probably his visa. Maybe the Czechs had a new secret marking, or something, that the agency hadn't tumbled to and learned to fake. The worst possibility was that there was a break, a leak, an informant.

It was something to worry about, all right; but what troubled Jake most was the way he was worrying. It wasn't just squirrels roller-skating around inside his chest. When you're nervy that way, at least you've got nerves.

Jake felt he had no nerves; or that they'd been all stretched out and gone slack, like rubber bands that haven't got any snap in them anymore. He'd been sitting in his room, his half glasses down on the end of his nose, dozing in the twilight, when the note was slipped under his door and the deliverer tapped twice and once and went away. An operation running! Him waiting there for the word; and he was half asleep!

He hadn't been sleepy. He'd just been tired. He'd been sitting with his book slipped down between his thigh and the chair arm. He hadn't turned on a lamp when sunlight faded outside and dusk settled. He hadn't been sleeping, but he'd wanted to take hold of the dusk and turn and pull it over his shoulder and over his head and go to sleep. A truck had passed on the road outside, but its noise hadn't roused him. It had come from nowhere, faded again to nowhere, and while it was passing merely obliterated any sound that might have roused him.

It was Milos, he thought: the business with Milos.

No, it wasn't. Like Steve McCluskie had said, what was so special about Milos? Nothing. Except maybe that he had been the most recent. The last straw?

To himself, Jake had never pretended that what he did

wasn't fun. You're not supposed to admit it's fun, because if you do they'll think you're a cowboy or a weirdo. One of those Catch-22s: if you get a kick out of hide-and-seek, you shouldn't play; if you're not all strung out, you're sick. You're just supposed to be a competent pro doing a tough job, in which you can take some satisfaction if you do it well, but you're not supposed to be having fun.

Jake couldn't point to the minute during the past two or three years when it had stopped being fun. He didn't let anybody he worked with see that he'd had it with the business. Sometimes—in the thick of it—he fooled himself for a while.

He hadn't gotten strung out, though; he wasn't scared. He just knew that underneath he didn't care much anymore, and for that reason they were going to get him.

It was that—about himself—that worried him most. It was seeing the man at the corner table, knowing he'd seen him before, and therefore assuming he was CIS, and only later—after calling in anyway—recognizing him as a highway engineer he'd met once in Znojmo. The recognition came too late. By then, Jake realized, he had assumed the game was over, and admitted to himself that he didn't care.

It was time to sell shoes.

"Just a second." McCluskie shifted the telephone receiver to his other hand, grabbed a pencil. "Okay." As he wrote, Deming came around the desk to look over his shoulder. But McCluskie wrote left-handed, covering the words as he scrawled them.

The message was brief. McCluskie didn't repeat it back for confirmation. He put down the phone.

"What did he say?"

McCluskie read,. "Rdv negative. Opposition engaged. Fall-back aborted. Prognosis negative. Will monitor."

"What does that mean?"

McCluskie looked up, then turned his palm to indicate the obvious.

"I mean, what's going to happen? What's it going to mean?"

McCluskie leaned back in the swivel chair. "What's going to happen? I don't know. Tom Talley is way out of his depth. But—as I have learned to my sorrow—he can be very resourceful. So I guess one possibility is that he'll make his way to the border, living on raw potatoes and turnips, tunnel under the dead zone, and come back to fly more missions. I guess another is that he'll cave up and starve himself to death rather than let them torture the secret formula out of him.

"What I figure is, they'll catch him, and after they pressure him a little he'll have sense enough to spill everything he knows, and then eventually we'll get him back in an exchange."

Deming sat in the other chair again. "Yeah. I see. Well, he'll be all right, then, won't he? We don't have to worry about him, do we?"

McCluskie swiveled left and right. "Paul, I really am not particularly inclined to worry about Tom Talley, personally. He has not demonstrated the kind of loyalty that would win mine. But he is our man; he did go over for us. We will do what we can for him. So as long as he doesn't think he's Chuck Norris behind the lines in a war movie, he'll be all right. All he has to do is keep putting his own self-interest first. He always does.

"Now, as to what it's going to mean: it's going to mean a score for us. If, by some miracle, they don't get him, they still—obviously—know who he is. So they must know he went in there on something to do with the Czerny thing; so the point's made. If—when—they catch him, it's the same thing, but better. He *tells* them why he's there. And then he tells them— For the past week I have been stuffing him like a turkey-bird with how important this thing is, and he's got it all worked out for himself that it's got to do with Murtaugh. So."

Deming drummed his fingers on the arms of the chair. "So. So it's really a good thing for us they got on to him. I mean, if he'd gotten in and done his thing and gotten out again the way it was set up, they'd never know. Then we'd've had to be real clever about that."

"Yeah, I guess . . . it's an ill wind that doesn't blow somebody some good."

"Okay, Steve, you're the chief, I'm just one of the little Indians. So maybe I shouldn't wonder about how the CIS got on to Talley right away."

McCluskie suddenly leaned forward. "You're wrong, Paul. You're very wrong. You think I set him up somehow? You're wrong."

"Okay. If you say so."

"I say so. I always tell the truth, Paul; that's why nobody believes me."

"All right. If you say so, I'm sorry. But then how did they get on to him?"

"Beats me. When Jake gets back, we'll go through his side. You can start a check on anybody here who knew anything. The only other possibility I can think of is . . . We ought to have a word with Talley's ladyfriend, Jane Boudreau."

At a little before eight o'clock, Talley rose from the dead. He peered carefully over the gravestones, then stood. He didn't see anything that didn't belong in a calendar picture.

Climbing the hill, and then lying on the ground after the sun had gone down, had stiffened his muscles. A little walking should limber them again, he thought. He could see he would be doing a lot of walking.

Light still filled the sky and reflected down over the landscape. Although the valley below lay covered with deeper shadow, the long hillside was in twilight, not dusk. The narrow lane wound clearly, gray-tan against the multicolored fields: anyone on it might be seen from a mile or more away. On the other hand, he couldn't cut across the fields—he might have if they'd been pastures like the ones around his house in New Hampshire; but you don't cut across fields of vegetables or grain. Not without attracting the displeasure of the farmers. To keep to the edges, going around one field and then another, would slow him.

He looked at his watch again. He had almost two hours; more than enough to walk to the town; not enough to wander. Better, he decided, to take the road and break across the fields if he saw anyone coming. At least he'd see them from as much of a distance as they'd see him.

He went down the path from the churchyard and onto the road.

With the sun gone, the air was cooling. Talley was glad of that as he worked the stiffness out of his legs and set a good pace. Under other circumstances he would have enjoyed the walk. Birds twittered; somewhere down the road a dog barked; by listening carefully he could hear vehicles passing occasionally on the road out of sight below the hillside; but all the little noises were accepted and contained within a stillness. During the time he had hidden himself in the graveyard, only two cars had gone by on the hill road, and a woman had come on a bicycle and locked the church. There was no sign of activity now. He might have believed the search had been abandoned, might have thought himself safe. He didn't feel safe, but the peacefulness and his own purposeful motion gave him a sense of assurance and hope.

He approached the first of the farms along the road. The main building was a single structure three stories high: the family's living quarters facing the road, the barn behind. A small tractor stood beside the barn, a man lay half under it. Intent on his tinkering, it seemed he wouldn't see Talley passing at all.

Suddenly a streak of black and tan shot toward the road with a rising roar. A German shepherd bounded out in front of Talley, bouncing on stiffened forelegs with the force of its barking. Instinctively Talley recoiled. The dog lunged, teeth bared, snarling. It might actually have torn at Talley, but he knew about dogs. He stepped forward, coming up on his toes, spreading his arms to raise his chest and shoulders, and roared. Ears down, the dog leaped to the side and back. Although chastened and wary, it didn't cower. Just out of range of a kick, it went on barking, and began circling as though for a strike from behind.

A shout! The farmer had come from under his tractor. A short man, stocky, black-bearded, he stood by the rear wheel and shouted again. His voice, his anger, sounded to Talley just like the dog's.

The dog's tail dropped. It wheeled and slunk toward the man.

The man called out to Talley. It sounded like the words had only consonants in them.

Talley waved a hand beside his head, and smiled to show he had taken no offense. He continued walking, briskly. He didn't look back.

By the time he reached the second farm, another half mile down the road, Talley's pulse and breathing were elevated only in keeping with his exercise. But then the same thing happened again—in a different way.

An elderly man sat on a bench beside the wooden door of his house, smoking his pipe. Talley avoided looking directly at him for as long as possible. Some exchange would have to be made, but if he held off he might get away with a simple nod. If they made eye contact at a distance, then there would have to be conversation. At least that was the way it worked in New Hampshire.

Peripherally Talley could see the man looking at him all along. He hoped the old farmer was only exercising his property owner's prerogative of watching anything going by his house; but, no, the man wanted to talk.

He said something like, "Boxey hedges."

Talley smiled and nodded and kept walking.

"Switching crackerjacks?"

Smiling again, Talley shrugged, and kept walking.

"Blackstrap molasses for tiny chicks."

Talley half turned, smiled and waved, and kept walking. When he was a hundred feet down the road, he sneaked a look back. The old man was still staring at him.

It wasn't going to work. He'd gone barely a mile, not halfway to the town, and already two people— Out here in the boondocks where there wasn't anybody around, *everybody* had already seen him and identified him as a stranger! He'd never make it to the fallback by just walking down the road!

But, again, what was his choice? He scanned ahead. Perhaps fifty yards away a dark line ran irregularly down the hillside to his left. As he came closer, he could see it was a little gulley, a stream running down to the river on the valley floor. It could lead him more or less directly through the fields and down.

When he came to it, he turned and started down. He looked, and saw the old man still watching him.

Only a foot or so across, the little brook took the natural course between two adjacent humps of the hillside. Its gulley wasn't two feet deep; but it was deep enough that the land on either side was worked as separate fields, leaving a grassy strip on either bank. Talley could see he wasn't the first to have used that as a path.

In five minutes he was out of sight of the farms. In ten he was hidden even from the church at the height of the hill. The track—it became a definite rut—crossed the stream, entered a narrow belt of trees near the bottom of the hillside, and went along the steepening slope at an angle. Finally it met another path, almost a lane, running beside the little river.

Talley had assumed he would come down onto the road that he knew went around the hill and to the town. He had tried not to dwell on the impossibility of walking on it unnoticed. But evidently, at some place out of sight from the observation point where he'd left his car, the road had crossed the river. Now it ran parallel to the farther bank. The river couldn't have been more than forty—maybe fifty—feet across. Cars on the road were right *there*. He could see them, they could see him. But trees had been planted in file along the roadside, and his side was screened irregularly by alders and willows growing from the bank.

Light was withdrawing from the sky, and down under the riverside trees it was murky. He began to walk toward town.

After he had gone a hundred yards the path rose slightly. While the flood-cut riverbank to his left fell as sharply as ever, now a slight shelf or bar projected into the stream six feet below the level of the path. A man was standing down there fishing. He was watching the water; and the river's noise covered the sound of careful footsteps. The path went down again, and there, leaning against a tree, stood the fisherman's bicycle.

Talley did have a moment's compunction about stealing it. But he wasn't taking it far, and the man would get it back.

Now he was really pleased. He could arrive at the near end of the appointed half hour, and under better cover: a bicycle identified him as a local citizen.

Talley hadn't ridden a bicycle in years. He wobbled and nearly fell at first, but (of course) the skill came back to him. By the time he'd gone another quarter mile he was pedaling steadily, moving smoothly, covering ground but not racing: the way a local who'd been out fishing would move.

He passed a break in the bushes on his side. A dark shape, across the river, was matching his speed. A car. Traffic was light: a car going one direction, thirty seconds, another the other way. So he was aware of the shape as a *particular* car, not merely one of a stream.

He passed behind another block of alders. When he emerged, the car was still exactly opposite, gliding with the menace of a cruising shark. He glanced quickly, naturally—not furtively, he hoped.

No pretense now: no shadowing at a distance in plain-clothes cars. This one had a big blue light on top, and the letters painted on the side began P-O-L. A man in the passenger seat was staring at him.

More bushes, screening him for ten seconds; then a long stretch clear. Tree trunks on the highway side would be breaking the watcher's view regularly. Maybe they, and the bushes on Talley's side, and the now swiftly gathering darkness, would prevent the policeman from making any kind of identification.

The lane was only a dirt path, bumpy, rutted; there were stones. He pedaled slowly, steadily. His heart pounded, he could feel his pulse racing, but he made his feet go 'round and 'round at the rate of a slow-motion walk. The little river flowed flat-bedded, shallow-pitched, with a surface unbroken by any splash, rippled only enough to reflect the sky, the bushes and trees, as a soft-edged mosaic, pale blue, purple-blue, light green and dark. And the police car's black shape glided along behind the bars of the poplars' trunks.

Talley approached another bank of bushes. Should he drop the bike, scramble up the hillside in the time it would take them to realize he wasn't on the path anymore? He could be well up the hillside before they could find a place to cross and get back after him.

And then where would he be? Up on the hill he'd just come down from, having shown them he was indeed the man they were hunting, having located the sector where he could be found. Right now, they were checking, just checking. A lone figure, out late in the evening: naturally they'd check.

Slowly, calmly, Talley made the sprocket go 'round and 'round.

And then he saw the bridge. Up ahead, fifty yards—he hadn't been able to see it before because of the bushes. Now they'd drive across the bridge and intercept him.

Their car began moving up on his left. They were pulling ahead, to reach the bridge before he got there.

Drop the bike and run!

To where?

Partly from despair, partly from stubborn hope, Talley kept going.

The car couldn't cross the bridge. The bridge wasn't any wider than the lane. The car paused at the far side, and the policemen continued to look at him carefully as he rode by. Then they started up again and sped away toward the town.

Talley nearly lost control of the bike. He had convinced them! By going on as though he were perfectly innocent, he'd convinced them that he was. He let out the breath he'd been holding in a laugh. He let himself coast down a little slope, sighing "Whooeee" and laughing.

Then he realized that they probably had identified him and had gone ahead to wait for him.

If they were waiting, Talley didn't see them immediately. The lane led out of the trees into a wide flat area. It joined a small paved road that came down from the hillside rounding away to his right: what must have been the road to the church up above. That road now ran straight through a double colonnade of poplars. As Talley proceeded, he could see the town beginning across the river. Another footbridge crossed from it. A glow showed through the trees on his side. Closer still, he could see that the light came from floods on poles around the playing field. The field seemed to be nothing elaborate, seemed to be like the one at home where the local softball teams played on summer nights. He heard a cheer.

Talley slowed, got off the bike, left it leaning against a tree in the darkness well away from the field. He could see benches under the trees along the road and a few strollers.

He looked at his watch. The time was nine-twenty. He was early. Shouting began again from the playing field. The crowd couldn't be large, the pitches of individual voices could be distinguished. Then the shouts flowed together, rose in volume and tension. There was a unison groan. A whistle blew.

A pair of strollers passed: an elderly couple. At a bench twenty feet away, Talley could see two other figures. They became one, then partially divided again. He didn't see anyone else close-by. Evidently the police hadn't gone ahead to wait for him there. He stepped out onto the paving and started to walk in the direction of the game. When he had gone far enough that the glow from the lights was reaching him, he sat on a bench.

Why stop there? he asked himself. For contact, for escape, he had to be seen. Why not go closer and be seen better? That would expose him more, but he was kidding himself, he admitted, if he thought he wasn't exposed already. By choosing that bench, he was neither really concealed nor really easy to see.

He ought to decide what he had to do, and then do it. But he stayed where he was.

His contact might come from any direction; probably would come from the darkness, from some place out of the way, where the contact could observe. Very likely that would be from the woods beyond the playing field, away from the river. Although he reasoned that way, Talley kept looking along the road toward the bridge that crossed from the town down beyond the field. When the cars crossed it, each one announced itself with a soft drum roll of loose planks.

Three cars. Together! Instantly he looked for escape in the other direction. A light flashed there, a powerful flashlight; someone had shone it onto the elderly couple. He realized there were two people behind the light. They must have come across the footbridge at that end of town.

Talley was caught between. His first thought was to run away from the river, toward the trees. But the floodlights gave enough glow that a moving figure would be seen.

Another cheer went up.

Talley rose and started walking toward the playing field.

It was like the one at home, except being configured for soccer. Blocks of open bleachers faced each other across the field. There might have been sixty people in one, half that many in the other. There was no entrance gate, no admission charge. One of the teams had red and white jerseys, the other yellow ones; both clearly were amateurs.

Talley walked behind the home team's bleachers, and then came up along one end, standing away from the front.

A referee blew his whistle, tossed the ball in. Talley stepped farther back as the play swept toward his end of the field. The spectators on the opposite side were coming to their feet, cheering. Then one of the yellow-shirts intercepted and started a charge toward the other end. The home crowd rose.

Talley went up into the bleachers. He stepped up onto the first row, then the second, then the third. He hesitated for another moment, then started toward the middle of the section: it wasn't going to do him any good to sit there on an end, all by himself. He went up farther to pass behind two men, then four men, then a family. Then he came down a row to take a seat at the far end of the gap between the family and a group of young men. There were nearly a dozen of them; they made one of the largest groups among the spectators.

One of the yellow-shirts passed the ball across to another, who spun a tight circle, faking out an opponent, and drove a kick toward the goal. The goalie lunged, slipped down on one knee to block and kick the ball out again; but the first yellow-shirt had dodged his man and was in position. His kick shot the ball straight back behind the goalie for a score.

Everyone on the home-team side was up and cheering, Talley with them. Then, as the teams trotted to their places to face off again, the spectators all sat. The young man next to Talley noticed him, shouted something, grinning with enthusiasm. Talley smiled and nodded. The young man pounded on the shoulder of the companion on his left, saying it again. All of the young men—boys: several of them were smoking with vigorous casualness, probably they were between sixteen and eighteen years old—were shouting and stamping their feet. Their rowdiness might have accounted for the distance other spectators kept from them.

Talley's neighbor turned to him again, as though the fact Talley was a stranger had just registered. He asked Talley something.

Grinning and nodding wouldn't be enough. They knew he was a stranger, they'd probably realize he was a foreigner; there was no point in making them think he was demented, too.

"I'm sorry, I don't understand."

The boy looked at him, astounded.

Talley decided he might as well go all the way. "I'm an American."

"American!"

Talley kept his smile and nodded.

The boy exclaimed to his fellows. The word passed among them. Those in his row leaned forward or back to see, the ones in the row ahead turned. Talley tried to draw himself down to keep out of sight behind them. But the red-and-white shirts were working the ball, and no one else seemed to have heard.

The boy turned back. "New York City," he said, demonstrating his geographical knowledge.

Talley shook his head. "No, I'm from New Hampshire."

The boy looked blank.

Talley wanted to keep the approval he had heard when he'd identified his nationality.

"New England. It's in New England."

The second boy over, who had been leaning forward to hear, said, "England? Englishman?"

"*New* England," Talley said.

"New England," the first boy repeated firmly to his friend. He must have translated it. He turned back to Talley and with authority declared, "Boss-tone."

Talley nodded and smiled.

"Boss-tone." The boy distributed the information among his companions with royal graciousness. Looking at Talley, he said, "Boss-tone," and another word in Czech.

Talley smiled and shrugged.

The boy repeated himself, slowly and more loudly.

Talley shook his head.

Suddenly the boy lunged, grabbing Talley around the throat with both hands, shaking him, and repeating the words.

"Boston Strangler!" Talley got out, the combination of words leaping from his memory to save his life.

The boy released him, sat back nodding and grinning.

The Strangler's terrorizing of Boston must have happened decades before this boy was born! Talley barely knew anything about it himself. How could this Czech kid know? Why would he think of—

But the boy had known about Boston. He enjoyed the admiration—or envy—of his fellows. Then a rising shout from the crowd took them all back to the field for a moment.

The charge was deflected, the ball went out of bounds. One of the teams called time-out.

Another young man got up from his place along the row, came around in back, and sat on Talley's right. He wore a leather jacket over a yellow T-shirt printed with the Grateful Dead logo.

"American, yes?" he asked.

"That's right," Talley said, wary again.

The newcomer looked out across the field. He narrowed his eyes. "The weather tonight it is very nice," he said gravely.

"Yes," Talley agreed. "The weather is very nice. Warm."

"Yes. It is warm."

Talley was looking to his right, at the young man. Suddenly he stiffened and shifted focus. A man had just appeared and was standing at the end of the bleachers, scanning across the field.

"My name is Istvan."

Talley swallowed. "My name is Thomas."

The first boy said loudly, "My name is Miki."

Talley turned. "Hello, Miki. I'm Tom."

Two other men had come to the left end of the seats.

Miki took out a pack of cigarettes, offered them.

"No thanks. I don't smoke."

Miki's eyes tightened.

Talley patted his chest and coughed. "But thanks, anyway." He smiled reassuringly. "I appreciate it. Thanks a lot."

Miki seemed mollified. Then he caught Talley's stare past him. He looked. He glanced quickly at Talley again, then said something to Istvan.

Istvan looked left, then right. He replied. He looked at Talley as he'd looked across the field.

"American," he said again.

"Yes."

"America is good country."

Talley nodded. His eyes went past Istvan's. A second man had joined the first at that end of the stands.

Istvan glanced that way again. "Czechoslovakia is good country," he said without turning.

"Yes," Talley said.

"Police are shit," Istvan said. He was wearing a blue cap with a black peak. He took it off and put it on Talley's head. He spoke again to Miki. A couple of the boys in the row ahead had turned to stare at Talley. Istvan snapped a command at them, and they looked front again.

Miki took the yellow scarf from his neck and put it around Talley's. "Police eat shit," he said, not to be second-in-command of the idiom.

A whistle blew. The teams took their positions. The ball went into play. The murmur of the crowd swelled. One of the men from the right end began walking slowly along the stands looking at the people. One of the yellows lofted the ball across the field. A teammate headed it toward the red-and-whites' goal. Another knee-bounced it, side-kicked it. The crowd came up to its feet.

Talley started to get up with them. Miki grabbed his arm, shoved him down again. Istvan said something, and Miki punched the boy next to him, and spoke, and that one and the next came around behind and stood beside Istvan. Miki leaned forward and spoke to his companions in the lower row.

Talley couldn't see out from the wall they made. The drive on the field must have been terrific. The home side cheered, then groaned as the other side screamed. Miki and Istvan and all of the boys were shouting and jumping up and down, and waving, so no one below would have noticed a gap in the rank. Then all the yellows cheered and screamed again. They all clapped. Then gradually some of the people at either side of the group began to sit down. The noise level remained high.

Miki pushed Talley's back, and made him lean forward as though tying a shoe. There was a flash below him. He gasped. The light flashed again. Someone must be going along behind the bleachers shining a light back and forth underneath. Still swinging, the beam moved off gradually to his right.

Miki tapped his back. Talley straightened. The boys were still standing, but Talley could see just a little between two of them. The man who had passed along the front of the stand had reached the left end. He was talking with the pair there. Then he and one of those men started back. Talley ducked again.

A whistle blew. The crowd shouted. Some of the other people whom Talley could see to the sides got up, too. Everyone began shouting and clapping.

Istvan touched Talley's back. "Okay," he said. Talley sat up.

Craning around first one way, then the other, Talley could see that only one of the hunters remained at either end of the stands. Istvan nodded toward the nearer one.

"No good, Thomas. He stay. Also," he jerked his head in the other direction. "Watch people when leaving."

The red-and-whites got the ball. They started a drive. Everyone on both sides was up. Suddenly a whistle sounded, and everyone screamed.

"All over," Istvan said, looking down at Talley. "We win." He looked across at Miki, spoke. Miki glanced down at Talley, then up and around at the policemen. He shrugged. He made a suggestion. Istvan shrugged.

"Look, guys," Talley said, "thanks for trying, but there

isn't any—'' Suddenly a thought came to him. ''Wait! They already looked underneath here. Do you understand? Down there.'' He pointed. ''They look, before.''

Comprehension came into both faces.

''Look, you stay there just a minute, okay?'' Talley waved his palms, building a screen. ''Okay?''

''Okay,'' said Istvan. He again snapped a command to his company.

''Go for it,'' said Miki.

Talley whipped off the cap and scarf. He lay on the footwalk, slipped his legs under the seat. Twisting, he stretched downward. His toe touched the ground. He eased his shoulders under. ''Okay. Okay, guys. And thank you. Thank you.''

Talley lay flat, squeezed under the seat of the first row, wishing he hadn't indulged in all that rich Viennese food, wishing he had dieted more at home, that he had taken off those ten pounds—even five. The footsteps of the people coming off the bleachers banged like a kettledrum being beaten next to his ear. None of them passing behind the stand saw him. Their line of sight would have been blocked by the higher rows; someone would have to be farther away, or squat, to see him. The two policemen who were farther away—standing off a hundred feet or so—whose silhouetted figures he could see head to foot, must not have seen him either. They were guarding the perimeter, watching the people who went off the far end of the stand and around behind to get to the road. Those people helped to screen Talley for a minute or two, and then the guards must have been watching for someone trying to slip away, rather than someone hiding.

Then, after the ten minutes it must have taken to impede the flow and check the spectators going back to town, the police came to do the playing area again. Talley heard them approaching. He tried looking down his body and past his toes, but the understructure of the stands made it difficult to see anything at an angle. After a moment, as they moved, he was able to make out several sets of legs. He could only hope he would be as hard to distinguish.

He had said to Istvan that the evening was warm; but it

wasn't. And he lay jammed against the damp ground. Yet he was sweating.

Two of the pairs of legs began to stride along behind the bleachers. A light flashed. It slashed in and out through the understructure's legs and complex diagonal braces and along the ground, hurling jagged shadows left and right. The men came to his bay. He could see their legs clearly. Then the light blinded him, stabbing at an angle from the pale earth under the stand.

The light went from his eyes. He opened them. When he could see again, the legs were two bays farther away. The men hadn't squatted.

When the clock in town struck two, Talley squirmed himself loose and crawled out. He had lain under the stand for four hours. During the first two, he had let himself fantasize that he would be rescued. This was the fallback contact place. There wasn't any other. Therefore, this was where his contact would be made. The person who was to have met him would know he must have arrived, since the police were looking for him. Since the police hadn't found him, then he must still be there; or would return. They would all simply wait until the coast was clear and then find each other.

It had been a little after midnight when he made himself recognize that no one would risk coming there to pick him up. A little later he realized that there probably would have been no contact ever, once the police started searching for him. He had been cut loose.

He emerged from under the stand, stretched and tried to limber himself. There might not be much hope, but he was damned if he'd let them get him without a fight. He would travel just by night, finding places to hide during the day, until he was far enough away to walk into a hotel, doing the Robert H. Dobson routine, and get the use of a phone. What else was there? He set off back the way he had come.

He planned to cross the little footbridge to the town side of the river and start along the highway. If he saw headlights, he'd hide down by the river.

The night was absolutely still, save for the slightest of breezes in the poplars and the faint ripple of the river. He walked on the grass beside the road so that his own footsteps wouldn't break the silence. When he came to the bridge, he trod lightly.

No cars had passed along the highway for over an hour. He had heard no one. He was sure the search had been abandoned until morning. Although he was sure about that, he kept himself as alert as his fatigue permitted, so it must have been because the man was sitting very still, in deep shadow under a tree, that Talley didn't see him until he was coming off the bridge.

It was too late to run. Talley continued walking—what else could he do? The man didn't seem to be pulling a gun or rising to accost him. Perhaps he was just a man who liked to sit by the river on a summer night.

Talley wished he knew some words in Czech, so he could say, "Nice night," to prove he was as innocent as he hoped the man was.

As he passed the bench and thought he might make it up the path to the highway, the man said, "Wait there, please."

Talley slept through much of the ride. He couldn't see out of the back of the van anyway.

The police and the nonuniformed men, whoever they were, hadn't questioned him in the town. They had taken his papers, and sat him on a bench, and pretty well ignored him. After fifteen minutes one had asked him if he was hungry, and brought him some coffee and a roll. Then they chained him to the bench in the van, put in there with him a man who didn't sleep, and started off.

Talley had asked the man where they were going, but wasn't answered. Wherever it was, he knew by the noise that it was in some city, and they arrived midmorning. He was taken through the basement of a building, up in an elevator, and delivered to a small, windowless office.

A man in uniform sat behind a desk there. To his right were Talley's false passport and visa, the identification cards from his wallet, arranged neatly. They were all there for Talley to notice, but the man didn't look at them. He remained silent for a moment, then said, as a greeting, "Mr. Talley."

Talley looked back, not surprised that his identity was known. "Dr. Benda, I presume."

CHAPTER 9

Talley met the old man's eyes steadily. Although the man wore a uniform, although his hair was cropped short, the mustache and the face were unmistakably as Larry Hovey had described them.

The man smiled ever so slightly. "Colonel Suk," he said. "The Dr. Benda you are thinking of is a kindly, elderly civil servant who comes sometimes to look after a certain sort of person among those who are brought here. I do not believe you are that sort of person, so we will not call on him.

"Now . . . that we know each other . . . let me begin by making clear to you your situation." He paused. "Something amuses you?"

"You may not be Dr. Benda, but you're starting the way Larry Hovey said Benda did."

Colonel Suk did not smile. "Acquainting a prisoner with his situation is a customary way of beginning."

"Assuming the situation can be made to sound bad enough to frighten him."

"I shall review the facts of your situation. You may decide whether they are being 'made to sound' in a particular way. Your name is Thomas Talley, not"—Suk gestured toward the papers without looking at them—"Robert H. Dobson. You have entered Czechoslovakia without permission, using fraudulent documents.

"Being in this country illegally, and using falsified documents, those two crimes—in themselves—are punishable by five years in prison.

"However, aggravating these crimes is the fact that you are an agent of the Central Intelligence Agency. You—"

"Was."

"What?"

"I was. An employee, not an agent. Seventeen years ago."

Colonel Suk paused for nearly half a minute. Talley was held by the colonel's stare, yet in the silence he could hear someone talking somewhere down the corridor outside the office. Although distant, the voice came not as a murmur, but with the sounds of words. Talley realized he could understand not one of them.

"Mr. Talley," Suk said at last, "what do you think we are doing here? What do you think you are doing?"

"Trying to set the facts straight." Talley had set himself straight: erect, but not rigid as though stiff with fear.

Suk glared at him from under those heavy eyebrows. "I think not. That is, I think you think you are doing more. I think you think you are proving to me that you cannot be intimidated. That you are sophisticated about interrogation procedures. That you concede to me no psychological advantage.

"You are making a mistake. A sophisticated, skilled intelligence agent would say nothing at all. You are merely proving yourself an amateur, which I know already. Please be silent until I have finished."

Talley felt himself flushing.

"To continue: you have been an 'employee' of the CIA; and you continue to be associated with them—even if on an irregular basis. Two years ago you undertook an assignment for them; you are currently on another. You know these are facts. You cannot successfully dispute them; we can prove them. They can add at least another five years to any sentence.

"However, I do know and accept the truth of the point you wished to make: you are not a full-time employee of the CIA, you are not an agent in the sense of being a professional spy. You do not have to make that point with me. To the contrary, I wish to make it with you.

"As you are not a professional spy; as you are not in this country to—let us say—obtain military information, there is no reason why you should pay the penalty as though you were."

Suk continued to stare at Talley. Finally he said, "So, Mr. Talley, have I made your situation 'sound bad' in order to frighten you?"

Talley started to lick his lips, caught himself. "No, I . . ." The man, Suk, was dealing. At least, he was trying to deal. At least he wasn't starting by throwing Talley into a dungeon. Talley made himself take a breath before replying.

"Well, yes, Colonel Suk; actually you have made it sound pretty bad. I appreciate also that you've suggested an alternative. I guess I'd be interested in hearing what it is."

Suk nodded once, sharply. "Good. We know—in principle—why you are in Czechoslovakia. You are continuing to investigate the Janos Czerny affair. We wish to know specifically what you hoped to find. From whom. We wish to know what conclusions you believed this information might enable you to make. We wish to know everything you know about the matter."

"And if I tell you?"

"We will not press charges against you. We will simply deport you."

"And if I don't tell you, ten years."

"Oh, Mr. Talley." Suk shook his head sadly. "There truly is no need for you to protest that you are not a professional agent. Everything you do proclaims it. An agent would know that your choice is not between freedom and ten years of prison; that is, between telling and not telling.

"Yes, if you tell us now, you will be released at once. However, if you do not tell us now, you will be sentenced to prison, and we will begin using the various methods available for extracting information. The professional person's choice is about how long he estimates he can withstand those, and whether the delay serves any purpose worth the cost to him."

The concrete wept. Talley couldn't sit against it; its damp chill would drain all his body's heat but never itself be any warmer, just as the walls consumed light from the naked bulb above and yet were ever the same dull and starving gray.

Talley sat on the edge of the metal-slat bench and wondered whether this cell was the very one Larry Hovey had been kept in.

He would break eventually, he knew. From what he'd read

he knew that "technical interrogation" by professionals was nowadays a highly developed skill: no sadistic punching or clubbing the victim to death before he can be made to talk. Perhaps they wouldn't begin with pain at all. Perhaps with drugs.

He accepted Suk's premise that anyone can be made to talk sooner or later. *Sooner or later* was the issue.

He wondered how late it was. They had taken his watch. He recognized that to be standard procedure—to disorient him, to keep him from having any outside reference. How long would Suk leave him there, giving him a chance to reflect and make a choice about a course of action?

Talley had already made his choice. Defining the issues made it for him. If a man is to respect himself, he must be responsible. He must not betray his country to an enemy out of fear or self-interest. He must withstand pressure—pain—to the limit of physical endurance. The issue is not whether a man can be broken, but what it takes to break him.

Talley sat, hunched, knees together, arms crossed, hands under his arms for warmth. He did not, he knew, present a heroic figure. He did not feel heroic.

No food was brought to him. His stomach growled, and hunger made him tireder. No sounds of other people reached him. For hours beyond his reckoning he sat and thought; and when they brought him back to Colonel Suk's office, he had determined what he would do.

"I came to Czechoslovakia to try to see Janos Czerny."

Colonel Suk looked almost surprised for an instant. "I am pleased that you have made the intelligent choice," he said.

"Thank you. Now I'd like to see someone from the American embassy. And I want you to be there, and I want us both to acknowledge that I'm assisting you with your investigation, and that in recognition of that you're not going to press charges, and you're going to release me. Then I'll answer your questions."

Colonel Suk fell back in his swivel chair and let his hands drop from the desktop into his lap. "Mr. Talley," he said in wonderment, "are you trying to play a game with me? Do you believe I will announce that you are to be released, and then you can refuse to cooperate?"

"No. Yes, I am trying to play a game with you, but not that one. I just want to make sure that if I do cooperate, you won't go ahead and throw me in prison anyway. I figure that if you agree to let me go—publicly—and then don't, it's going to be pretty embarrassing for you and it'll be hard for you to get anybody else to make a deal in the future. I don't know much about this business, Colonel; but I guess this sort of situation must occur frequently enough for you not to want a reputation for bad faith.

"On the other side, if I don't talk, then you've always got your 'other methods.' You can break me, and make me talk, and then let me go, and I can't really make any complaint—the only reason for you to hurt me would be because I tried to cross you."

Suk stared across at Talley out of wide eyes, the hint of a smile on his lips.

"Now," Talley went on, "here's the game I'm willing to play: I was sent here to investigate the Czerny-Hovey thing. That's obvious, I'm not telling you anything. I've just told you one other thing that ought to be obvious, too: I was trying to get to talk to Janos Czerny. I told the CIA guy in charge of the investigation that Czerny is the only person whom we haven't talked to who really knows about this thing. But, of course, I was wrong. You know about it—better than anybody else.

"So, Colonel Suk—Dr. Benda, whoever you want to be—I'll cooperate with you as a way of getting you to cooperate with me. I'm not going to try to be clever, or think I can trick you and you won't know what I'm doing. Let's just recognize that we both know that when a person asks a question he also is telling something."

Suk leaned forward again, his forearms on the desk. He rubbed his hands together and clasped them. "That is not entirely true, Mr. Talley. I have told you that I wish to know everything about your investigation. I could let you talk on and on, taking down all you say, without indicating which statements are of particular interest. Should I wish to ask questions, I might ask dozens, only a few of which are pertinent."

"Yeah. Maybe so. But I won't play that way. I'll answer your questions, but you'll have to ask them specifically. I won't just talk from a single lead."

"Mr. Talley, I cannot decide whether you are childlike in

your naïveté or one of the shrewdest agents I have ever met. In either case, you are a delight. Please tell me—I can hardly wait to hear your answer—why you think I will play your game instead of simply . . . tickling your feet . . . until you tell me what I want to know."

"I don't know, Colonel. I guess you have some reason, since you offered to deal in the first place. Maybe you think breaking me would take a while"—Talley looked directly into Suk's eyes—"and I would certainly try to make it take a while, and you figure to get what you want quicker if I help."

Suk continued to stare at Talley for a moment, then turned, pressed a button on the telephone, spoke into the receiver, hung it up again, turned back.

"The American embassy is being called. Someone should be here within two hours. In the meantime, you will be given something to eat, and you may wash." He pressed a button under the edge of his desk. Instantly the office door opened and the guards who had brought Talley in reappeared. Suk spoke to them.

Talley rose.

"We shall play your game, Mr. Talley." Suk was smiling, but he looked up at Talley piercingly. "However, there will be penalties for cheating."

Talley ate the coarse bread and honey, warmed his hands and insides with the big bowl of thin coffee. He washed at the little sink, then lay on the bed. This new cell was warm, its walls painted a creamy beige. It even had a little window. Talley could hear birds cheeping in the courtyard outside. He recognized that he had moved up in the world.

Despite all the comforts, he still felt ill. He felt as he had once as a young child, able to dog-paddle but not yet really to swim, when he realized he had gotten himself to the deep end of the pool.

While waiting for the American embassy officer, Colonel Suk filled sheets of ruled paper with questions he might ask Talley. He was delighted. This man not only would give information but would eagerly accept and carry back what Suk told him. Of course, the telling must be concealed in such a way that Talley could neither fail to find it nor doubt he'd done so by his own cleverness. Colonel Suk selected his words and set them down slowly with his old fountain pen. From time to time he paused, and let his mind drift in search of other ways he might make use of Talley. None came at the moment; but he felt sure that they would.

The guards brought Talley to a different office. It was spacious, with a couch and armchairs on one side opposite a row of windows. A desk and visitors' chairs stood at the end before a wall covered with shelves of books. Colonel Suk sat behind the desk. Another man, seated in front of the desk, turned and then rose as Talley entered.

"George Tillinghast," he said, "from the American embassy."

"I'm Thomas Talley." Talley extended his hand.

Tillinghast hesitated, looking questioningly at Talley as though giving him time to withdraw the identification before a handshake confirmed it.

Talley nodded, Tillinghast shook his hand, and they both sat.

"Colonel Suk has acquainted me with the allegations on the basis of which you are being held; namely, that you entered Czechoslovakia using false—"

Talley interrupted. "I'm here on behalf of the CIA."

Tillinghast's mouth remained open for a moment. "I . . . ah . . . Well."

"Mr. Talley has agreed to cooperate with us on an investigation we are conducting. In return, we have agreed to drop all charges against him, and to allow him to return to Austria as soon as we no longer require his assistance."

Tillinghast looked at Talley carefully. "You have agreed?"

"Yes. When you report this, tell the people who'll want to know that I think it's the best way for me to continue what I was working on."

"Well." After three years' duty in Prague, Tillinghast had learned that in matters concerning any intelligence services it is impossible to imagine what invisible wheels may be turning secretly within other wheels. "If you say so." He shrugged a pin-striped shoulder.

Shock had not dulled his carefully trained sensitivity to nuance, however. "Tell me, Colonel Suk, do you have any thought about how long you might require Mr. Talley's assistance? I shouldn't think Mr. Talley would want to commit himself to an open-ended situation."

"It is difficult to say. But that does not mean Mr. Talley's commitment is without end. In return for his cooperation, we have agreed not to bring charges. There are laws limiting how long a person may be held without charges."

"I understand that there are, Colonel. I also understand that sometimes they are not strictly observed."

"If any unfortunate lapse should occur in the case of an American citizen, Mr. Tillinghast, I am sure your embassy would call it to our attention."

Tillinghast raised an eyebrow to Talley. "Is this okay?"

"I think it's the best choice I've got."

"Okay. I hope you know what you're doing. We'll try to keep in touch."

When Tillinghast had gone, Colonel Suk motioned for Talley to take his chair again, and went around the desk to his own. He sat, took a sheet of paper from the stack at his elbow, uncapped the fountain pen, and nodded. "Shall we begin?"

Talley had set both feet flat on the floor, his hands on his knees. He was ready. "Sure. The sooner the better."

"When did you begin working for the Central Intelligence Agency?"

"You mean this time? I guess last week."

"When was the first time?"

"1967."

Colonel Suk wrote each answer on a separate line, forming the words carefully and without haste.

"What were your duties?"

"I analyzed product from Southeast Asia."

The first questions were routine: queries to which Suk must already know the answers. Talley recognized that they were asked merely to establish the habit of his answering, and to set a rhythm.

"You did not work in the field—gathering intelligence?"

"That's right."

"And you resigned?"

"That's right, in 1971."

Talley had expected the interrogation to be tape-recorded, with questions coming one upon another so that he wouldn't have time to think about his responses, so that any hesitation would itself be noteworthy.

"You resigned in anger? There was bad feeling between you and your superiors?"

"That's right."

Although the venetian blinds were tipped, light was bright behind them. The windows were open: a breeze stirred the blinds from time to time, and Talley could hear the courtyard birds clearly again.

"And you had no further contact with the CIA until two years ago?"

"I kept in touch with a couple of people who were personal friends. Just occasionally. It wouldn't have looked good for them to be close to me. I had no official contact with the agency. I wasn't employed by them."

"But you were called upon two years ago to assist in the Czerny-Hovey investigation?"

"Yes."

"Why? Since you had had no contact, since you had parted with bad feelings."

"That's exactly the kind of person Walter Simson—the man I had worked under—wanted. It was suspected that there was a mole in the agency. Walter wanted help in investigating that from someone he trusted, but someone who people outside the agency would also trust not to cover up."

"What further contact have you had with the CIA since then?"

"None."

Suk looked up. "None at all?"

"You must know how it ended. I took Hovey away from them. They sure wanted nothing more to do with me after that; and I never had wanted anything to do with them."

"Yet they called you again for your help . . . when was it?"

"Last week. Tuesday. About eight-fifteen in the morning."

"Why—if there was such mutual antipathy—why did they call on you?"

"Because I'd worked on the original investigation."

"But you had betrayed them."

"No. I took Hovey away from them, but all my investigating was sound. My conclusions were the ones they adopted. They don't like me, but I guess they put some value on my judgment—about the facts, anyway."

"Who called you?"

"Walter Simson."

"He is in charge of this investigation?"

"No. He's actually retired from the agency now. They got him to call because he's an old friend."

"Who is in charge of the investigation?"

"I don't know." Talley hesitated for one instant. Although Suk's face was as blank as ever, Talley somehow realized the man knew the answer, that the question was a test. "The man in charge of the part I'm doing is Steve McCluskie."

Suk wrote that, then asked, "What were you asked to do?"

The atmosphere, the rhythm of the interview gave Talley a sense of confidence. He had decided to think about his answers, but not to analyze the questions. He would repeat each question to himself to set it in memory, but not think about what they might tell him until later.

"To look over the Czerny-Hovey material to see if there might be anything we'd missed. To come over to Vienna and talk to D'Avignon again."

"Why was the matter raised again?" Suk asked without pausing to write.

"I wasn't told."

"Didn't you ask?"

"No."

"Were you not curious? Did you not think the reason for reopening the investigation must be itself evidence you should analyze?"

"It wasn't my job to deal with it. My job was very narrowly defined."

"How was it defined?"

"As I told you, it was only to look over the material I had dealt with previously."

"You assumed that other people were looking at other material?"

"I assumed so."

"Why?"

"It seemed reasonable to assume that."

"Do you *know* that other people are investigating other material?"

"Put that way, no, I don't."

Suk looked steadily at Talley for a moment, then poised his pen again. "What material did you look over?"

"Everything that we'd had before."

"Of what did that consist?"

"The report from the attaché in Vienna. Report from our Prague embassy. Report from our man in Paris. My interview with D'Avignon. Hovey's debriefing. My own report and conclusions."

Suk continued writing for several moments. Beyond the bird sounds the steady city traffic hummed. A propeller-driven airplane droned over at a distance. "Nothing new?"

"No."

Suk held the pen ready again, but didn't write. "Nothing new. And yet the matter suddenly is reopened. Why do you think that would be?"

"I told you, I don't know."

"I know you did. I asked you what you think might be the reason."

Involuntarily Talley caught his breath. "I didn't think about it. That's one of the things you learn: compartmentalize, don't think about what you're not supposed to think about."

Suk put his pen down. "Mr. Talley, you are trying to cheat. You are not cooperating. Our compact is based on your agreement to answer my questions. If you tell me you did not think—speculate, privately—about this matter, I must tell you I know you are lying."

Sweat suddenly ran down Talley's ribs, chilling him. He almost shuddered. "Okay. I did speculate. Walter Simson called me the morning after that guy Murtaugh was killed trying to defect. I told you what day the call came, you've already got it figured out for yourself. My private speculation was that the agency thinks Murtaugh might have been the one who gave Czerny away—that it was an inside job after all."

Suk nodded, picked up the pen. "But you were given no material relating to Murtaugh to consider?"

"No. That would have involved me in things I didn't need to know about."

Suk wrote, then asked, "So you looked over all of the old material. Did it suggest that your previous conclusions had been in error?"

"No."

Suk wrote. "Did it suggest lines of investigation you had overlooked?"

"No."

Suk wrote. "Not even in relation to M. D'Avignon? Then why did you wish to question him again?"

"Because he was always the one we suspected. If there hadn't been a penetration in the agency, then D'Avignon had to be the one who'd betrayed Czerny."

"And what conclusion did you reach after talking with M. D'Avignon again?"

"When we talked with him, he told us a different version of his story, so we were more suspicious. When he tried to kill us, well, then we were pretty sure."

"So you now are satisfied that he was the person who betrayed Janos Czerny?"

"Yes."

Suk didn't write. He looked at Talley. "I detect equivocation."

"We have no doubt he was working for you."

"But? And? However?"

"I tell you—unequivocally—that we're sure he was working for you."

"Then why did you wish to speak with Janos Czerny?"

"We're thorough."

Again Suk laid down his pen. "I may become annoyed. If you were satisfied about the role of M. D'Avignon, then why undertake an adventure so full of risk as attempting to speak with Czerny? 'Thoroughness' does not justify such a risk if the conclusion is already certain."

Talley recognized the question as reasonable. He nodded, more to assure himself that he could handle it than to show Suk he agreed. "Even though D'Avignon was your man, you could also have had someone inside the agency. Czerny—supposedly—sent a duplicate of the material you fed him. I'm not telling you anything: even if you didn't plant that material yourself, you knew about it. Your killing Alexandrovitch proved that. Czerny supposedly used an alternate network not only to make sure the material got out but also to tell us he had been betrayed by a mole. By talking to him, I could find out whether he really did that. If the duplicate is news to him, then you planted it to shake up the agency—which it did. But you wouldn't have made us look for a penetration if there really was one, so that would prove Murtaugh wasn't working for you then."

Suk leaned back, looking at Talley levelly. "So that is what you were sent—at such great risk—to discover?"

"Yes."

"Again: your conclusion two years ago had been that M. D'Avignon was the betrayer, not someone in the CIA?"

"Yes."

"You were shown no new material to make you doubt that conclusion?"

"That's right."

"Yet the CIA has you return to question him again; and sends you to talk with Janos Czerny: all this effort and risk to reinvestigate a conclusion that there is no reason to doubt."

"They doubted this one, Colonel. The reason has to be that they discovered you did have an agent inside—Murtaugh."

"What would lead the CIA to believe that Murtaugh was our agent two years ago?"

"Finding out that he was now, I guess. I don't know. I really don't."

"But does it seem reasonable to you that discovering Murtaugh's defection, which *could only* have happened recently" —Suk seemed to catch himself, then went on hurriedly— "according to our evidence, would cause the CIA to doubt soundly based conclusions made two years ago?"

"Yes. That seems reasonable to me."

"Would you have doubted those conclusions? They were your own conclusions, were they not? Did learning about Murtaugh's defection cause you to doubt them?"

"I would certainly have wanted to look into it."

"Did you doubt your conclusions?"

"No. I didn't doubt them. But I still would have looked them over again."

"Thoroughness."

"That's right."

After a moment Suk leaned forward, forearms on the desk. "Does it strike you that this investigation is excessively—even ostentatiously—thorough?"

"What do you mean?"

"Does it strike you that the CIA is making a great show of not knowing when Murtaugh became our agent?"

"I . . . no, it doesn't."

Suk stared long enough for Talley to feel the force of his own pulse.

"You are lying again."

"No . . . I . . . No, I'm not. That suggestion shook me, because I wouldn't want to think I'd been sent in here just for some kind of show. And because I'm realizing that there's a lot going on here that I don't know anything about. I really don't. What I do know—I believe this to be the absolute truth—is that the agency is really serious about this investigation."

"That is what you believe?"

"That's what I believe."

Suk nodded as though he had noted the answer without necessarily accepting it. "What would you think if I told you that Murtaugh was not our agent two years ago; that Czerny's entrapment—and the entire affair—was totally executed from here?"

"I guess I wouldn't believe you. I'd probably think Murtaugh or somebody else on our side must have been involved."

"The principle of reversal: any information your enemy gives you must be false."

Talley shrugged.

Suk shuffled back through his notes. "So let us go back a little: again, what—exactly—what evidence caused the CIA to doubt the conclusion that we had no mole inside it two years ago?"

Talley took a quiet breath. This is how it would be, he had known: the same questions repeated to see if they would bring the same answers. He tried to reassure himself: he'd told the truth, he had nothing to fear. "To go back: again, I saw no new evidence. The discovery of a defector now would, I think, be reason enough to review the conclusion."

Suk's eyes gleamed. "You do?"

Talley tried not to be alarmed by the sharpness. "Yes."

"Reason enough to send someone—someone who is not

even a regular, professional agent—into danger? Was the conclusion thrown that much into doubt?"

Why was Suk pressing him? "We doubted it. I doubted it."

"You doubted it? I thought you said . . ." Suk shuffled again. "Yes, here, I asked you if anything in the old material caused you to doubt your former conclusion. Your answer: 'No.' I asked you whether your conclusion two years ago had been that M. D'Avignon was the betrayer, not someone in the CIA. Your answer: 'Yes.' I asked again, 'You were shown no new material to make you doubt that conclusion?' Your answer: 'That's right.' And here I ask, 'You were given no material relating to Murtaugh to consider?' Your answer: 'No.'

"In short, you have said over and over that you have no reason to doubt your conclusion, but now you say you doubt it. I say I believe what you have told me over and over. I say there is no doubt. I say this investigation is a hoax!"

Talley sat still for some time. The deep end of the pool was far deeper than he had thought. He had to float before he could begin paddling again. Finally he said, "Colonel Suk, if there is a hoax, I'm not part of it. I really want you to believe that. I sure as hell did not come in here, risking ten years in prison, and—what? having my balls electrified?—to play some trick on you.

"I'm here—frankly—because I think *you* are trying to trick *us*. I told you I didn't doubt the original conclusion. I don't, even though I can see that Murtaugh's defection brings it at least up for review. The thing that made me doubt what's going on was D'Avignon nearly killing me to prove that my conclusion about him was *right*. I can't make any sense of that, not even by trying to reverse it. But I believe it's part of some hoax that you're pulling, and I wanted to find out what it was.

"Now, I don't know anything about Murtaugh. I don't have any theories. I don't know what the CIA knows, or thinks, or is doing, or thinks it's doing. I just knew something was fishy, and I wanted to find out about it because I am thorough. I get hooked on problems, I want to know everything—in other words, because I'm a stupid, stubborn idiot, and I've let it get me in real trouble again."

For several moments Suk glared at Talley. Then suddenly he sat back and smiled. "Mr. Talley, I believe you! You are indeed a delight. I cannot tell you how unusual it is in my business to meet a man like yourself, a man who speaks frankly and tells the truth."

Suk positively beamed, and—despite himself—Talley felt pleased and proud.

Without turning his favor from Talley, Suk stared away toward an upper corner of the room. "Yes, yes," he said. "So." Then he looked at Talley again, his eyes gleaming. "Yes. Such a virtue should not go unrewarded, Mr. Talley. I think you should be allowed—I think you should be *assisted* in reaching your goal. I think you should have your meeting with Janos Czerny."

For a moment Talley stared back, stunned. "You're going to let me see Czerny?"

"Certainly."

"Why?"

"Because we have the same goal, Mr. Talley: to learn the truth!"

CHAPTER 10

"Hello, Professor Boudreau. How are you?'' McCluskie was standing in the small lobby when Jane rushed down from her room.

''Where's Tom? What's wrong?''

''Tom's just fine, just fine. Everything's—''

''Where is he? He said he'd be back late this afternoon, and it's eight o'clock!''

''He's been delayed. That's why I came to see you. I wanted to let you know everything is okay.''

''Where is he?''

''Could we step outside? I've got a car parked just down the street. Could we talk there?''

Jane hesitated for a moment, then started for the door. Without seeming to rush, McCluskie reached it in time to open it for her. He gestured, ''Just over there. This is really a nice-looking hotel,'' he said before she could demand anything of him. ''Small, but it has real character. How did you and Tom find it?'' He walked beside her, yet turned toward her in a way that made it seem he was leading and following her at the same time.

''I had been here before,'' her nonanswer the best resistance she could make against the force of his apparently sincere interest.

''Terrific location, right here in the old city. You know that church—up there at the top of the steps—that church is the oldest one in Vienna!''

"Yes, I know."

McCluskie's car stood in a no-parking zone just beyond the entrance to the little plaza. "Here we are." He opened the door for her.

He went around and got in on the driver's side.

"Now, what I wanted to ask you, Professor, was—"

"Tell me about Tom!"

"Okay. Of course. Sorry, I should have said right away that we've gotten a message from him, and he's fine. There's been a delay in his getting back, but he is perfectly all right."

"You mean he's still in Czechoslovakia?"

"That's right. You knew he was going to Czechoslovakia?"

"Of course."

"Tom told you."

"Of course," she said even more firmly.

"When was that?"

"Yesterday morning, before he left."

"Did he . . . Do you think he told anyone else?"

"Certainly not. Who would he have told? No. He was being so conscientious about your damned security that he wasn't even going to tell me! What's wrong?"

"I told you, Professor, Tom's okay. But we've learned that the fact he was going to Czechoslovakia did leak out. Naturally we want to try to find out how that happened. Now, did you and he discuss this—where he was going—talk about it in public, say?"

"No. We were in our room—in the hotel. We had a fight about it, as a matter of fact. And then he left."

"And of course you wouldn't have told anybody about it, yourself. We can be sure about that, can't we?"

"You certainly may."

McCluskie nodded vigorously, as though in full agreement with her assertion. "Well, then, the leak is probably someplace else entirely. However, we may just want to check to see who's staying in the rooms next to yours, and above and below. Or look at the view from your room. It's amazing about these long-range mikes these days. They can pick up a conversation from a distance, even through window glass."

"You mean they might have been spying on us the whole—"

"Probably not, Professor. It's just a possibility to be considered. I'm sure there's not really anything to worry—"

"Nothing to worry about! I don't believe you. You've lied about this. . . . You've done nothing but lie from the very beginning! You told Tom there would be no danger, and someone tried to kill him! You told him there would be no danger with this trip, and now you say— Where is he? What's happened?"

McCluskie held up both palms. "Professor, Professor . . . You've got every reason to be upset, but I am telling you the truth—as best I know it. I have all along. Now I'll tell you about Tom: we've received word from our embassy in Prague. A man from the embassy spoke with Tom this afternoon. He's fine. He's being well treated. He's cooperating with the Czech authorities, and they've promised to release him as soon—"

"He's been arrested!"

"Not exactly, I guess. I mean, he was intercepted; but apparently—"

"When is he going to be released?"

"We don't know exactly: as soon as they've gotten whatever information they think he can—"

"So he is under arrest! They're holding him—as a spy; it must be. You said he was all right!"

"He is all right. Now, Professor, I'm telling you—"

"You lie! All you do is lie! You use people, and you lie— Let me out of here!" Jane flung the door open.

"Professor, wait just a minute!"

But Jane was out of the car and running back to the hotel.

"Jane? It's me.

"Yes. I'm okay, I'm—

"He did? Well, it's true.

"No, I'm okay. I'm in Prague.

"Well . . . Czech intelligence.

"Yes. Somehow they knew I was coming.

"Maybe. I guess they could have found out that way. I'll ask them." Talley glanced at Colonel Suk, who stood a few steps away, looking out the window of his office. Suk had explained the call could not be private; he seemed to be trying to be as discreet as he could.

"Yes, really. They're treating me just fine. I've had hotel rooms that were—

"No! No, Jane. Don't do anything. There's nothing you can do.

"No, I don't think Senator Kennedy could. Now, this is a bad situation, but it's not too bad. I've made a deal. I can't talk about it, except that it's turning out better than anybody could have hoped. And in a couple of days it'll all be over, and they'll let me go.

"I can trust them because they wouldn't have any reason—

"Jane, please. No, you can't come here. That wouldn't do any good.

"Absolutely not! The press would be the last thing—

"Listen to me! There is nothing you can do, and you'll only mess things up if you try to do something!

"I'm sorry. I know you were.

"I know you are. That's why I got them to let me call you; so I could tell you I'm all right.

"Yes. Really.

"Yes. Try not to worry.

"I know. Try.

"I don't know if they'll let me, but I will if I can. But if you don't hear from me, that doesn't mean anything's wrong.

"Yes. I will.

"Yes.

"And I love you, Jane."

Talley put the receiver down. He sighed.

Colonel Suk waited another moment before turning to speak. "So," he said. "I hope your friend was relieved."

"Yes. Thank you."

"She must be extremely concerned about you."

"Yes, she is."

"It seemed"—Suk cleared his throat in what might have been an apology for knowing what had been said—"that she was determined to attempt something on your behalf."

"Yes. I think I convinced her there was nothing she could do, and that she shouldn't try."

"Yes. That is best. Still, her concern and determination must be very deep."

For an instant, Talley thought Suk's look was not merely appreciative, but appraising. Then the old man smiled warmly. "And admirable," he said.

* * *

At four-thirty Jane fell asleep again over her book, but a noise in the street startled her at five-fifty. She put the book aside and turned out the bedside lamp and lay there for another fifteen minutes. Then she gave it up, got up, showered and dressed. When she came downstairs, the girl was just setting tables for breakfast.

Jane ate two *Brötchen* slowly, since she wasn't hungry, and since taking time over breakfast gave her something to occupy her. Afterward, because the city offered nothing to do at that hour but bustle with the people going to work, she tried reading again. Finally she went out to walk.

Clouds scudded low overhead. The air felt clammy. In the entire past week rain had fallen only once at night, and—in a brief shower—one afternoon. Clear weather couldn't last unbroken. It would have been presumptuous to believe the weather had changed because of her mood.

Coming out of the hotel, she turned left to the street, the Tiefergraben, and then left again, intending to wander up to the Burgring. Without registering the fact as significant, she noticed that a man got out of a car on the other side of Tiefergraben just as she turned onto it. Then, when she turned once more to take the enclosed stairway up to the Wipplingerstrasse, which crossed over Tiefergraben there, she saw the man had come to her side of the street and wasn't far behind her.

All concrete—steps, walls, ceiling—the stairway stank and always seemed dank and dangerous to her. There was no real reason for fear. The passage ran straight without turns or alcoves that might conceal an assailant. Morning light came in from both ends. Passersby could look up or down it. Yet she hurried whenever she used it. This time she went up even quicker, then paused three quarters of the way to the top. The man turned in behind her.

Jane whirled and dashed up the remaining steps. She whipped around the railing at the top, and, half running, headed in the opposite direction from the rise of the stairway.

Through the railing, the man had seen the direction she took. He sprinted up the last steps, and as he came to the top grabbed the railing to come around after her—and there she was! She had spun and was bearing down on him.

"Are you following me?"

For an instant the man looked nonplussed. "Yes, m'am," he stammered.

"Why!"

"Mr. McCluskie thought we should just keep an eye on you."

"Why? Mr. McCluskie has been at great pains to assure me there is no danger to anyone. If that's true, then why should it be necessary for you to keep an eye on me? If it's not true, then I'd like to be told exactly what the danger is."

"Well, m'am, I'm sure that what Mr. McCluskie said is the truth. We're sure not *expecting* any danger to you. But I mean, I guess it's just *possible* that the people who are holding Mr. Talley might want to find a way to put pressure on you so as to influence him. We don't *believe* that's so, but Mr. McCluskie's the sort of man . . . well, he wouldn't want to be wrong about something like that and not have been prepared. That's all it is, m'am."

"I see. So I'm to have the pleasure of your company wherever I go."

"I hope you won't find that offensive, m'am. My partner and I will try to stay out of your way. If you'd just tell us where you're going to be going . . ."

"What's your name?"

"Parker, m'am. Bob Parker."

"Well, Bob, I do find your following me offensive. Nothing personal, of course. I know you're just doing your job, and you're trying to be polite about it. But I hate the idea of being watched; and—in my actual experience—the only reason the CIA takes an interest in people is to use them. And your using people puts them in danger, it doesn't protect them."

"Well, I'm sorry, m'am. But it's something we have to do."

"What if I decline your company? What if I tell you to stop following me?"

"I'm afraid it wouldn't make any difference, m'am. We'd still have to do it."

"What if I make a scene? Call a policeman?"

"I don't know, m'am. I'd identify myself, of course. And then the police would want to know why we were following you—whether there really was a danger: that'd be of concern to them. And Mr. McCluskie would have to talk to them. I don't know how it would turn out: whether they'd make us stop watching out for you, or say you had to leave the country to solve the problem that way. I just don't know. But it would pretty well shoot the day, I would think."

"I see." Jane looked at the man steadily for a moment. Then she smiled. "All right. I'm going over to one of the department stores on Tuchlaben. I suppose you might as well walk with me as trail along behind."

"Thank you, m'am. Just a minute while I call my partner." Parker touched his jacket lapel and spoke, as if to no one, "Scott, want to bring the car around?" To Jane he said, "And if we can take you anyplace, m'am . . . we've got the car."

"Thank you, Bob. That's very kind of you. Perhaps later. Maybe this won't be so bad after all."

On the four-block walk to the department store, Jane chatted pleasantly enough with Bob Parker. She explained again that she did not find fault with him personally, only with the idea of being followed. He said he understood completely.

When they arrived she said, "I'm going in to buy some lingerie. I'm going to be trying things on in the fitting room. I'm afraid you can't come in with me there, but I suppose you can stand by the counter."

"I think I'll just stand out here, m'am. I think that'll be all right."

"All right, Bob. I'll probably be fifteen minutes or a little longer."

"Okay, m'am. Thanks."

For the first fifteen minutes after coming out of the store's other entrance, Jane had been filled with the excitement of the game and the glee of winning it. She had gone around the clock museum, down an alley, through the arch and out at the front of the Am Hof church, wound through side streets, and finally come to the Volksgarten. Certain by then that Parker and his partner would never find her, she sat down on a bench at the edge of the rose garden. Gradually her elation left her, and—perhaps in reaction—she found herself falling into despondency again.

A small party of appallingly energetic early-rising tourists read to one another from guidebooks about the Theseus temple. They thought the building was very nice, but it was a shame they let people write things like that on it. Jane shoved her hands farther down into her raincoat pockets.

Tom had said there was nothing to worry about. He'd sounded confident.

He'd told her there was nothing to worry about when he left to go into Czechoslovakia! Damn him! Damn him.

Damn him for his ridiculous sense of responsibility, and his insistence on finding out everything, and his infantile macho masculine pride—all of those things she loved him for—that McCluskie had snared him with, and used to make him—

Damn McCluskie! Damn the CIA! They'd let Tom rot in a Czech prison forever, for all they cared about him!

She took a breath and sighed and shook her head. There she was, going around it all again: worry, then anger, then worry again. She had to do something other than think about it.

She decided to go back to the art museum.

First she scanned around, just to be sure the CIA men hadn't caught up with her, or that there wasn't another team of them. God, she was getting paranoid, she thought.

She saw no one loitering who didn't look like a legitimate sightseer. Two kids with backpacks stood studying a city map. A man wearing a burgundy turtleneck and a camel-colored jacket that set off his dark handsomeness was beyond the temple, coming along the path to the right in her direction. An elderly woman sat on a bench feeding pigeons and sparrows. Those people, and the few others in the park at that hour, looked innocent. Way over past the rose garden, near the café, was a man in a spylike leather jacket, but he was reading a notice on a kiosk, not looking in her direction at all.

Abruptly Jane rose and went out to the Ring and turned left to go to the museum. She passed where leather-jacket had been, and peered through the bushes to see if he was still reading (which she would have thought suspicious). He wasn't there at all. She did see him again when she reached the pedestrian crossing and stood out at the curb looking toward oncoming traffic. He must have left the Volksgarten before she did. He was down the Ring, nearly two blocks ahead of her. He didn't look back.

* * *

In agony the women implored the soldiers to relent. Those doing the work ignored them, or held back, or dragged the children from their hands, looking angry about the difficulty the mothers were causing. A pair of red-tunicked men on horseback—probably officers—watched from one side with no apparent concern except to see that the operation was carried out thoroughly.

Jane had gone first to the Breughels. The museum had just opened, so she had a chance of looking at them again before the bus-tour people were brought through. But she turned from *The Slaughter of the Innocents* almost at once. The lusty peasants on the other side of the room didn't jolly her. Supposedly festive, they looked to her deadened by drink and the dullness of their lives.

She went to see if the Italian masters could cheer, or at least distract, her. They certainly tried to do so. On every side they offered to sweep her away in sensation, passion. She drifted toward the center of the room, glanced slowly around as though deciding which particular invitation to accept. Her attention was caught, though, by a man examining a picture next to the archway through which she had entered.

She would have noticed him in any case, because he was tall and dark and sharply handsome, and carried himself with an inner elegance. He was wearing a burgundy turtleneck and a camel-colored jacket.

For a few moments she looked at Mars importuning Venus, or Venus enticing Mars (it was hard to tell); or perhaps it was Venus and Adonis. Or another couple entirely. She strolled farther, and saw St. Someone and some angels regarding each other with the same kinds of expressions as the people in the previous painting. She glanced back toward it. The man had moved to it. He stood at the far side, so she could see his face. His look was of deep admiration. She saw his eyes shift from the painting to her. His expression didn't change.

She turned away and went on into the next room. He didn't follow her. That is, he might have spent a moment more with the picture he seemed to like before coming to see what further delights could be found. He glanced at the painting on the wall by the archway, then to the one on the wall to his left. Jane stood in front of a picture farther down that wall. Moving slowly, the man passed two canvases, paused at the third. Jane went to the next one over. The man moved to the one next to her.

Other people in the room whispered as they discussed the pictures. Their footsteps scraped softly on the parquet floor. Light came into the room from the large central skylight, colorless, almost directionless.

The man came to the edge of the painting she stood before, as though to join her in looking at it. She turned her head, he smiled slightly—no more than might have been a polite acknowledgment of their proximity. She did not return even that courtesy. She looked at him coldly, then pivoted and went on into the next gallery.

But she wasn't going to let herself be driven from the museum. She would not allow this man to control her, even negatively by making her avoid him. She went to the circle of straight-backed, gray velour-covered couches in the center of the room, and sat.

For a moment she put her hands behind her, stretching her back against stiffened arms, then composed herself and prepared to wait. Ten minutes? Fifteen? An hour? She had nothing else to do. He'd certainly be able to appreciate the paintings thoroughly before she got up again. And make himself more and more ridiculous.

Jane had no fear of the man, other than the usual one of a really tacky advance. More and more people were coming into the museum. And if—by that peculiar working of the law of averages in galleries—at some moments after the room had been almost crowded it then emptied completely, a guard standing at the far end of the next room had her in sight.

The man came in. He did study several of the paintings extremely carefully, but not to the point of making himself a fool. Finally he simply paused at one side of the room until one of those empty moments, then came over to her.

"I beg your pardon," he said. He had a good voice, nicely modulated, very suave. Excellent English, although he was European.

She wondered what line he would use. She opened her arsenal of rejoinders.

"I believe we have a mutual acquaintance," he said.

Ah, yes, that one.

"Thomas Talley," he said.

Jane stared up at him, dumbfounded.

"Permit me to introduce myself," he said. "My name is Anton Korda. I am a captain in the Czechoslovak Intelligence Service." He tipped his head in a way that was almost a bow. "May I sit down?"

Dazed, Jane moved sideways. Anton sat, politely on the edge of the couch and not too close to her. "Thank you." He adjusted the creases of his trousers, then laid one hand over the other on his thigh. "Now, the reason I have—"

"How . . . how did you . . ."

"Know you were here? We followed you from your hotel. I do apologize for that; but I wanted to speak with you without the presence of . . . third parties."

"But I . . . *How* did you follow me? I . . ."

"Yes. The way you evaded the CIA: that was quite clever. But not to think badly of them. They were not trying to hide their presence from you. We used many more men, spread widely: it didn't matter what evasions you took within a given area, we had it ringed. I tell you this so that you will see I am being completely honest with you. Now, are you over your shock?" Anton smiled encouragingly. "May I tell you why we have done all this?"

"Please."

"Good. Your friend Thomas is assisting us with certain investigations. He is being very helpful, and we are grateful to him; and I have no doubt that he will be able to return to Vienna in the very near future. However, we believe his return can be made most quickly with your help."

"How!"

"By coming, briefly, to Czechoslovakia yourself."

"What! Why?"

"These affairs are extremely complex, and some aspects of them are of a confidential nature. I'm afraid I cannot . . ." Anton caught the sudden intensifying of mistrust in Jane's face. "Of course you will be suspicious of whatever I tell you. Naturally so. But may I ask whether there is anything in particular that causes you to mistrust me?"

"How do I know you don't just want to get me in there to put more pressure on Tom?"

"Yes, indeed. I can well understand why you might fear that. I assure you that although our business has its unadmirable aspects, we do not countenance acts like—"

"Oh, bullshit! Bullshit, Mr.—Captain—Korda. Whoever you are. I do not believe a thing you say!"

Anton rocked back before her anger. He spread his hands and shrugged. "You may believe me or not believe me, Professor Boudreau. This is what I have to tell you. We do not need to put pressure on Thomas Talley. He is cooperating with us fully. He will be released. However, there are complexities in this situation. He may be released soon, or he may be released later—at some unforeseeable date in the future. The chance of sooner rather than later will be immensely improved by your spending about twenty-four hours in Czechoslovakia. You will be returned to Vienna at the end of that time, because it is to our purpose that you should be. What you wish to believe, and what choice you make, is entirely up to you."

CHAPTER 11

Janos Czerny again laid aside the weather map and report. He certainly had no need of the report to tell him a drizzle descended steadily from the close and lumpy sky. The printed information that a complex low extended over most of Western Europe from the Netherlands to Poland merely defined more exactly what he already knew. Dampness made his knees and fingers ache, and low pressure weighed on him like a sodden overcoat. The meteorologist's prediction that this weather would continue for several days only agreed with what he could see for himself as he looked out the window of his room in the Post Hotel at the unmoving clouds.

Despite the weight of the day, and his pain and fatigue, he held himself erect. That doing so allowed him to look down on most other men wasn't the point. Indeed, as an actor had once said viciously but accurately, Czerny would look down on everyone else even if lying in a hole in the ground. At this moment, in fact, he was alone. He kept his spine straight, his white-bristled head high, and looked slightly down his beak of a nose because to slump would be an offense against himself.

He had been looking at the weather map. The report's long-range prediction was good: a broad high-pressure system over the Atlantic might be expected to arrive in about five days. It was perfect. A high-pressure system would bring the intense, clear sky and the brilliant "sun of Austerlitz" he had to have. Moreover, after all the warmish wetness, a cold front would mean morning fog—real fog—which the fog machines and animation (if needed at all) would merely supplement.

Napoleon's strategy at Austerlitz had been to appear to be withdrawing from the superior force of the combined Austrian and Russian armies. He had left the heights of Pratzen unoccupied—a sure sign he had no intention of holding his ground. His opponents quickly took that dominating position. From it, on the morning of the battle, they marched down into the fog-banked bottomland expecting to cross the river and fall upon the flank of Napoleon's retreating army. To their surprise, they found the French on the near side of the river. To their horror, they found the French attacking. The French cut through their enemies and took the heights. Partly by dividing the Austro-Russian forces and gaining the superior position, more by demoralizing opponents who found themselves attacked when they had thought they were attackers, Napoleon achieved a quick and stunning victory.

The battle had taken place on December 2. Czerny's re-creation would be filmed in June. Perhaps winter had been late coming in 1805: Napoleon wrote of the battle as taking place on "one of the finest autumn days," and there was no mention of snow or of particular cold in the descriptions. The decision to film in a warm month would therefore not violate historical authenticity drastically, while providing overwhelming practical advantages: in cold weather, bivouacking the twenty thousand soldiers would have been far more difficult and costly.

In Czerny's film the egoism and pretentiousness of the armies' commanders—strutting and sweeping in panoply and retinue—would be portrayed with scornful irony. However, directing his own forces put Czerny in a frame of mind much like theirs must have been. In addition to those twenty thousand men supplied by the Czech army to be his soldiers, he commanded the hundreds of townspeople from surrounding villages who would play their historical counterparts, the professional actors who portrayed the principal and supporting characters, the corps of costumers getting all into clothes that fit well enough for whatever distance they'd be from the camera, the squadrons of set decorators who had been anting over the landscape for two weeks already, moving, hiding, or painting anything less than 180 years old. There were the makeup artists, the electricians, the sound technicians, the special-effects people, the horse handlers, and, of course, the camera crews. Behind all of these were managers, messengers, assistants, clerks, the providers of food and lodging. Although the total was but a fraction of the host present at the actual battle of Austerlitz, it still was larger than the army with which the Greeks had taken Troy.

Czerny ordered his forces, as a supreme commander must, through his own marshals and generals, adjutants, aides, staff officers, unit commanders, and noncoms. For filming the battle, this chain of command included the second, parallel one of the Czech army units that had been involved since planning the scene began.

Coordination would be especially critical when the battle was restaged and filmed, because that could be done only once. Scenes that would appear in the finished film before and after the battle could be handled in the usual two units: Czerny, himself, directing the dramatic parts with the actors; the second unit getting the landscapes and atmospherics according to his instructions. There could be time for rehearsals and retakes. But once the battle scene started, once the sun rose above the hills and the mist started to drift, and those twenty thousand soldiers began marching, there would be no calling ''cut'' and going back and making them all do it again just slightly differently.

Some battle-scene shots could be isolated: the close-ups of soldiers waiting, a wall of figures solidifying through the fog, men flung back or crumpling, blood pellets splattering on their white waistcoats. Czerny and his staff had spent days listing every shot to be taken and identifying the ones that could be done separately. The rest—those to be taken in real-time continuity once action had started—were divided among seven camera units. Three of them would cover the Austro-Russians, three the French, and one in a helicopter would get the sweep of the battle as a whole. (Seven cameras shooting simultaneously might be unprecedented, Czerny thought. He had forgotten how many Bondarchuk used for the battles in *War and Peace*, and felt it beneath his dignity to ask.)

Czerny had never before filmed ''an epic.'' Indeed, he had originally conceived this picture—this testament to the indomitable, simple strength of common people that enabled them to suffer and eventually triumph morally over the power of the state—without any large-scale scenes whatever. He had thought to present the three emperors, the great armies, the famous battles only by report: as his common people heard of them and were affected by them. The Ministry of Culture had persuaded him differently.

Someone in the ministry evidently felt that Czerny's film would have greater "impact" if it contained some scenes of spectacle. Czerny suspected this person meant the work might enjoy greater commercial success, or (a motive only slightly less despicable) wanted, as a matter of national pride, to have it compared with *War and Peace* and Kurosawa's *Ran*, which had just been released.

Czerny had had no choice but to attend the screening of *Ran* that was arranged for him. He would have wanted to see it in any case, of course. He agreed that the battle scenes were stunning technically. He had always agreed that Kurosawa was one of the better cinema artists. However, he felt that *Ran* was deeply flawed, and did not accept that critics should call Kurosawa "the greatest living director" on the basis of his knowing how to stage a fight.

Janos Czerny was too secure in his own artistry to care about designations such as "the greatest." He held such comparisons in contempt. He did care about critical standards, though, and was angered that so much importance should be attached to a skill for handling crowd scenes—something which any director of the first rank could do if he wished.

This thought led Czerny to consider how he might have filmed *Ran*'s battles. He agreed that Kurosawa's device in the castle-taking scene—where the camera views every gory detail while sound is suppressed—was striking. However, he thought, how much more effective if the device had been reversed: if the raging battle had been heard, but not looked at: if the eye of the camera had detached itself from the petty fray and gazed over the vast, untroubled landscape.

The scene came alive in his imagination. That Olympian eye of the camera might take some notice of the fighting: look down from time to time at some particularly appalling folly—there could be close-ups, cuts from shot to shot while it did—but then the gaze would drift off slowly. The timing would have to be exquisite, of course. If he were doing it, he would direct that camera—from a helicopter—and let assistants handle the ones on the ground according to his storyboards. And he would edit them all together, as always. He saw the picture. It would brilliantly expose the inconsequentiality of power. At that moment, Czerny decided that the person in the Ministry of Culture had been right for all the wrong reasons. Yes, he would film the battle.

And so, in a way that Czerny considered appropriately Tolstoyan, forces were set in motion. Over the course of a year all the personnel and matérial were prepared. And now, after having received the report promising a cold front in five days, he and his staff had made the decision to assemble them. Most of the film people had already come to the area. Now—in three days—the twenty thousand Czech soldiers would be encamped in units all around the district.

Talley and Colonel Suk arrived at a few minutes before six in the evening. Their destination turned out to be a house set behind its own wall—it might even have been called a small villa—on the outskirts east of Brno. Talley knew where they were because Colonel Suk had told him the names of places, and all about them, as they were driven down from Prague. Colonel Suk had originally said they would fly, but the rotten weather forced a change in plan.

The house looked as if it had been built sometime in the eighteenth century to be the home of a well-to-do merchant. It must now be in the service of the state: there were uniformed guards inside each entrance, the rooms on the ground floor seemed to be offices, and large bulletin boards had been mounted over the rococo paneling in the downstairs hall.

Suk led Talley up two flights. On the landing at each floor a guard sat behind a small desk. As they reached the third floor, Suk explained, "We will spend the night here. There are facilities here for visitors." He proceeded along the hallway, then paused. "I have a surprise for you," he said. He opened the door and let Talley go in.

"Jane!"

"Tom! Oh, Tom!" Jane sprang from the couch in the small sitting room and threw herself upon Talley. "Are you all right!"

"What are you doing here?"

Jane was clutching Talley, pressing herself against him. He

twisted to look at Suk and demanded, "What is she doing here! What's going on!"

Suk raised a calming hand. "Professor Boudreau has come here voluntarily. She will be here for this one night only. She has come to help us ensure that you will be able to leave, yourself, as quickly as possible."

"What do you mean? What's going on?"

"I will explain everything to you both tomorrow. For tonight, let me simply assure you—"

"You're pulling some trick!"

Suk stared at Talley incredulously for a moment. Then he spoke slowly and patiently, as though to a child. "I am proceeding on a plan that I believe will serve my country's interests, Mr. Talley. Of course. I will explain at the appropriate time, which is tomorrow. For the present, I do assure you that Professor Boudreau's safe and speedy return to Vienna tomorrow is an essential part of my plan; so you need have no apprehensions about her being here.

"This little apartment"—he glanced into it—"is pleasant, I think. There is a bedroom and bath through that door. Supper will be brought to you soon, with a wine that I like myself. Please allow yourselves to be at ease. All will be well."

Talley would have exploded with anger at Suk for involving Jane, but the colonel smiled, bowed slightly, and stepped back into the hallway, closing the door behind him.

"You shouldn't have come!"

"I had to."

"You can't trust these people. How could you think you could trust these people?"

"I had to. You're trusting them."

"I'm not trusting them. I just think I have an angle, that it's in their interest to let me go."

"They said it's in their interest to bring *me* back to Vienna."

"But you don't know why. You can't figure an angle. You had to *trust* them!"

"All right! I had to trust them. And I *don't* trust them. But I *had* to! How could I refuse, when he said it would help get you out of here . . .?" Jane turned her head away. She put one hand to her face and sobbed. "Why are you angry with me?

I've been just sick with worry. And he said . . . and how could I refuse . . . and why are you angry at me?''

Talley moved to the end of the couch, where she had gone, and put his arms around her. ''I'm sorry. I'm not angry at you. I'm angry . . . I'm worried sick, myself, about you, that's all.''

Supper was brought to them. Talley and Jane dined at the little table set in front of the room's large window. The food was good. It was served on fine china. They drank from crystal. They tried to pretend they were enjoying themselves, but the darkness did not quite obscure the steel grating over the window, and they knew the room must be bugged.

''I don't understand it,'' Talley said, telling Jane no more than the Czechs already knew. ''I come in here doing the whole cloak-and-dagger, secret-agent thing—counterfeit papers, rendezvous with unknown contacts, fallback procedures—to sneak a meeting with Janos Czerny and expose a Czech intelligence ploy; and what do they do when they find out about it? Set up an interview for me. Put me up for the night in a suite, with room service and wine. I don't understand it at all.''

Jane shook her head. ''I can't understand any of it. It's just too devious. It folds back and forth on itself so many times, I can't see how any of them ever think they can know the truth about any of it. I'd think after a while they'd give up, and just do whatever they think they have to do, and stop trying to trick each other about it. Because, after they've twisted it so many times, how can they tell *what* the other side is going to believe?''

''I don't know. I think for some of them it almost becomes an end in itself. I think Colonel Suk . . . Well, of course he's got a plan; he thinks he can accomplish some objective goal by playing my game; but I think he may also have agreed to it just because he was taken by the idea. I think he could—''

Talley stopped suddenly, looked back into the sitting room.

''What's the matter?''

''I think I'd better not talk about this.''

Jane also looked about the room. She tipped her head and smiled with one side of her mouth. ''Do you suppose they have hidden cameras, too?''

Talley shrugged. ''Could be.''

''Well, maybe that's why they brought me here, Tom.

Brought us together.'' She spoke loudly. ''Maybe that's how they get their cheap thrills. All of the men I've seen here look like such repressed deviants, I could believe it. If I'd known, I could have brought along a case of Ping-Pong balls and our electric paint sprayer.''

''Yeah,'' Talley said. ''Well, we'll have to restrain ourselves. I think I'm doing enough for them already.''

''What are you doing, Tom? What is this 'game' you think you're playing with them?'' With a jerk of her head she indicated the suspected microphones. ''Obviously *they* know what it is already. So there's no reason for you not to tell me.''

He considered for a moment, then nodded. ''Essentially it's simple. They wanted some information from me. Realistically I had to recognize that . . . they could get it.''

For an instant, as he said that, he tried to avoid Jane's eyes. Then he met the look of horror in them. She nodded.

''So I agreed to give it to them the easy way, but in a way that would get me information *from* them that *I* wanted; and in an agreement that would get me out of here.''

He looked down at the table again.

''But . . . What I wanted to tell you about this . . . the reason, why I decided to try to do it this way . . .

''At first, I thought I had to be heroic. 'A person has to do certain things—even if they're hopeless—in order to keep his self-respect,' I told myself. I still believe that. But . . .

''There's a joke a Jewish friend of mind told me. A group of scientists have been working on an international atomic energy project, and something goes wrong, and they're exposed to radiation, and they're examined by the project doctor, and they're told they're all going to die in a week because there's no cure. So the director of the project offers each his last request. And, of course, what each scientist asks for is supposed to reveal his ethnic character: the Frenchman wants to spend a night with Catherine Deneuve, and so forth. Well, when they get to the Jewish scientist, he says, 'Thank you very much, but if you don't mind, what I'd like is to see another doctor and get a second opinion.' ''

Jane smiled at Talley. He had raised his eyes to look at her as he told it.

''Well, I sat there through that night, thinking. They had put me down in a dungeon so I would do just that. And for a while, I thought about what I had to do, and how I'd do it, and I got myself ready to bear as much pain as I could, and hold out as long as I could."

Jane nodded. "And then you thought that maybe you could get a second opinion."

"Yes. I wasn't going to sell out my country just to avoid pain. But maybe those didn't have to be the alternatives.

"And I realized I'd been doing just what you said I do: putting things in terms of absolutes and ideals. I thought about you—and us—a lot that night. It was a very long, cold night.

"And so I thought that maybe instead of spending all my time preparing myself to suffer for my ideals, maybe I should work on figuring a way that I wouldn't have to. Dealing with the problem, working at it, not having it be all or nothing."

Without speaking, Jane nodded several times. For a moment Talley was silent again, but she knew he hadn't finished.

"I . . ." he began, ". . . I wanted to tell you this because . . ." Without looking at her face, he slid his hand across the table, and touched hers with a fingertip. ". . . Because it seems to me to relate to us. I don't know . . . I think I've learned something through this. I don't know if I can apply it . . . But at least I can try to do something. At least I've got the idea, and I can work on it."

Although the rain had slackened the next morning to a fine mist, cloud obscured the Pratzen heights and also the tops of lower hills around. Even the open and shadowless landscape along the river seemed murky. All colors were dulled, but the greens less so than others. The thickness of the air seemed to absorb what noises were made by those few people who had ventured out, and—except for the rush of the nearby river—there was silence. Altogether, the atmosphere had an undersea quality.

When Colonel Suk, Talley, and Jane arrived at the meeting place, Janos Czerny was already there, waiting in the rear of the car that had brought him. In his former life (as he thought of it) meetings began at the moment when Czerny arrived. Since his arrest two years ago, he had learned to enlarge his spirit by accepting the yoke of humble attendance on others. That inferiority was emphasized, not contradicted, by his guard's waiting until Suk, Talley, and Jane had emerged from the car that brought them before opening the door and allowing him to get out.

"This is Janos Czerny," Suk said. "This is Thomas Talley and Professor Boudreau." Suk had waited while Czerny's guards brought Czerny to him. They had halted at a distance that precluded any shaking of hands.

"It's a great pleasure to meet you, Mr. Czerny," Talley said; and Jane said, "A great honor, Mr. Czerny."

Czerny tipped his head with the humble dignity of a deposed monarch.

To Czerny, Suk said, "Mr. Talley was sent into Czechoslovakia by the American Central Intelligence Agency for the purpose of asking you some questions. I wish that he should ask them, and that you should answer them fully and truthfully."

Then, including Talley and Jane, Suk continued, "Now, please let me explain what is to occur. Mr. Talley and"—he allowed the slightest pause to undercut the honorific—"Mr. Czerny will stroll together along the riverbank. You may go as far as that bench, if you like." He indicated a bench facing the river, perhaps fifty yards away. "You may speak as long as you wish; but—given the unpleasantness of the weather—perhaps no more than half an hour?

"Professor Boudreau and I will wait here, in the automobile, from which location we will be able to see you clearly, at all times. By this observation, Professor Boudreau will be able to attest that the two of you have met and conversed and that your conversation was free and unmonitored. That is, that Janos Czerny has been able to reply to all your questions with complete truthfulness since there can be no question of our knowing about, and possibly being displeased with, any of his answers.

"This is why we asked Professor Boudreau to come here, Mr. Talley: to provide an independent verification of your interview. I told you I would explain her presence, and I am doing so. I will explain further—and completely—after you have spoken with Mr. Czerny.

"Have you any questions?" Suk waited for a moment, then gestured to indicate that Talley and Czerny might begin walking.

"You're making a movie about Napoleon?" Talley wasn't going to ask his serious questions until they had reached the bench, and until he had gotten some sense of the situation and of Czerny.

"No. I am making a film about the common people. Napoleon is a minor character who appears in the story briefly."

"Ah. I see. But you are restaging the whole battle of Austerlitz."

"Yes."

"That seems to me an incredible undertaking. I've always marveled at something of that scale. How do you do it? I mean, how do you organize it?"

Czerny had always detested those people who—with expressions of wide-eyed wonder—asked naïve questions about his art. But—looking down and sideways—he saw that Talley's eyes weren't wide. They had the narrowed sharpness of a dissectionist. Czerny began to explain his planning for the battle scenes, the organization that would realize it.

They reached the bench and sat. Still, Talley prompted with questions about the film. They were not unintelligent, and Czerny continued answering. Clearly Talley was attending; but as he did so he stared off into the distance in a way that was both casual and yet methodical, eventually completing a 360-degree survey.

Talley saw no place within half a mile where anyone could be hiding, using a long-distance mike. As Czerny responded to his next question, Talley leaned forward. Directly in front of the bench, people's feet had worn away the grass and left a patch of bare earth. As Czerny talked, Talley wrote in the dirt with his finger, "Are they listening?" He looked at Czerny, touching himself here and there in places where a microphone might be hidden on one's body.

Czerny knew he hadn't been wired, but he understood Talley's desire for an answer that couldn't be overheard if he were. He shook his head as he went on speaking about costumes made of paper for the troops in the rear ranks.

Talley rose, walked around the bench looking carefully into the short grass. Finally he squatted and looked under the bench. Suk would see that, he knew, but Talley didn't care.

"So," he said when Czerny had finished, "you're making a film about how the Czech people survive Western imperialism."

Czerny looked stern for a moment, as though offended. Then he smiled slightly, scornfully. "I am making a film about how the common people survive oppression. In this particular case, the oppression is that of Western imperialism personified by Napoleon. Those scenes in which such statements are explicitly made are being filmed in a manner—the lighting, the position of the camera—such that anyone of artistic discernment will recognize they are apart in style from the rest of the work, and could be—perhaps will be eventually—excised from it. My masters in the Ministry of Culture do not possess such discernment. They will be pleased with what they see. Others may see that my statement relates to all emperors, governments, state systems that oppress the people.''

Talley smiled, enjoying Czerny's joke and also his own satisfaction that if they were being monitored, Czerny didn't know it.

Jane watched the two men fixedly, as though if she looked away they might vanish into the mist. She didn't notice when another black car came up and parked behind Suk's.

Suk respected her concentration, remaining silent and unmoving for ten minutes, and then speaking softly at first.

''They seem to be having a good discussion,'' he said. ''So, Professor Boudreau, let me explain further why I have brought you here to witness this conversation.

''When it is ended—when we see them rise and start back to rejoin us—you will be taken away, back to Vienna.''

Jane jerked forward, but Suk put up a hand and went on before she could speak. ''No, you will not be allowed to speak with Mr. Talley again. Please listen. The point of your being here—as I have said already—is so that you can attest this interview occurred, that Mr. Talley spoke with Janos Czerny under circumstances which guarantee his questions were answered fully and freely. That, presumably, Mr. Talley now will have the information for which he came: the information, presumably, which is of such importance to the Central Intelligence Agency. However, I cannot permit any contact between you and Mr. Talley in which he might—even by a single word, a single gesture—indicate to you any of the content of that information or any conclusion that he might have drawn from it.

''We assume, of course, that the CIA would want to secure Mr. Talley's freedom in any case. However, now that he possesses this information that is supposedly of such vital importance to them, they should be even more anxious to have him back.

"I shall be informing them of how his release will be made.

"For your part, what I hope you will do is, first, testify to the CIA that Mr. Talley is now in possession of the truth they seek. Secondly, in the almost—but to me not entirely—unimaginable event that the CIA does not move at once to secure Mr. Talley's release, I trust that you will . . . prod them. I know that when you and Mr. Talley spoke on the telephone the evening before last you then suggested you might take the matter to Senator Kennedy and might inform the press about it. In your wonderful country a citizen has so many ways to question the activities of your governmental agencies, to bring them to public accounting. I have absolute confidence that your deep concern for Mr. Talley, and the firmness and determination one senses at once in your character, will lead you to make use of all of them—become a thorn into the side—should there be any unreasonable delay in achieving his freedom."

"Where's Jane?"

"On her way back to Vienna."

"Why! Why didn't you let me see her?"

"Because—"

"What's going on here? What are you pulling? How do I know I can believe you? Goddammit . . . !"

Suk met Talley's growing fury with steely silence. He waited until Talley's concern to know overmastered his rage.

"You do not know that you can believe me," Suk said then. "But if you will listen for one moment, I will explain so that you may."

"Okay," Talley said. He shoved his fists down into his trouser pockets and made them stay there by keeping his arms rigid.

Suk repeated what he had told Jane. When he finished, Talley took a deep breath. He let his elbows bend, and loosened his shoulders, because it was clear to him that the ground wasn't where he'd thought it to be, and he was going to have to be loose to keep from breaking when he hit it.

He looked at Suk a little sideways. ''Okay, Colonel,'' he said. ''What is it? What is the CIA going to have to do to get you to let me go?''

''We shall release you no matter what the CIA does, Mr. Talley, because that was the agreement made between us. We agreed that you would be released as soon as you had provided us the information we wished to have from and/or—perhaps I should have said this more explicitly—*through* you. If the CIA does not meet our terms for your immediate release, then—after six months or a year—we will be satisfied that their refusal, in itself, answers our questions.''

''Six months or a year. And what do they have to do to get me out right away?''

''Send us, in exchange for you, Mr. Steve McCluskie.''

CHAPTER 12

"You've got to be kidding!"

"Not at all, Steve. May I call you Steve? You call me Anton. And it seems our destinies may be interdependent."

McCluskie sat back. Anton had gotten to the church first, and when McCluskie came in, he had sat one row behind the younger man. McCluskie had been leaning forward, his forearms on Anton's pew. For a moment after sitting back he was silent, getting over some of his shock at the condition the Czechs had set for Talley's release.

Finally McCluskie nodded and smiled. "Sure, Anton, sure. We are old buddies, aren't we? Now, come on, old buddy, be serious. I'm supposed to exchange myself for that idiot Talley?"

"Is Thomas Talley an idiot, Steve? We have sometimes suspected the mental competence of your agents, but I would not have thought you employed such people knowingly."

McCluskie heaved a sigh of theatrical exasperation with Anton's humor. "Okay. Come on. What's the program?"

"Professor Boudreau has already told you of Thomas Talley's meeting with Janos Czerny. Presumably you—the CIA—wish to know the outcome."

"If that's what you want to find out, you should be in touch with Langley. What if I—just for the sake of my own skin—don't want to go? I don't even tell them about this. What do you learn then?"

"We are communicating with Langley, too. While your superiors might veto your visiting Prague if you wanted to, they can't make you go if you don't. One of the differences between your service and mine. At this moment, Steve, I am interested in seeing *your* reaction to our proposal."

"Okay. Well, my personal reaction is that I don't care enough about this that I should go to Prague and let you put splinters under my fingernails and make me tell you about everything I know. I mean, we're not going to do that, no matter how much we want to know what disinformation you've pumped into Talley."

"Not disinformation, Steve. You have been assured of that by Professor Boudreau. But of course you're right. We could not imagine you being willing to exchange all you know for what Talley knows, no matter how valuable the latter might be. That is why we offer a proposal that will guarantee that our discussion with you will be limited to one subject. We also offer assurances about the methods of inquiry—no splinters, Steve, nothing like that. Oh, I do assure you."

"Try harder."

"Yes. What we—" Anton paused as a pair of English-speaking tourists halted at the end of his pew to examine an inscription on the wall. He and McCluskie were sitting at one side of the church, about three-quarters back from the high altar, isolating themselves from tourists, who mostly stayed in the rear, and from the half-dozen worshipers who sat near the front. Although the lamps in the chandeliers over the center aisle had been turned on against the dimness of the rainy afternoon, the men sat in a gloom that seemed out of time—neither lit by any living source nor having the finality of total darkness. Scores of votive candles in their red glass cups gleamed with hope, but they were distant.

"What we propose," Anton began again, "as I said, is that we will question you only on one subject: your investigation of the Czerny affair and the business of George Murtaugh, to which the investigation obviously is related. To assure that you will answer our questions fully and truthfully, we will use some technical aids—polygraph, drugs, and so forth—but we will not do anything to you that would be injurious or even painful. As soon as we have finished discussing with you that one matter—say, two weeks?—we will return you safe and sound across any border you wish.''

Anton paused, then nodded, smiling slightly. ''I see that even your admirable control of expression is inadequate to conceal your skepticism. Indeed, how could you believe this assurance?''

McCluskie smiled in return. ''I guess you're going to tell me; and I can hardly wait.''

''I said, Steve, that our destinies might be interdependent, yours and mine. To guarantee your safety, we will pledge mine. If this exchange is made, you get not only Thomas Talley but me. While you are in Czechoslovakia, I will be here, in custody of your people. As we promise to ask you about this one subject only, you will promise to ask me nothing at all. At regular intervals—say, each twelve hours—each of us will be put in direct telephone contact with our respective colleagues. Simple word code. In that way, either of us could signal if the agreement is not being observed. If one side breaks it, then the other would be free to do as it wishes with the one of us it holds. While with all modesty I recognize that I might not be as valuable to your side as you would be to mine, nevertheless, I have served in several stations, and do possess a great deal of knowledge that we know you would like to have, and that we prefer you should not have.''

Still leaning back against the pew with his legs stretched under the one in front, McCluskie folded his arms high across his chest and stared at Anton. ''Well,'' he said at last. ''Well. Words really do fail me.'' He shook his head in amazement. ''You really are serious about this?''

''Oh, absolutely.''

''I mean, you seriously expect that I'd take it seriously? That I'd do it?''

Now Anton withdrew into his own apparently relaxed containment. He let his hand slip from the seat back and down to lie over the other loosely in his lap. ''I'd rather not talk about our *expectations*, Steve, other than to say that we would expect you to want to get Thomas Talley back: to get this information you sent him to find.''

''You promised to let him go.''

''We will. Eventually. From our point of view, the matter

will not become embarrassingly urgent for a while—some months, at least. How urgent is it to you?"

"I see." McCluskie put his head back and gazed upward at the dome, where blessed saints ascended amid cherubim into glory. "Neat," he said. "Very neat. Nice. Colonel Suk?"

Anton offered no response.

But McCluskie nodded as though they shared an understanding. "Very nice. Give him my compliments, will you?" He suddenly sat upright, his hands on his thighs. "Well. Obviously I'll have to talk this over with the big boys back home. With any luck, they'll think it's the craziest thing they ever heard of, too. I'll be in touch, okay?"

"Alert signals there's going to be heavy traffic back and forth to Langley." McCluskie spoke even as he swept into the office where Deming waited.

"What's the deal?"

"You won't believe it. I don't believe it." McCluskie dropped into the chair behind the desk, tore a sheet of paper from the pad. "Alert signals, and then call that damn Boudreau woman, and get her in here again." He began to write. "I'll tell you the whole mess when you get back; but—essentially—they've grabbed our going after Czerny, and they're using it to throw us over . . ." He paused. "Wait. Wait one little minute," he said, drawing out the words.

Deming halted on his way to the door.

For another moment McCluskie stared into space. "Yeah," he said. "Goddamn yeah! Do that stuff, Paul; but first, get through to Linz. I don't care what he's doing, I want Jake Kaz here now!"

Late into the evening, and long past midnight, Talley sat up trying to understand. He had been put again into the relatively comfortable cell, the warm one with a real bed and its own john, and the window. Colonel Suk had said he hoped Talley would be comfortable there "for a day or two," while the details of his release were worked out.

Suk had maintained his cordiality despite Talley's surliness. The effect didn't really reassure Talley. When Talley hadn't responded on the journey back to Prague to the kind of information and pleasantries Suk had provided on the trip out, Suk stopped offering them; he merely took a sheaf of papers from an attaché case and spent the rest of the time reading and making notes on them.

Why was Suk still holding him? Talley had protested, arguing that McCluskie would never come; the man knew too much about too many things ever to be exchanged for what Talley could report about Janos Czerny. Suk had smiled and said no; that under some ironclad guarantee, McCluskie would be questioned for a limited time about this one affair only. But he'd refused to respond to Talley's demand for a further explanation.

Once again, Talley realized he'd been led out onto a battlefield at night, and there were mines, and booby traps, and ambushes set by the enemies for each other, and he was wandering blindly among them. If he could only understand what was going on, perhaps he could see a way to extricate himself.

He decided he should start from the beginning.

The beginning, for him, was being asked to reinvestigate the Czerny-Hovey affair.

He'd explained to Suk that the CIA would want to reinvestigate because of the business with Murtaugh: to find if Murtaugh had been an agent two years ago. Since Janos Czerny had confirmed that Czech intelligence had planted the idea of a mole in the CIA, Talley knew now for certain that Murtaugh hadn't been.

Why did the CIA care? Murtaugh was dead now. He wasn't doing any harm.

The question would be, what harm had he done? What material had he given the Czechs during the time he was an agent?

Suk said he suspected the investigation was a hoax. Why would he think that? Why would the CIA only *pretend* to want to know if Murtaugh was a Czech agent two years ago? They should—truly—want to know.

Answer (according to Suk's speculation): they must already know when Murtaugh became an agent. If the CIA did know that, then they also knew what information he might have given. To conceal knowledge of when he became an agent would be to conceal knowledge about the information.

Doing that would allow them to change things—play who knew what kind of games—without Suk knowing it. Or, if he suspected their game—which he did—they could make him unsure about everything he'd gotten from Murtaugh.

The issue for Suk, then, would be: is the information he received reliable? How would Suk's ploy of demanding McCluskie in exchange for Talley answer that?

If the CIA really didn't know when Murtaugh became an agent, then the information he gave between the time he started and his discovery would be true. In that case, the CIA's primary goal would have to be to find out what was given. If they did know what had been given, then their goal would be to hide that fact so Suk wouldn't know what games they might be playing.

And then Talley understood Suk's ploy, what the exchange meant. Talley's information would be exchanged for McCluskie's. If the CIA had nothing to hide, then getting Talley's information would move them toward their primary goal at no cost. Conversely, if they cared less about what Talley had to tell than about what McCluskie had to hide, then the reinvestigation was a sham, and Suk would know the CIA had been trying to make him believe something that was false.

From having been able to analyze the problem, Talley felt a sense of triumph that lasted long enough for him to lie down and fall asleep. It wasn't until the next morning that he began considering which goal the CIA was pursuing, and whether McCluskie would come in for him.

When McCluskie got upstairs to the room where the skeletons stood, Jake Kaczmarczyk was inspecting closely the left rear ankle of the brontosaurus. A teacher was lecturing a group of schoolchildren gawking up open-mouthed at the head, half the length of the long, narrow room away from him. McCluskie stayed by the door exchanging stares with the remains of a creature that reared high above him, but demonstrated—for all its terrifying toothiness—that simply being mean doesn't guarantee survival. After a minute or two, the children were led away, and McCluskie went to Jake. Before he could speak, Jake turned to him.

"I got to talk to you, Steve."

"I got to talk to you, Jake. That's what we're here for."

"But I got to talk to you first. I mean, this pulling me back, sending me here to see you 'imperative, immediately, repeat, immediately.' There wasn't any warning put on it; it wasn't to tell me the shit's hit the fan and to get me out of the way of the spray. I've been around long enough to know there probably is dung flying in all directions, but what you want is for me to find a big mop."

"Yep."

"Yeah, that was as easy to see as the wart on Cousin Karl's nose. But the thing is, Steve, I . . ." Jake had been standing solidly, feet spread, as he always did, so he could weave or come up onto his toes to emphasize a point; his hands were shoved down to the thumbs into his trouser pockets in the way that had stretched all of his pants and made them baggy. He pulled his hands out and turned them upward and looked down at whatever wasn't being held in them. ". . . I can't."

McCluskie stood absolutely still.

"I . . ." Jake went on, the comedian's flat tone and fast delivery gone. ". . . You told me to tell you whenever I wanted to quit. I . . . it's time."

McCluskie slipped his own hands into his back pockets. "What's the matter, Jake?" He spoke calmly, seriously but not heavily. "When you look under your bed, are they there? Or do you keep waking up and having to look every hour?"

"No, I . . . They're not on to me—I mean, they're not any closer than they've ever been. No, it's not that I'm strung out. Well, yeah, Steve, maybe it is; only not the way you'd think.

"What can I tell you?" He put his hands back where they were used to being. McCluskie waited for him.

"A couple months ago," Jake began, "I had to go see somebody. Not a project you have anything to do with. No big deal; I just had to see him right away, though. It was out of the district I was working that week on my BigOx itinerary. No problem. The CIS tabs me, but they don't keep on me. I can disappear off my route and go someplace and be back—if it's a quick trip—and they don't know. A couple times I've gotten caught and had to use a story I had ready; but most of the time they never know, because I know how to do it. I mean, like for example, on this particular trip I had to make, there's a place where, if they're setting up a random road check, they always put it there. It's like a speed trap: you come around a curve, and there they are. Only, if you go up a side road to a hill a couple kilometers before you get there, you can look down and spot them. If I go that way, and I care about it, I check.

"Well, this time I didn't check. I mean, I cared; I should have. I forgot.

"How could I forget a thing like that? That's something . . . I mean, I do things—checks—like that all the time. It's a habit, I don't even think about it. In the time I've been in this business, I must have done checks like that ten zillion times. So maybe after ten zillion times, I just couldn't remember whether I'd done that one.

"I only realized I'd forgot when I came around the bend. They weren't there. That day, they weren't there.

"But the thing is—I realized after I pulled over and was breathing again—was that when I came into the bend and remembered that I'd forgotten to check, I knew they *would* be there; and what I thought was, 'So they finally got me.'

"What I mean, Steve, is that I know they're going to get me. I mean, down inside, I'm so sure about that that it doesn't even make me nervous anymore. I think that's why I forgot to check. I mean, I didn't really forget. Just, down inside I was saying to myself, 'Why bother? They're going to get you anyway.'

"Maybe I even wanted to have it over with.

"That's why I need to come out, Steve. That's why I can't do this whatever-this-is you have to have done. Not because my nerves are shot, not because I'm scared. I'm not scared. If I was scared, I'd be okay."

Jake shook his head. "I'm making mistakes, Steve. That—that I told you—that was just one. I'm not paying attention to the details. I mean, I try. But I can't trust myself. You can't trust me."

He sighed. "My hair's going gray, I need glasses to read—should wear them all the time—I . . . I haven't got it anymore, Steve." He had been looking to the side, away from McCluskie, not at anything. For an instant he seemed to focus on the skeleton. Then he brought his eyes back to McCluskie's face. "You'll have to take me out. I'm sorry."

McCluskie remained solidly silent. Finally he said quietly, "Okay, Jake. I can't argue with that. I wouldn't try to get you to do something you honestly think you can't do. And I sure as hell am not going to try to make you feel bad about it. You've paid your dues. You've bought your gold watch twenty times over, and you can have it anytime you want."

"Thanks, Steve." Jake's eyes were full. He continued to stare straight ahead. Pretending to scratch an itch on his cheek, he wiped beside his big nose.

"I mean it," McCluskie said. "It's okay. But I would appreciate it if you would at least give me your advice. We're going to need that. We're going to need that kind of help from you—all we can get."

"Sure, Steve. Anything."

"Well, what we have to do—it's this business about Janos Czerny that you set up. They did take our man."

"Jesus."

"He's okay. Actually he's doing fine. But there is a problem. A big one. As usual, you don't need to know the details; but what it comes down to is this: we've got to snatch Janos Czerny out of Czechoslovakia."

"It isn't necessary. Colonel, it just isn't necessary." Talley's intensity thrust him forward in the chair across the desk from Colonel Suk. "You really can't believe that I came into Czechoslovakia, knowing I was putting my head under the ax, just to pull off some trick. I mean, I didn't want to come here anyway; I only did it because I was convinced the investigation was important."

"Yes. I believe you, Mr. Talley. We are not questioning your motive."

"Well, I'm not questioning the CIA's."

"Perhaps you should."

"No. There's a lot I don't like about the agency; but I just don't believe they'd put me in this kind of a position . . . I don't believe that of them.

"But that doesn't mean they'll send McCluskie in. You may have it figured wrong. They don't know when Murtaugh became your agent. They don't know what material he might have given you. Okay, so by keeping McCluskie away, they make you doubt it all."

Suk regarded Talley for a moment, his chin resting on two fingers steepled from his clasped hands. "Your analysis of this matter has been very interesting, Mr. Talley. Particularly since you have . . . yes, I accept that you have really little factual knowledge about it. But although impressive, your logic is faulty. If the CIA truly is ignorant of what material was given to us, then they can have no confidence that I would doubt it. I might be able to corroborate one piece or another. They might indeed seek to mislead me, to discredit this item or that; but first they must know what the items are.

"They really *must* know. That should—if we are to believe they are not practicing a deceit—that *must* be of greatest importance to them. So I am afraid you cannot persuade me that Mr. McCluskie's failure to redeem you—should he fail to do so—would prove nothing, and therefore that I should release you now.

"Besides, Mr. Talley: I should think you would want as much as I to wait and see what will happen. After all, if the CIA is attempting to deceive me in this matter, then they certainly have deceived—and exploited—you."

"Holy shit! Snatch Czerny!" Jake stared at McCluskie as though the dinosaur had walked off its pedestal.

"Have to, Jake. We have to do it. Colonel Suk has our balls in an electric vise, and the only way we're going to get out is to send somebody around behind him to pull the plug."

"Holy shit," Jake said again, more quietly, deeply awed, and then was silent before the enormity of what McCluskie had told him. Finally he asked, "Snatch him, or break him out? I mean, does he know, does he want to come?"

"We haven't asked him. We're not in contact, that's the point. We naturally assume he'd like to be a free man, but we're not going to try to discuss it with him. We just have to reach him and grab him out, like fast—right away."

"How you think you're going to do that?"

"Well, I had thought I was just going to say, 'Jake, go get him.' Now I guess I have to start by asking *you* that question."

"I told you, I can't do it. I told you, I'm sorry."

"I told you it's okay. It's okay." McCluskie paused, then said it again. "It's okay."

Jake's eyes filled, and he had to look away. Then he sighed. "It's not okay."

"It can't be helped. You can't do it, you can't do it. What

you can do is tell me, help us, run it from here. You work out a plan: you tell us what you'd do if you were there. You tell us who to see, what to tell them to do. That you can do. You know the terrain. You know the people, better than anybody else in there; better than anybody else in the world. If you can't be in there yourself . . . well, you can mastermind it from here. Now, give me some ideas: how do we do it?"

"Right away: you want him out right now?" Jake's shoulders rose as though grateful to bear the burden.

"Time is of the essence."

"You know where he is?"

McCluskie shrugged. "I know where you said he was four days ago; where we sent Talley—up at Austerlitz."

"He's still there. At least, as far as I know, he is. He's going to film the battle there, and he hasn't done it yet."

"That should be good, shouldn't it? I mean, you have people there—you had a way to slip Talley in to see him. And it's out in the country. I'd think that would make it easier than if he was in the middle of Prague."

"Yeah. Except for one thing. The word is that he's doing the battle with help from the Ministry of Defense—you know, for all the extras. I mean, from what I hear, what he's going to be in the middle of is about a division of the Czech army!"

McCluskie gave that intelligence a respectful moment of silence. "Let's walk," he said at last.

The men turned and began strolling along the wall opposite the skeletons.

A couple and two children came into the room. McCluskie and Jake went out to a corner of the great, marble-floored foyer.

"Well," McCluskie offered, "that does add to the challenge of the problem, doesn't it?"

"Yeah." Jake pursed his lips appreciatively. "Of course, it might not be as bad as it seems. The only thing dumber than a company of the Czech army is two companies. When you get up to the regimental level, the IQ goes down to about that of a bushel of potatoes. I mean, not that they're really stupid; it's just the only thing they know to do is fire up the tanks and roll straight ahead. Anything else—left, right, stop and scratch their asses—they check all the way back to Moscow first."

"Makes the problem more interesting, though."

"Yeah." Jake considered it, then said "Yeah" again and

went on speculatively but with authority. "What you'll have to do is, you'll have to move even faster than you usually would try to. Once you're in motion, you keep going: no grab, go to ground, then wait to sneak out in the dark of the moon. I mean, you give them a chance to deploy—take positions, put a perimeter around you, set up checkpoints, lay out sectors and search—you're done for. That they can do really well. But you move fast enough, they won't have a plan, and they haven't got the flexibility."

McCluskie nodded agreement. "So it would have to be done, really professional, real style. The kind of operation they'll call one of the classics and put in the training manuals." The idea seemed to take him, and he enlarged on it. "The Czechs, too, once the heads stop rolling. It'll make them all look like a bunch of thumbsuckers; but after the stink's fanned around and collected in a few places, the ones that are left will want the operation put down and studied as an object lesson. *The Jake Kaz Snatch*. What a finale for you. Of course, you've already made your place in history, Jake: your whole career in there. But this one will really take you out in style.

"That is, of course, assuming you can figure out the minor problem of how to do it. What do you think? You think it might be possible?"

"It might be, yeah. With him out in the country. Bound to be a lot of confusion with all those out-of-towners for the movie—who's going to notice a couple more? Yeah, it'll be a really tough one, but . . . The key is going to be how to get out. I mean, like I say, moving up to him probably won't be too bad, or the moment of snatch: he's not like under heavy security. But then it's got to be *so* fast; and there's no way of running for the border and going out barefaced with a cover—even if he'd be willing, which he may not.

"Like you say, Steve, it's an interesting problem. But . . . yeah . . . there might be a way to do it. I'll have to think about it. Maybe . . ." Jake stared off somewhere beyond the stairway.

After a moment McCluskie said, "Since you're not going back in there yourself, there's no reason for us to keep on meeting in places like this. You're not under cover anymore, you're going to be a staff officer now. You might as well come to the office with me. You can start getting used to working at a desk."

McCluskie spoke slowly, as though thinking it out. Jake stared at him, dismay growing darker across his face.

McCluskie went on, "We'll look over the charts and see who we have who could go in there, and maybe start some people moving so they'll be ready when you tell them what to do. You don't have any preliminary ideas, do you?"

"How the fuck could I, Steve? I'm not used to dreaming up plans just in my head without knowing . . . I mean, I found somebody who could get your man in to see Czerny. Breaking Czerny himself out . . . I need to have people who'll come right into overt play, maybe take out some opposition if they have to. I got to know where Czerny is—I mean, *exactly*: his schedule. I got to see the lay of the land, estimate the possibilities. You're right: this is some special problem; it really has to be a class action. I don't know if it can be done at all, but I think maybe I could . . . if it's sanded and polished, and fit together just right. I can't do that in two minutes after you tell me about it."

McCluskie put up his hands as though surrendering. "I didn't mean to push you, Jake. I'm sorry. But—like I said—this has to happen right away if it's going to be done at all. And it really has to be done."

"I'll do what I can, all right? But what can I tell you off the top of my head? I'm not used to sitting in a swivel chair and firing off orders about something I don't know anything about to the grunts who are out there up to their asses in the mud!" Jake glared at McCluskie for a moment, then turned his eyes down as though he had been the one scolded.

Then he began again half angrily, half contritely. "If I was going to do it myself—given you want it right now—I probably wouldn't even try to work it all out ahead from a distance. I'd line up my people, and when I saw a way, then I'd figure how— If I saw a way and my instinct said it would work, I might just go for it on the spot. That's what having been around and having experience is for. But to try to give you a plan from this distance . . . Close up, I could probably . . . But . . .

"Oh, fuck it," he said.

"Ingenious, Colonel. Absolutely ingenious. You should be very pleased with yourself."

"Thank you, Comrade Director," Suk said, as though the

director had said he himself were pleased. Suk sat upright, not stiffly but correctly, in an armchair.

The director leaned at casual ease, with one arm up along the couch back. He had received Suk in the informal "conversation area" of his office. "This will be a brilliant coup for us, if the device succeeds."

"Thank you, Comrade Director."

Only Suk and a few others of the old guard continued to put "comrade" in front of every title. Or rather, as the director had noted, in front of the titles of their superiors. The director did not recall having heard Suk address anyone as "Comrade Lieutenant." The director parried Suk's point by seeming not to note it, just as Suk had ignored the director's conditional.

As the meeting's purpose was merely to give the director an informal report, the men were alone. Suk had no doubt, though, about its being recorded. Since the recorder was the director's, he did not attempt to plant his own lines. He attended in silence.

"The attempt on the lives of the CIA agents in Vienna might be thought excessive, Colonel. And this entire procedure with Janos Czerny and the exchange you have proposed is certainly unorthodox and might be questioned. However, if the result is as you hope, your methods would be completely justified. We shall simply have to wait and see."

"Yes, Professor, you do have a right to know. You have every right to know. But I am not going to tell you." McCluskie stood beside his car, his hand on the top of the passenger's door. He had opened it for Jane, but she had balked at entering. "I came here to tell you we are going to do what's necessary to get Tom released, and that's all I'm going to tell you."

"How can I believe you?" She held her arms crossed, partly against the chill—she had come down from her room without her coat—but more to fortress herself against McCluskie. "I told you I would hold off making this public only on the condition you get him out of there at once."

McCluskie absorbed her anger with the blandness of a feather pillow. "And I told you we would, just as fast as we could. Which is what we're doing. And I appreciate how worried and upset you are, which is why I came, to keep you informed. But I am not going to give you any details. You can have as much scorn as you want about our concern for security, Professor; but if security hadn't been broken, Tom wouldn't be in there right now. And if you hadn't taken it upon yourself to go there, the Czechs might not have been able to pull what they're pulling, and they might have let him go by now."

Instantly fury shot up to shield her from that accusation, but before she could retort, McCluskie went on.

"That's a fact, Professor, and you'd better consider it instead of just denying it. You know, there can be more to things than just the way you see them.

"Now, if we don't have Tom out of there soon, I know there's no way I'm going to be able to stop you from making a public issue of this. I would like it, personally, if you believed I wouldn't disappoint you. But you won't, and you've got your secret letters out to whoever you sent them to. So you know I can't stop you. But you can wait, and I'm telling you, you'd better. Having a big public inquiry about this thing would suit the Czechs fine; and if one gets started, they'll keep Tom longer just to keep it going.

"Think about it. Does it occur to you that they didn't involve you and put you up to this just purely for Tom's sake?"

That thought had indeed occurred to her. The guilty suspicion that she might in fact be helping the Czechs against Talley's interest doubled the simple fear she felt for him.

"I don't know what the Czechs want," she snapped back, still fighting it. "I don't know what you want. I don't understand any of it, and I don't care. All I care about is that I'm not going to let him be just swallowed up in there, and abandoned, and nobody . . ." Her voice started to break, and she tightened and controlled it; but she couldn't stop her tears. "I just have to get him out. I just have to do anything . . ."

McCluskie knew his wasn't a shoulder she would accept to cry on. But he did try to make his voice both gentle and confident. "I know, Professor, I know. I sure don't blame you for that. So I want you to know we are doing something; so just hold on and wait for just a couple more days. It's going to be all right. Just hold on and wait."

CHAPTER 13

It was going to be a lot harder than usual, Jake realized as he passed through the border check. And—because of that—easier, too.

The guard, Karoly (Jake knew the first names of all the men at all the crossings he used regularly), grinned at the offer of a share in the profits if he didn't search the van and report the pornographic photos of Bulgarian beauty queens Jake was smuggling in. But the grin was tight, and so were his eyes; and when Jake started to pull away and then paused for a moment to put his papers into his jacket pocket, he saw Karoly picking up his phone.

The CIS would be snug on him. It figured. With the ploy Colonel Suk was pulling, they'd figure the CIA would try something of their own. They probably wouldn't expect Jake to be in any overt action; but they'd know he might be involved somehow.

By the time he'd driven twenty kilometers beyond the border, he'd begun to understand how really hard it would be. No one was following him. By then Karoly's call should have had them on him.

He did his mirror checks. He did his speed variations. He did his customary bored-traveler stare at anybody who passed him. He pulled off just past the crest of a hill and got out to piss. Nobody was following him.

They were watching him, of course; he never doubted it.

Not following him meant they were doing it the costly way, with spotters in buildings along the highway or parked on crossroads far back from his route. They weren't close on top of him; they were staying back where he couldn't see where they were. They were inviting him to try something, so they could find out what it was.

That kind of surveillance, and their caring enough about him to use it, meant it would be hard to break free. Impossible. He'd never do it, he'd never be able to slip out and do a number and get back in again.

But that was the way they were making it easy for him, too. He wasn't going to try to get back in. Jake Kaczmarczyk the BigOx rep would go out of business. Jake Kaz the secret agent would have to move without cover, pop up out of nowhere with his guns blazing, snatch Czerny, and beat the posse to the pass. If they held back far enough, tagging his van, watching him try to maneuver within the rules of the BigOx game they'd all agreed to play, he might do it.

The entire operation was full of such contradictions. Because he was having to move so fast—it was only the afternoon after the day he'd talked with McCluskie in Vienna—there had been no time to make detailed plans; but that meant there was no way for the CIS to get on to them. He'd have the element of surprise. Because he had no plan, he was free to take any opportunity that came up. McCluskie was arranging the transport to the Austerlitz area. That worried Jake, because it was a link he couldn't control. But aside from that link, having no support meant nobody else could be caught or foul up and blow him. Everything cut both ways.

The steady rain on his windshield kept the landscape blurry. Each time the wipers swung across, for a moment the view straight ahead was clear; but even so, moisture in the air veiled and took away the farther hills. "That's the way it is," he thought, "that's the way it's going to be."

It would be strange to be speaking English most of the time.

Maybe the agency would make a place for him in northern Austria. The look of the country on either side of the border was about the same, of course. It would still feel like what he was used to. He'd miss that look if he had to go back to the States.

No, what he'd miss would be the people. The farm families that hung on to their identities, their pride, even when they had to work as part of a collective. Old Maryk. The Hrádecs. Little Lotti Zuk's sixth birthday was coming up in August. He'd planned to bring her a present. He'd known her family since her father was twelve.

Shit!

What he should do is leave the fucking agency altogether, and go back to Iowa, and get a BigOx field rep's job there. Then he could keep on doing the part he really liked.

Maybe he could find a way to send Lotti's gift in to her. Maybe he could find a way to keep in touch with people, get some news from time to time. He wasn't even going to be able to say good-bye to anybody.

His eyes were a little watery and puffy anyway, so it only took a small sniff from the packet of black pepper he'd brought to make them stream, and make him sneeze and blow all the time he was checking in.

Maria, going behind the desk to get his key, commiserated. In this terrible weather everybody was catching colds. Yes, the best thing would be for him to go straight to bed and sleep through the night, and sleep late tomorrow, too. No problem about making up his room. He could sleep until noon. She would bring him some chamomile tea if he wanted, otherwise she wouldn't disturb him. Yes, if he wanted, he could stay another night as well and rest, simply let her know by midafternoon tomorrow.

Jake did go straight to bed, although it was only five in the afternoon. He was going to need his rest. Three hours later he got up, used some pepper again, went downstairs and had a bowl of chicken soup and two glasses of tea with rum. Then he went back to bed for another three hours.

Low clouds and drizzle obliterated the view through the window of Talley's cell. He sat on the bed and read—or at least looked at—the book Suk had loaned him. The heavy weather actually helped him: it obscured the landscape he couldn't go into.

Anyway, he was trying not to take the long view. He told himself just to work at getting through one day, and another. There was no point in trying to see further. He couldn't believe

McCluskie would be exchanged for him, but he couldn't be sure. Although he suspected he now knew where the winding road he'd been lured onto came from, he couldn't be certain where it was headed, or what twists it might take to get there. He understood Suk's purpose in holding him. But—if McCluskie didn't come—would Suk consider it achieved and release him within days? Or would he play out the game for months?

Anger was the only thing he had no uncertainty about. He was angry at McCluskie. He was angry at Suk. Both of them had misled him, tricked him, used him. Most of all, though, he was angry at himself for letting them do it.

The noise of the local people leaving the bar when it closed at midnight woke Jake. He got up and dressed, except for his boots, using the glow from the lights outside the hotel to see by. At twelve-fifteen they were switched off, too. For another fifteen minutes he could hear Willi and Maria moving around downstairs, and then there was silence. He sat on the bed and waited.

The feel of the black wool sweater against his skin was less an itch than a tingle of excitement. Putting it on, and the dark gray trousers, laying the black anorak over the foot of the bed and standing the farmer-style rubber boots beside it, had brought back a kind of thrill, a sense of high adventure he hadn't known for years. He hadn't operated black since the late cold-war days when (as he thought of it now) he was still a kid, before they set him up with his permanent cover.

A lot of water under the bridge since then.

How had he ever gotten away with that run to Žatec to pick up Sykora's list, as fresh out of the shell as he'd been? Well, he'd been green, but he'd been sharp.

Now he was worn and ground right down. He was an old bird now; a tough old bird; but maybe a wise one. He'd have to be. He'd have to use all his experience to make up for—

But what the hell? Why was he running down his own price? He was good. They didn't come any better. Hanging up his suit in the wardrobe and putting on these clothes had really given him a charge. For the first time in years he felt like he was having fun again. Yeah, he was scared. Yeah, he wanted to hang it all up. But how can you not get a thrill about going in for one last run when you're the ace?

* * *

At two o'clock he thought it all through one more time. He couldn't check the room again in the nearly pitch-black, so he had to do it in his head. Yes, he had gone through his old briefcase before starting this trip. There was never anything in his case that would incriminate anybody, but this time he had made sure there was nothing that could give Colonel Suk himself any idea that could even remotely, wildly, compromise anything or anybody. Yes, he had checked his battered suitcase and his clothes. He had left the packet of pepper on the dresser so they would know how he'd made his nose run and not accuse Maria of being in collusion. He felt in his fingers exactly how the door handles had to be pressed to prevent the latch from clicking. He saw exactly where he had to walk along the edges of the hallway—where to cross from one side to the other—to avoid the squeaky boards in the floor.

At ten after two he got up, put on the anorak and the peaked cap. He put on the boots. He would have to walk carefully so as not to scuff the tops together, but the soles would be as quiet as sneakers. He stood for a moment in the darkness just beyond the foot of the bed, his fingertips touching the footboard. He had to be correctly oriented, to get to the door without bumping into anything. When Maria quietly told him, while she was putting the soup down on his table, that she hoped the men who had taken the room next to his wouldn't disturb him, he had known what she meant and hadn't been surprised.

He made his way to the door. He put his ear against it. Then, pushing it slightly, as he had practiced, he pressed down on the handle. He opened the door a crack, listening. He opened it fully.

One light burned, down by the WC. Going to the WC might have been an excuse if he'd been caught out in the hall now, except not in this costume.

He released the inner door handle very slowly, pressing down on the outer one. Then, using his right palm to ease the door closed, he let the handle up.

He paused, listening. Someone in a room down the hall was snoring. In the one next to his, someone sighed as though yawning.

Carefully, but not so slowly that he might lose his balance between steps, he went down the hall to the back stairway. On the floor below, he did go into the WC, and out through the window there. It was a small window, but Jake was a small man.

When he hit the ground, his boots came down on a puddle; but that single splash could not be heard over the rain and the constant rush from the downspout if anyone was nearby to hear. Nobody was.

Someone was probably watching his van from a steamed-up car somewhere in the parking lot. Jake cut around an outbuilding behind the hotel and away from the lot.

Because the night was so black, it took him the full two hours he'd allowed, using side roads and—mostly—lanes between the fields, to cover the three kilometers down the road to the hotel the truckers used. He came up on the floodlit parking area carefully, took another fifteen minutes to be sure there was only one watchman, and that he and his dog were staying inside their booth. The watchman was supposed to patrol, of course; but on such a night, who could blame him for trying to keep dry?

Jake was pretty well soaked himself by then. The anorak's imitation-leather yoke actually did keep his shoulders dry, but the steady rain had gone through his cap and run down his neck, and from the sopping thighs of his trousers down into his boots. The wool of his clothing at least kept his body heat in.

Although it was dawn, the heavy clouds, the steady rain, held night down; and the floodlights drove it back and concentrated it until it seemed as thick as the trucks it lurked behind. That depth of darkness and the hard shine of blue-white glare on wetness made every shape and surface dense and hard as diamond or obsidian.

Nine trucks stood in the lot, five in one row, four in the one behind them. One was a tanker, two were general haulers, the sides of their trailers unmarked by any lettering. Jake had seen at once the sky-blue tarp with the white logo of the truck he wanted. It was third from the left in the second row. That was good. It made him feel good to know the driver had picked the best place he could, the one that would give Jake the most cover possible.

Jake swung off to one side, to put all the trucks as a block between himself and the guard's booth. Then he ducked low and ran to the trailer, the shape of his dark-clothed body and his shadow writhing across the gleaming glass of the pavement. He had to figure no one would be looking. He had to hope the hiss and rush of rain, its steady drumming and rattle on the trucks and the guard's booth itself, would cover the sound of his footfalls from the dog's hearing. If the animal did wake, if its ears pricked, would the guard notice? Would the dog growl? Would the guard pull on his poncho and come out to see, or would he consider duty done by simply looking through the rain-beaded windows?

Jake hunched, his neck turtled down into his shoulders, and ran and tried not to think about any of that.

The back right corner of the tarp was untied, the way it was supposed to be. He crawled up under it and into a space between cartons that hadn't been packed as closely together as they might have been.

After a while the body heat generated by running left him, and he shivered and huddled into himself as much as he could.

At a little past five the sound of the rain on the tarp slackened, then stopped entirely. A few minutes later Jake heard the voices of two men. One must have been a driver, the other the guard. The driver expressed his gratitude for the guard's having stayed outside all night in the rain looking after the trucks. The guard said it was no trouble, that the cloth of his uniform had been manufactured in accordance with a state regulation that prohibited it from being wetted by rain.

A truck door slammed. A starter whined, the engine caught and rumbled steadily as the driver warmed it. Jake heard other voices. More drivers were coming out. They also were talking with the guard. Evidently, the rain having stopped, the guard was showing his diligence by making a last tour around the trucks before they all pulled away. A second starter screamed, another engine caught and roared, then a third.

Jake could hear nothing above the engines for a minute. Then—less by sound than by sixth sense—he realized someone was at the rear corner of his truck.

Jake tried to pull his knees up closer to his chin. He could move them only two inches. The space between the cartons was barely wide enough for him to have wormed into. His head touched another one that blocked the end of his tiny cave. He lay in total blackness. If someone lifted the tarp just enough to peer in, would they see him—the soles of his boots?

"What's the matter?" A voice spoke from somewhere toward the front of the truck.

"Your tarp's loose here."

"What? Let me see. Yeah, must have come loose in the wind. Thanks."

Jake heard a scratching sound, then a metallic click coming through the truck's frame. The driver must be tying the tarp to a ring.

Jake held his breath, held himself still. The guard might be satisfied by the driver's unconcern; would the dog be?

"There. That'll hold now."

"Where you going?"

"Brno."

"Rotten day to be on the road."

Jake let his breath out very, very slowly and then slowly filled his lungs again.

"Aren't they all?"

"They say it's supposed to break tomorrow."

"Fine by me. Well, see you next week."

Jake heard the driver's footsteps alongside the trailer, heard the door open and slam again. Then the truck started. He continued to lie as though dead, barely breathing, until the truck began to move.

What was it he had forgotten?

The truck jounced and jolted too much to let him doze, so Jake had gone over it all in his head again—every preparation he'd made, his getting away from the hotel, his plan for when he got out of the truck. The more he assured himself that he hadn't forgotten anything, the more convinced he became that he had.

There was no reason for him to think so. Everything (except the truck) was running as smooth as a wagonload of wheat going down a shoot. The pickup had been arranged out of Prague by some agent or net he knew nothing about. He and the driver hadn't seen each other, and never would. When they got as far as he was going, the truck would stop, the driver would loosen the tarp again and get back into his cab and enjoy his semmel and thermos of coffee. It would only be midmorning then. The CIS men back at the hotel would only be beginning to wonder when he was coming out of his room.

The bicycle and guns and false papers would be waiting, hidden behind the abandoned chapel he'd told McCluskie about. He'd get on the bike and pedal away, and by noon, by the time the CIS were finally beginning to worry, he'd be long gone, carried out of Bohemia completely, sitting in Moravia, in Jan Hrádec's kitchen.

After that . . . Well, that was the part he should be worrying about. Jan's first son, Little Jan, had been one of those kids who died throwing rocks at the tanks back in '68. Antonin had been only five then; but he wasn't ever going to be allowed to go to a technical school, or be employed at any work but common labor at the collective farm. Marthe had married him last year, anyway; but they'd vowed not to have children who wouldn't be free.

If Jake had tried to get out everyone he knew who wanted out, he'd have had to charter a bus full-time. And he wasn't in the underground-railroad business primarily. So he thought of it not as any exploitation, but as doing two good things at once. He could offer the Hrádecs (as he had Milos Nagy) a way to help the agency that would take them out, too.

Thinking about Milos made him wince again. Well, it was their choice, it was always their choice.

If Antonin and Marthe chose not to help him this time, then he didn't know what he'd do. He didn't know what he was going to try doing with their help, either. But knowing nothing about Czerny's situation made it impossible to think about that, so he kept thinking about everything else; about what it was that—the stone in his stomach getting colder and heavier—he was sure he had forgotten.

The good thing was that the rain had stopped. The bad thing was that he had to walk for three kilometers, not knowing if he'd have to walk fourteen more, not knowing if he'd get there at all.

The truck driver hadn't even tried to turn off onto what was a reasonable secondary route for him, the road that went by that chapel. When he'd seen the plank barrier and the two soldiers there, he'd picked up speed again and continued on the main road until he was beyond the next curve. Then, as he'd been supposed to do on the other road, he stopped and got out and untied the back corner of the tarp. "The army's blocking the turnoff," he said. "Not a check; they're just not letting anybody in. I bang twice, you come out." Then he got back into the cab and started to open his coffee.

Jake scrunched himself down toward the end of the trailer, and when the driver banged twice on the door of his cab, came out fast, dropping to the shoulder and moving as though he'd been walking and simply passed the truck. He was a half-dozen meters away by the time the next car came around the bend.

As Jake covered the two hundred or so meters from the bend to the side road, he saw two cars try to turn in. The driver of the first car showed papers, and the barrier was moved for him. The second was ordered away. The driver tried to argue, but the sentry drew himself up and snapped an arm and pointed finger to full length. While that was happening, a boy on a bicycle went in and neither soldier looked at him.

Jake came up to the junction with his hands in his pockets, and turned in as though it never occurred to him not to. One soldier nodded, merely acknowledging his presence.

Okay, they weren't looking for anyone. They weren't keeping everybody out. It was just vehicles. He was pleased with himself for having arranged to travel in the area on a bicycle; pleased enough not to worry about the extra walk to reach it.

He did worry a little when first a jeep and then two army trucks passed him while he was walking. None of the soldiers paid any attention to him, though. He thought he might just get through the whole thing without any trouble, until he saw the tents.

A large group of them had been pitched in a pasture off to his left. Then there were four big ones on the grassy strip at the edge of a wood, and little ones in under the trees. Several soldiers lounged just inside the open doors of a barn at a farm he passed. All of those were back from the road, not really a problem. But then Jake came over the little rise and saw the abandoned chapel off ahead, beside the road on the right, and the tents—enough for an entire company—in the meadow down the road beyond it, and the three soldiers on the broken steps in front of the chapel, and the other soldiers, in groups, strolling up and down the road.

Without the bicycle he would have to walk the remaining fourteen kilometers to the Hrádecs' farm. He was already forty minutes behind schedule, and walking all the way would take him over two hours longer than he'd planned. And his rubber boots weren't right for steady walking—a tender place on his heel would be raw long before he got there. And he'd have no papers if he was stopped. And no weapons to use in trying to snatch Czerny.

Of course, if the soldiers had been close to the chapel last evening, the bicycle might never have been left for him.

One soldier was leaning against the chapel, the other two sat, smoking. With idle curiosity they watched Jake approach. They were very young. The one standing had his first stripe. Jake guessed they were conscripts.

He nodded to each of them as he let himself down heavily onto the step and sighed. "Somehow, it stopped raining," he said. "Somehow, the message wasn't delivered that I'd have to walk." Grunting, he pulled off his boot, pushed down his wool sock, touched the sore place on his heel. "When did they begin turning back the traffic?"

"I don't know. Sometime this morning, I guess," one of the soldiers answered.

"Six-sixteen this morning," Jake said. "It must've been. I went past there at six-fifteen and there was no block. The message that I'd pass at six-fifteen did get through. If they hadn't waited until after that, if the block'd been in place before I went, I wouldn't have gone. Or I'd have made a different plan to get back without having to walk."

"You think they timed it just to get you?"

"Of course. What else? You wouldn't suggest that in this country things happen by accident, without a plan, would you?" Jake pulled up his sock and—with more grunts—his boot again.

"If you'll excuse me, Comrade Colonel"—he nodded at one of the men beside him—"Comrade General" to the next, "Comrade Field Marshal" to the one standing, "I've got to take a leak."

He rose and, reaching for his fly, went around toward the back of the chapel. Wild elderberry bushes had grown up around it. Looking in, he could see the bicycle leaning against the back wall, behind the bushes there. He pulled it out.

"Thank you for guarding my bicycle," he said as he came around again. "I'll give a good report on you to the Minister of Defense next time I see him."

"That's your bike?"

"Of course it's my bike. You think I've got magical powers, I can just walk down a road and reach into the bushes and pull out a bike that I didn't put there already this morning?"

"Why didn't you ride it this morning?"

"Why would anyone ride his bicycle in the rain when a friend comes by and offers a lift in his car? Do I look like a thirty-year corporal? How did I know they'd close the road as soon as I'd passed so I couldn't get a ride back with a truck driver? Come to think of it, that explains it: getting the lift wasn't planned, so they had to move so fast to close the road they forgot to send word to keep the rain going."

He wheeled the bicycle up to the road, climbed onto it. "You wait and see: when they find out what happened, heads will roll."

CHAPTER 14

McCluskie had gotten word that the bicycle had been put in its hiding place. When he heard that the truck driver had left Jake off, he sent out the teams to Poysdorf, fourteen kilometers south of the Czech border. Since Jake had no idea how he would try to snatch Czerny, he couldn't say which way he'd go to try to get out. But the nearest border to Austerlitz was straight south, so it made sense to have some people near it.

"They'll call in to confirm when they're in position," Deming reported.

"Good. Well, now we wait."

"Anything else you want me to do, Steve?"

"Yeah. Anything you can think of that you can do. I can't think of anything else, myself."

"You going to stay around?"

McCluskie sat back, shrugged. "Well, there's no reason to. Jake's got to get there, figure a plan. It's going to be hours, maybe a day or two before he can move—assuming he tries it at all. We could go out, have a nice lunch, have a nice dinner, catch a show. Yeah, I'm going to stay here."

"Yeah. I hate waiting. I think the waiting's the hardest part."

McCluskie nodded. "Of course, Jake might not see it that way."

*   *   *

Going to the concert had been a mistake, Jane decided. The music didn't distract her. She couldn't really listen, couldn't follow it, hardly knew what they were playing. But the loud and agitated parts underscored her anger at the CIA, the Czechs, at Talley himself; and in the soft and lyrical passages she ached with love and longing for him.

Walking back to her hotel, undressing, sitting in bed staring at the wall, she recognized that her anger, and her love and her fear of losing Talley, had merely been focused by his arrest. He would be released soon—she wouldn't let herself think otherwise—but the conflict of emotions would remain. When she saw him again, she would throw herself into his arms. And then?

She shook her head. That was the trouble with both of them: they thought too much, looked ahead too far.

Talley had said—on the evening they were together in Czechoslovakia—that he would try to live by compromise. Could she?

Even at ground level the thick fog glowed from the radiance of the moon unseen overhead. The fog was so filled with light and yet obscuring, so dense yet insubstantial, that anyone out of doors might imagine himself in the depths of a dreamed ocean. The constant distant whine and roar might have been its tides.

At three in the morning the trucks had been rumbling for a full twelve hours. The first companies of soldiers had been dressed in their costume uniforms after their midday meal, driven unit by unit up to the heights throughout the late afternoon, fed their field-ration supper there. The trucks swung around on alternate routes to other staging areas and were loaded again. They made a continuous chain around the circuit, crawling slowly because of the fog. The soldiers who would play the French, down on the lowland, began marching to their positions at eight P.M. The last of all of them would be in place by four.

At the town's soccer field the floodlights intensified the fog with yet more light, a warmer, slightly amber light that made it seem still thicker. The sentry there had given up trying to see into it. He sauntered, shoulders hunched and hands in pockets, 'round and 'round the helicopter.

He had not been able, though, to make himself stop listening. Convincing himself that there was nothing to hear other than the trucks going up to the heights, he would drift for a while in his own thoughts and then halt suddenly, ears pricking. Had he heard something? A footfall, the soft pad of a heavy paw, a slithering? He would stand, rigid, his hand on the sling of his submachine gun. He would hear nothing. He would not be able to hear again in memory whatever he thought he'd just heard. He would persuade himself he'd heard nothing, and resume his patrol.

At three o'clock, with great relief, he heard the van coming along the road from the town, as he'd been told it would.

The driver of the van had realized that in such fog less light meant better vision. He had used only the amber running lights, and crept all the way in first gear. He knew when he was approaching the soccer field by that warmer glow in the air around it, and then he saw the fence and the arch of the entrance. The glow from the floodlights was strong enough to cast shadows from the fence out into the fog, making a phantom three-dimensional barrier across the road. He stopped the van without bothering to pull to the side.

He and his partner had gotten out and opened the rear doors when a voice shocked them both as though a were-creature had risen out of the earth behind them.

"You the people with the things to unload?"

The driver's partner gave a kind of yelp, and the driver gasped. Both of them were too startled at first even to curse. Then the driver managed to gulp out, "Who the fuck are you?" He stared at the three figures who had materialized there. One was a short middle-aged man, another taller and younger. The third looked to be a tall teenager wearing a sweatshirt with a hood, but he stood back of the others, where his face couldn't be seen well. The driver did have the impression that the youth was as pretty as a girl.

"We were told to come here," the older man said. "To help."

"Who told you?"

"I don't know. Somebody who was hiring people to help."

"Why did he send you here?"

"To help you unload," the man said in a patient tone that

suggested he was a simple man used to explaining simple matters to domestic animals.

"We didn't ask for any help. We don't need any help."

"Then why did he send us out here?"

"That's what I just asked you!"

"Well, how do I know? We were sent out here to help you unload. If you don't need any help, that's all right. As long as we get paid for coming out here. But you're supposed to give us a paper—write it down—that we helped you, and how long, so we can get paid. Now, if you don't want us to help you, that's all right. But you should give us a paper anyway to say that we came like we were sent, and we should get paid even if you—"

"Okay, okay. You can help unload. Why not? Just don't touch anything until I tell you. Jiri, let 'em carry the film cans."

The sentry heard the voices. He knew the people were coming, expected to see them, yet was startled when the hulking figures appeared and solidified.

"Nobody stole it," the driver said to him.

"Oh, they tried. If I hadn't been watching every minute . . ."

"Oh, yeah, yeah. Watching. You been inside sleeping. You been in there all night playing with yourself."

"On duty, on guard, on the alert."

"Yeah, yeah."

The driver opened the hatch at the waist of the helicopter, stepped up and in. "Okay, hand me those. One at a time."

The man and the youth who had followed passed up the aluminum containers they had carried. The driver secured them inside. He dropped to the ground again.

"On the alert. You know they stole the bleachers. You think there are bleachers there?" He gestured to one side and the other, shook his head. "They're gone. While you were inside here having wet dreams, they stole them. They stole the clubhouse, too." He jerked his head at his helpers. "Come on."

"I wasn't guarding the bleachers," the sentry said; but the men were already vanishing.

After several minutes he heard the driver's voice again. Then a strange shape emerged from the fog and resolved into five men and a large box on wheels. Two of the men were pushing the box, a third walked beside it, his hand resting on it. The youth followed at a distance. The driver walked on the other side, giving a steady stream of directions.

At the door of the helicopter they stopped. The men pushing stepped back, and the driver and his helper opened the box. "We'll put it in ourselves," the driver said. They lifted the camera from its case, set it onto the floor of the helicopter. It was shrouded with a black leather-looking cover.

One of the men who had pushed the box had stepped back and was looking at the helicopter in wonder. "I never saw one of these things before," he said. "Not close up, on the ground. I still don't understand how they can fly without wings. Can I look at it?"

"Sure," the guard said, and the man walked slowly around the machine.

When the driver and his helper had secured the camera to its mount in the hatch, they came out again. "Okay," said the driver, "you can take the case back." To the sentry he said, "You know, they stole the fence, too. While you were on guard."

"I'm not guarding the fence."

"Somebody should have been. I just hope when we get back out there we won't find they stole our van. We'll be back in an hour, unless you let them steal the road, too."

"Are you the one who makes the movie?" the older man asked as they were pushing the case back to the van.

"Well, yeah, you could say that," the driver answered. His helper snorted. "Well, yeah," the driver insisted. "We handle the camera. There's somebody else who tells us the stops and . . . the technical stuff he wants. But we actually take the picture." For another moment the driver deliberated between impressing the yokels with his individual responsibility versus his importance as a part of a great machine. He found a way to do both.

"Actually there's six other crews like us. Seven cameras altogether. And there's a guy in charge of each. But there's one chief director over the whole operation—he's the one whose idea the whole film is. And he's going to be in the helicopter, and we're the ones who're running the camera directly for him."

"Ohhhh," the older man said, nodding appreciatively. "And when does he come?"

"Just before five, I think. Everything starts at five, just before the sun rises. He doesn't like to wait around, so he'll probably come just before then."

"Ohhh. Could we wait and see him?"

"I don't think so. I don't think they'll let anybody be close around here."

"Oh. I would like to have seen him. And see that machine go up."

"Sorry."

They reached the van. The helpers lifted the camera case into the back.

"Thanks," the driver said. "You see we didn't really need any help, but thanks anyway. Now, I'm supposed to give you some kind of paper?"

"Yeah," the older man said. He was the only one of the three who had spoken at all. He reached inside his anorak. "I got something for you here."

"You have not forgotten anything," Jake insisted to himself. "It's just nerves. You just got to have something to worry about, and it's all going so well you got to make it up."

He was glad, now, about the road to the chapel having been closed, and about all the soldiers being around. Getting the bicycle and riding it all the way to the Hrádecs' had been true problems. They had kept him from fretting about imaginary ones. There had been no trouble, though. The soldiers obviously considered themselves to be on a kind of holiday. Except for the ones who had been closing the district to traffic, none of them had any interest in the civilian population at all. At least not in an old man on a bicycle: they did whistle and call to girls who went past.

Still, fear of the soldiers took the curse off the operation being hopelessly, forebodingly, flawless. That and the half hour when it seemed the Hrádecs wouldn't help. Antonin's and Marthe's faces had started to glow as soon as Jake began to tell them he might get them out. But then Big Jan said he wouldn't go along. Only after he and Antonin had walked outside, and both came back with their eyes wet, had they assented.

Everyone around the village knew of the helicopter, of course. Antonin told Jake about it almost at once: trying to use it was so obvious. Marthe worked as a chambermaid and waitress at the Post Hotel. She was the one who had been supposed to get Talley in to see Czerny. She knew Czerny would be filming from the helicopter. There really had been nothing for Jake to figure out. They had merely had to reach the soccer field at midnight and wait for a way in to present itself.

What was it, Jake tried to remember, that he had been told? Every profession has its nightmare? Actors dream of going on stage, and they don't know the name of the play or what they're supposed to say. Teachers dream they've forgotten to go to a class throughout the entire semester. Maybe surgeons can't remember which part they're supposed to take out, or how to close the cut.

Antonin and Marthe sat in the front of the van, holding each other. Jake sat in the rear, his back against one side. The two film men lay tied and taped, their faces turned to the other side. Jake glanced at them from time to time, to make sure they weren't wriggling. Mostly he stared ahead, telling himself he hadn't forgotten anything, going over it all again to convince himself.

At four-fifteen he looked at his watch again and said, "Okay, let's go."

". . . Wings don't go 'round and 'round. I don't understand it at all."

The sentry heard the man's voice approaching, so he wasn't alarmed when the three figures formed in the mist and came toward him.

"Maybe when I see it go up . . ." The older man was speaking. He nodded to the sentry. "So. Pretty soon now."

"Yeah. You're still here?"

The older man came up to the sentry to talk to him. The younger one halted a meter away. The pretty youth drifted on toward the helicopter—not too close—trying to look inside the open hatch.

"They told us to wait. I don't know why, they really didn't

need much help to load those things; but they wanted us to help, and they said to wait here in case they need more help when the chief director comes. You been on duty here all night?"

"Since midnight."

"That's a long shift. When do you get off?"

"I don't know. After five. After they take off."

"Did you ever ride in one of these machines?"

"No."

Jake gazed thoughtfully past the sentry's shoulder at the helicopter. "I don't understand . . ." He fished in his pocket, brought out a packet of cigarettes, took one out, then seemed to come back to awareness with a jerk. "Oh. You want a smoke?"

The soldier glanced away, into the fog. "Well . . ."

"Who's going to know?"

"Thanks." He took a cigarette.

Jake brought out matches, struck one, held his cupped hands out. The soldier leaned forward.

At four thirty-five a vehicle came up the road. It stopped, two doors slammed. After a moment the voices of two men approached. As they neared the helicopter, the man in uniform standing by it called, "Who's there?"

"At ease, Captain, at ease. I'm the pilot."

"Who's the other one?" The guard seemed to be taking his duties most seriously. He had his submachine gun slung ready-to-fire across his chest, his hands on the stock and grip.

"I'm the cinematographer." The man spoke with a tone suggesting that the sentry should be impressed by that title, but that he would be too ignorant to know what it meant. For all his show of alertness, the soldier had probably been sleeping. His uniform seemed rumpled and ill-fitting. He was an older man, but without rank; a career man, probably many times broken, probably for alcoholism.

"Where are the cameramen?"

"They went to the clubhouse, sir. To use the toilet, sir."

"They were supposed to stay here."

"They said they'd be right back, sir."

"They were supposed to stay here." The cinematographer climbed into the helicopter. "I'm not going to take the cover off or put the lenses in until we're up," he said. "Not in this fog. If we're going to be ahead of the sun like we're supposed to be, we'll have to take off as soon as Janos comes—to give me extra time. If those bastards are late . . ."

"I'll warm her up," the pilot said. "Stand clear of the rotor," he told the sentry. "I'm going to start the engine." He climbed into the machine and went forward. After a few moments the starter screamed.

At four o'clock the thousands of soldiers up on the heights, and those down by the river, had been formed into ranks according to the diagrams their officers and noncoms had been given. Then they had been allowed to sit in place. The first units were to begin moving at five o'clock exactly; so everyone was ordered to his feet at fifteen minutes before. All the thousands of them were standing within two minutes after the whistles began blowing and the first commands were shouted, but they were gotten up that far in advance to be sure they'd be ready. They were allowed to stand at ease for a few more minutes, though.

At four-fifty—to be sure they'd be ready to move ten minutes later—the next order was given. It might have seemed they'd all been called to attention to honor Janos Czerny, who, at that moment, stepped from his car outside the soccer field.

In the early days of his career, Janos Czerny had always arrived at the theater before anyone else, with his notorious checklists and pages of notes. In time he had learned that while genius may be an infinite capacity for taking pains, authority depends on delegating the execution of details to others.

His cameramen's van was parked up ahead, the car in which his pilot and his cinematographer had driven stood behind it, the helicopter's motor was running. In three minutes he would be strapping himself into his seat. In four the helicopter would lift. Emil, his cinematographer, would have five minutes—more than enough—to ready the camera as he obviously would not have done on the ground in the fog. At five o'clock the soldiers would begin marching. At seven after, the sun would rise. Everything was following Czerny's plan. He was pleased. Scowling slightly, he strode across the grass toward the soccer field entrance without deferring to his two guards. They seemed to accept the shift in positions and fell in behind him.

Now, with dawn advancing, turning the sky a brilliant blue

high above, the fog had lost its moony whiteness and become gray. The floodlights barely tinted it out on the field. Still awaiting the warmth of the sun that would dissipate it, it was as thick as ever. Slowly revolving, the blades of the helicopter's rotor churned it, but couldn't blow it away. The three men saw the shape of the machine and began to pull down their heads well before reaching the radius of the rotor's sweep. They saw also the silhouette of the army sentry standing to one side. Czerny made out Emil's figure by the camera in the open hatch. He ducked and scuttled toward the ship. The guards paused to let him reach it.

One foot on the step, his hands reaching up to the handholds, Czerny saw the wide-eyed fear in Emil's face. Momentum was carrying him, and before that fear could register and stop him, someone reached out and grabbed his upper arm and helped him in through the hatch. Then the guard who was to go up, too, crouched and approached.

Jake had wanted to do it clean and nice-guy, as he had with the cameramen and sentry. Slipping the submachine gun's safety to "off," he shouted, "Halt! Halt! Halt!" But the noise of the engine covered his voice. The guards couldn't hear him. Doubled over, the submachine gun leveled, he ran in under the whirling blades in a way that both of them might see he had them covered, and let him back them off. He didn't expect to be able to do it that way, but at least he tried.

Whatever particle of time it took them to comprehend that the sentry was not a sentry wasn't sufficient for them to realize they couldn't be quick enough. Or maybe they instantaneously assumed Jake was going to shoot no matter what they did, so they might as well try. The nearer one was pivoting, reaching into his jacket, the farther one throwing himself to the side and reaching, when Jake held the trigger, swinging, and cut both of them down.

He put an extra burst into each, then spun and ran for the hatch.

Czerny, still staring at Emil, was sitting in the swivel bucket-seat, the hand of the man who'd pushed him there on his shoulder, when Jake came through the hatch. Czerny's jaw dropped. He started to try to rise, but the hand forced him down again.

Jake grabbed Emil's arm. "Out!" he said, "out!" half shoving the man, half allowing him to jump. Emil hit the ground, dropped to hands and knees, began scrabbling away.

"Buckle him in!" Jake shouted. As Antonin started to do so, Czerny tried again to rise. "What is the meaning—"

Jake grabbed at the submachine gun, swung it to point at Czerny's head. His finger was well away from the trigger, but he didn't think the man would notice. "Quiet!" he shouted. As soon as the belt had been made fast, he unslung the gun and handed it to Antonin. Then he went forward.

He took the pistol from Marthe's hand without allowing the muzzle to leave contact with the back of the pilot's head. "Go on back," he shouted.

He put his head down by the pilot's ear. "Okay," he said. "When I tell you, then we're going to go up. You're going to fly this thing the way I tell you. We're going over the border, to Austria. You can come back then, if you want to. Maybe you can stay. Either way, you're okay. You do anything wrong, I'll blast your fucking head off, okay? We may die, but you'll go first. Okay? All right, do it!"

The pilot hesitated not one moment. He advanced the throttle, tipped the blades, and the ship leaped upward.

Instantly they were above the fog that lay as though in frozen waves like a white sea. From it islands of blue hilltops rose. Janos Czerny stared out the window next to the open hatch through which the still-covered camera pointed. Even at the distance, even before the first rays of the sun touched the Pratzen Heights, he could see the patches, the black blocks that followed the contours of the hill yet were not natural to it. Second by second, as the horizon brightened ever more yellow-white, those rectangles stood in sharper, darker contrast to the green behind them. And then they started to move.

"They're marching!" he said.

The helicopter was swinging south and east, just the path Czerny had planned for its first sweep. As he had envisioned it, the masses of troops were flowing down to disappear into that softness that might seem a mist of enchanted, innocent sleep spread over the valley. The roar of the helicopter was deafening; it was the silence he had imagined.

"My film!" he said. "My film!"

Antonin put his head down close to Czerny's.

"My film!"

Antonin straightened again. He shook his head, not understanding.

CHAPTER 15

Suddenly, yet not all at once, the single blue-white surface of the fog brightened with palest yellow streaks as the sunlight touched it, and where shadows of the hills were cast, it deepened to purple patches. The helicopter was a black speck, a tiny damselfly, skimming close across a mottled lake. Then a phantom companion appeared, its shadow, racing with it, away to its right, vanishing whenever the helicopter passed through a dark patch, there again when it came into light, drawing gradually closer.

Jake made the pilot fly barely above the fog, below hilltop level. There was no way radar could see them. He guessed they'd have ten minutes, anyway, before anybody back at Austerlitz knew something was wrong. It would take at least that long for the cinematographer guy to get himself together and back to town. Maybe more. By the time somebody official had his mind around the fact that the helicopter wasn't where it should be, and he'd put out an alert to watch for it, before any air interception could be called for and scrambled and could find them by visual contact, they'd be at the border. That's where the trouble would start.

Not, he figured, in the going over. Although the fog was thinning as they went south, they still might find a patch hanging in across the line and be able to go over without actually being seen. Even if they were spotted, they could shift at the last minute and pass between tower points, or hop over out of small-arms range. Jake wasn't worried about them being shot at, so much. The problem really wasn't getting out of Czechoslovakia at all, anymore. The problem would be with the Austrians.

If this white-haired old guy showed up at, say, the West German border being driven on his way to, say, Paris, and this nice young couple appeared at the Vienna airport and were put on a TWA flight to the States, and they all had valid-looking documents, nobody would have to take official interest in them. Nobody would have to notice they'd passed through neutral Austria at all.

On the other hand, the government of neutral Austria would have to notice—and would be bound to be pissed off about—a CIA agent and two criminals who'd murdered, stolen a helicopter, and snatched away a convicted traitor, who might just say (before he'd had a chance to think or be talked to about it) that he wanted to go back and finish making his movie. The Austrians would have to take action if they saw those people coming in. If they caught them.

How to avoid getting caught was the problem Jake had worked at all through the night, while he and his friends waited for the camera crew to come, and then for Czerny.

If he could get them all to Poysdorf, they'd be okay. McCluskie had men waiting there for them. If he could just get Czerny and Antonin and Marthe holed up and find a telephone, they'd be okay. Now, on the face of it, that didn't seem like a hard job. They'd be coming down out in the sticks. Maybe nobody would see them land; and if it was a farmer out in the middle of a field, so what? There was probably an average of one cop per every five hundred square kilometers around there. If that.

The problem was going to be the goddam helicopter.

The helicopter had been God's gift to get them out of Czechoslovakia, but once they landed, it was going to be like a great big ball and chain. Put it down close to a town or a highway, it'd be spotted before they could get far away from it. Put it down away back behind some hill, it'd take longer to locate and get to; but they'd have to go farther before they'd find a way to contact the guys in Poysdorf.

Now, if the pilot was a buddy, he'd drop them and then keep going and take the pursuit after him. Jake didn't think he should count on the guy's being a buddy. Jake thought about that, and finally figured out what to try.

In the last couple minutes before they reached the border, he leaned close and shouted into the pilot's ear.

"When we get on the other side, this is how it's going to be: I'm going to tell you where to land. It's going to be close to a road. We're all going to get out—you, too. Then you're going to get right back in—or I'll blast your head off—and take right off again—or I'll blow the thing up with you inside. We've got a bomb aboard, back there. It's radio-controlled. I can set it off at a range of anywhere up to ten kilometers. You're going to fly away from the road—off to the east—for at least five. I'm going to be able to see you at that distance. Then you set down again. Then you can get out and get away wherever you want. If you don't set down, if you turn back toward the highway . . . boom! You got it?"

The pilot nodded. He looked even sicker. Jake felt sure that whether he believed the story or not, he'd give it the benefit of the doubt.

Now fog lay only over streams and rivers, tracing their courses as though with white chalk lines on a green board. The helicopter swept at barely a hundred meters across the Brno-Bratislava autobahn, and Jake directed the pilot toward Lednice and then straight along the road past the mist that covered the lakes, to Valdice. When he saw the steeple of the church rushing at them, he gestured, and the pilot lifted the ship and they flashed toward the border, up and over the fences and dead zone, as though in a bound.

There wasn't a car in sight as far as they could see north toward Drasenhofen or south toward Poysdorf, so Jake had the pilot come down right on the highway. Why not?

He'd been tempted for an instant to have him take them clear down to the Poysdorf outskirts, but decided that would be pushing it too far. Instead, he got them off just at a crossroad, so if anybody did see where they landed, and they weren't caught right there, there might be some question about which way they'd gone.

The pilot proved either credulous or prudent. He got directly back into his ship when Jake told him to, hurled it upward, sped off to the east for a distance that Jake estimated to be just barely beyond the five kilometers he'd been ordered to fly, and set down abruptly. He was hardly on the ground again before they heard the jets.

The thunder swelled up out of the south and around to the west. A hill rising at that side of the highway blocked any sight of the jets until they pulled around at the border, streaking along it toward the east. There were two of them, black specks clear against the bright sky.

Jake and the others turned to watch the planes, but he didn't let them stop. At first, even as the helicopter was rising to leave them, Czerny had started to protest. He had gotten out something about no right, and outrageous, when Jake took a step forward and shouted directly up into his face, "Shut your fucking mouth!" Perhaps it was the sight of the little man looking at him like an angry terrier who might leap and bite his nose, perhaps it was merely hearing anyone speak to him in that way, but it shocked Czerny into momentary silence.

"You're a free man!" Jake shouted. "Goddammit, you're free!" He glared up at the great man. "You want to go *back*?"

Jake took the second of silence that followed for acquiescence. He put down the submachine gun, stripped off the Czech soldier's uniform from over his country man's clothes, grabbed uniform and gun, and said, "Let's go," jerking his head down the road toward Poysdorf.

He didn't imagine that they would all just walk the five or six kilometers into town. He only figured to get them headed in the right direction until he spotted a hiding place. But then—just a second before they heard the jets, as Jake was turning from watching the helicopter land—he spotted the booth and the sign.

Across the road, on the southbound side, was a small, three-sided shelter with a bench, and the yellow sign with a black H on it sticking out from a pole. A bus stop. As the jets swung around the border, now following it south again, he crossed the road and read the notice that listed the times when the bus was due to stop there. He looked at his watch. He considered. "Come on over," he called to the others.

On their next pass, the jets roared directly over the highway. Austrian radar would have picked up the helicopter as it came high over the border, then lost it when it dropped again. The jets had swung around a possible outer limit first. Now they would work inward. They were starting to turn east the second time when they must have seen the machine. They banked more sharply and then flew a tight circle. Then they spiraled outward again, keeping surveillance from a circuit nearly as wide as they'd made on their first time around.

In the shelter Antonin and Marthe sat close together, gripping each other's hands tightly. After Jake had hidden the submachine gun and the uniform in the ditch behind the shelter, he sat on the other side of them, next to Czerny.

"We are going to take the bus," Czerny said incredulously.

"That's right," Jake assured him. "Another seven minutes, about."

"We will be recognized."

"How? Nobody here's ever seen any of us before. I mean, even though you're a famous man, Mr. Czerny, I doubt any of the people out here would recognize you by sight."

"But they will know we are strangers. I suppose this bus must be for people who go to work in the town. The same people, every day. They will know we don't belong here."

"Well, yeah. But they won't refuse to let us ride. This is a free country, Mr. Czerny. You'll have to get used to that kind of thing. Of course later, when the police have gotten out a public alert and inquiry, somebody'll probably remember and report us. We'll be long gone by then."

Jake spoke with a tone of absolute confidence. What he said, after all, was perfectly plausible, and they'd all do better if they acted like it was true.

For another three minutes they sat in silence, all looking east, watching the sunlight slip brightness down over the hillsides facing them. Three times the shrieking roar of the jets rose and hurricaned over them and faded to distant rolling thunder, incongruously—surrealistically—out of the pale and fairest-weather sky. A truck rumbled north in that time, a car passed going south. Neither driver regarded them with any but the idlest curiosity.

Then they heard a helicopter coming and—looking south to watch for it—saw in the distance the flashing blue lights of the cars speeding up the highway.

The helicopter was angling east, heading directly toward

the Czech copter the jets were spotting for it. It would get there before the cars.

A minute and a half later the Austrian chopper was a dot in the sky starting to descend toward its objective, and the police cars raced up doing at least 150 kph. Their engines screamed and their brakes squealed as they decelerated and skidded right, onto the side road. The men in the cars must have been focused on making the turn at high speed. If any of them noticed the four people waiting patiently for the bus, the sight wasn't provocative enough to halt them.

"They didn't stop," Antonin said in wonder; "they didn't stop," in hope.

"Sure. Who expects anybody to be making a getaway on a bus?"

"But when they find the pilot," Czerny said portentously, "he will tell them who to look for. He will describe us."

Jake looked at him as though considering the feasibility of returning him to Czechoslovakia straightaway, himself. "Well," he said after a moment, "it won't matter. We'll get away before they can get back to us again. Here comes the bus now."

"Ah, Mr. Talley." Colonel Suk was standing at the windows when the guard opened the door and showed Talley into his office. All the shades had been raised, and midmorning brilliance filled the room. "Please come in." He turned to face Talley and tipped his head, indicating one of the armchairs across from the windows. He kept his hands clasped behind his back.

Suk waited for Talley to sit with what seemed to be his usual benign patience. Talley didn't like the look in the man's eyes.

"I have some good news for you," Suk said. "You may go back to Austria."

Surprise brought Talley upright in the chair.

"Yes, Mr. Talley, it is true." Suk came across the room slowly, smiling, as though enjoying the pleasure of making another person happy. "I have no further reason to hold you here." He nodded, began to pace to the other side again. "No, Mr. McCluskie has not exchanged himself for you. He has found a different solution to the problem." The tone of Suk's voice was good-humored, but Talley could see his hands gripping one another, clenching in regular spasms.

When Suk reached the windows again, he stood facing them while continuing to speak. "I had foreseen that he might attempt to do so by the obvious means of sending another person to contact Janos Czerny. We had taken further steps to isolate Czerny; he was never alone. But Mr. McCluskie was more audacious than ever we imagined he might be."

Suk half turned to look at Talley again. He forced his smile to broaden. "When you see him, please extend my compliments.

"So," he shrugged, "the question of whether this investigation of the Czerny affair was genuine or part of a ruse remains a question. You still believe—after all your thinking about it—you still believe it was genuine?"

"Yes."

"Yes?"

"Yes."

"Mr. Talley, may I offer you some friendly advice? Never, never try to conceal your true feelings. To your great credit, you lack the skill."

"I . . ." Talley tried to think of something to say, but Suk put up one hand to stop him.

"It is of no matter. I believe that when you came here you were convinced the investigation was genuine. I believe that you doubt now. In neither case do I believe that you *know*, so I will not pursue the issue with you further. However, I should think you would wish to pursue it with Mr. McCluskie when you see him again."

"I will."

"Yes. Well, it has been a pleasure to become acquainted with you. Too bad you had no opportunity to see Prague while you were here. It is a beautiful and interesting city. Perhaps someday you will come again—purely on holiday. If so, do let me know so that I may see to it you are well taken care of."

Talley could almost believe the man's warmth was genuine.

The director had a complex role to play. Like Suk with Talley, he had to maintain a façade of equanimity, even good humor.

"Right out of the middle of twenty thousand soldiers," the

director said, shaking his head as though amused at an outrageous prank played by some schoolboys.

Suk merely nodded.

"Which means they had to get into the middle: through the army first." The director kept all anger from his voice. He recognized that Colonel Suk was older than himself and with considerably more experience, a brilliant officer, a master of his craft, invaluable to the state and to the director's own career, and powerful. The man was not to be rebuked or chastised for having lost one round in a long and constantly shifting game.

"Supposedly the area around the town was sealed," he added.

"Only to vehicles. Only to people who didn't live there," Suk reminded.

"Yes. Of course. Just to reduce traffic during the filming. The army wasn't conducting a security operation. Actually their presence may have made it easier. Inevitable confusion, the regular police involved with traffic, and so forth."

On the other hand, as surely as the director would claim credit for every one of Suk's successes, he could be tainted by any failure. "However, I'm afraid the army is not accepting their lack of blame with good grace. After all, it *would* at first seem that it is they who have been made to look like fools. Although everyone in the government has been assuring them that no one does take that view, the army staff has been demanding that responsibility be clearly fixed elsewhere."

Suk tipped his head slightly, as though to show he was attending politely to a matter of little personal interest.

"I have had a rather unpleasant two hours," the director confessed. "The outcome—in a nutshell—is this: results speak for themselves. I am required—I have been directed—to tell you, Colonel, of the extreme unhappiness of the minister and the Council about this event. However, it has been agreed that the situation in which we find ourselves will not be regarded as the ultimate result of your operation." The director turned up both palms. "Everyone awaits, eagerly, your findings as to the truth or falsity of the NATO battle plan."

They all came up to the border, one car with security men ahead of Talley's, one behind. The car ahead stopped. The driver got out, spoke to the guard, then waved Talley through. Except for that, for not having to show his papers, he left Czechoslovakia just the way Robert H. Dobson had been supposed to. Suk had had him flown by helicopter from Prague to a village near the border. The rental car had been brought there, too. He had been told to get in and drive. That's all there was to it.

He wondered if anyone in Austria had been told that he was coming. The Austrian border official looked at his papers and waved him on without in any way suggesting Talley was known to him. Talley imagined himself simply driving to Vienna, going back to the hotel, and calling out to Jane, "Hi, honey. I'm home."

But then he saw her, getting out of the black Mercedes that was pulled over at the roadside just ahead. He actually recognized her before he realized a man standing by the front of the car was waving at him.

Pulling up behind, Talley barely had time to step from his car before she had reached him and thrown herself upon him.

"Oh, Tom! Oh, Tom! Oh, dear love!"

"Yeah, well," McCluskie said, "I knew you'd like to see her. And frankly, bringing her along was the only way I could keep her off my back." He was beside the driver, turned to look at Talley and Jane, who sat, arms still around each other, in half the back seat.

"Thanks," Talley said again.

McCluskie said to Jane, "You will make those phone calls as soon as we get back to Vienna?"

"Yes." She explained to Talley, "I wrote letters to some friends, with instructions about turning them over to certain people if they didn't hear from me by a certain time. I was *not* going to let them get away with just leaving you in there."

Talley raised Jane's hand and kissed her fingers.

"I kept telling her we weren't going to do that, but the professor is a very determined woman. Keep her on your side, Tom, that's my advice."

"I'm going to try to," Talley said.

McCluskie smiled and nodded as though bestowing his blessing on the happy couple. Then for a few moments he stared out the window past Scott, the driver. Turning to look back again, he asked, "Well, what do you think you'll do now, Tom? Stick around Vienna for a few days? Go see some of the mountains? I mean, I think you've earned some more holiday, if you want. What the hell? It's only the taxpayers' money."

"I think I'd like to go home," Talley said. Jane nodded vigorously.

"Yeah, I can understand that. We can probably have you on your way in another day or two."

Talley looked at him sharply.

"I mean, naturally, we need to talk a little. You know, routine debriefing."

"Yeah, sure," Talley said. "Okay, let's talk. I don't think it'll take a day or two, Steve. I think a half hour ought to about do it, and it's going to take at least that long for us to get back to Vienna, so let's talk."

"I don't think this is the time, Tom. I don't think this is the place."

"Sure it's the time. You always want to debrief as soon as you can, while it's all still fresh. There's nothing wrong with the place. It's secure, isn't it?"

"Come on, Tom."

"No, I mean it. You said, 'keep Jane on my side.' I intend to. I'm going to tell her everything I tell you. Now or later, it doesn't matter. She knows most of it—the background—already; and I want her to know more while she's still got those letters out." Talley turned to Jane. "That was brilliant. God, I love you."

He looked back at McCluskie. "I think I've got this thing pretty well figured out now, Steve. Colonel Suk was right: this whole Czerny reinvestigation was a fraud. I understand now why you might pull that. But it means you were using me. You damn near got me killed in that theater. You sent me into Czechoslovakia with the risk of prison and interrogation and maybe getting killed there, too. And all the time you knew it was a fraud. You didn't need me to find out anything. You didn't need Czerny to tell you he didn't send that duplicate material out of Russia. You knew Murtaugh wasn't a mole then. You were just playing a game with Suk, and using me and my stupid, compulsive curiosity. And you didn't care what the fuck happened to me!"

McCluskie pursed his lips for a moment. Then he took a quick breath and let it out in a quick sigh. "I did care what happened to you. I had no idea anybody would try to kill you—*us*—in that theater. I really didn't think you'd get caught in Czechoslovakia. But—yeah—I didn't care enough to not use you. That's the truth."

"Nice to know it, at last."

"I knew it all the time!" Jane said. "That they didn't care about you."

"I haven't told you anything that wasn't the truth, Tom. Not one damn thing. You think it over. I told you that carrying out the investigation was important. It was. I told you we wanted to be doing everything anyone could think we could do. We did. I didn't tell you the real reason, the entire truth, but why should I?"

"So that I could have made an informed choice."

"Yeah, well, I figured I knew what your choice would be. Look out for yourself, and don't get involved. Okay. Why not? Why should you get involved? You're not in the agency. You want to get rid of your garbage, you hire a garbageman. You want to live in a free country, you hire people to keep it that way. But you don't handle any of the mess yourself."

"You could have tried me! If whatever this is, is really important, if my living in a free country depends on it, you could have tried telling me about it!"

"Sure. Maybe I'm wrong. Maybe *this time* you'd have put something beside your personal concerns first. Okay. Suppose you did know what was going on, and you did agree to go in there, and then you got caught. Think about that. The very fact that you knew enough to convince you to go—if that's what it would take—would mean you knew too much, so you couldn't go. Use your head.

"I did tell you that this was important. I did tell you that. Over and over."

Talley was silenced for the moment.

But Jane responded, "How do we know we can trust you? How do we know what you say is important *is* important? You people have been wrong again and again. Why should we take your word for it?"

"Because you have to. You don't have to take our word for everything, forever. But it is a fact of the real world that there have to be secrets, and not everybody can know everything all the time. You have to take some things on trust."

"No, I do not have to! All right, Mr. McCluskie, there have to be some secrets. I'm not totally out of touch with the 'real world.' But I am not ever going to *trust* you. The reason America is a free country is that our system is founded on *dis*trust of the government."

"Yeah. Well, that's a great analysis, Professor. And you're right: checks and balances, the people are sovereign, never trust anybody who'll work for the government. I believe it. But now, just how do we operate on a day-to-day basis, applying that theory to everything we do? You're so goddammed smart, Professor, tell me that! I just asked Tom what more I could have told him so he could give his 'informed consent' to work for us—what I could have told him that wouldn't have made it impossible for him to work for us. I haven't heard him say a word since then."

"I don't know, Steve," Talley answered. "I don't know. I have to think about it, because—you're right—it's hard. But there has to have been something. If you had told me— Goddammit, I did help! Walt Simson called me and said it was important, and I came over here! You said talking to Czerny was important, and I agreed to go in there! Why can't you give me credit for that? Why did you think you had to trick me to get me to do it? There must have been something you could have told me so that I'd feel proud now that I did it, instead of feeling I've been screwed.

"You know, the way I feel now—I feel about you just the way I feel about Colonel Suk: both of you tricked me and used me. I don't feel there's any difference between you. And I could almost hope this whole operation—whatever it is—blows up in your face and comes crashing down and buries you! God damn you all!"

"You don't see *any* difference? You really can't see *any difference—any difference at all*—between Suk and me?

"I want to tell you, Tom, that makes me feel pretty bad—both for me and for you."

McCluskie held Talley's eyes for a moment, but then Talley couldn't do it any longer. He looked down, and McCluskie shifted to look through the windshield. They sped down the highway in silence. Then slowly McCluskie tipped his head to one side, then to the other, as though seeing how whatever he was looking at appeared from different angles. He nodded, turning partway back, but not actually facing Talley again.

"I can see how you might feel pretty angry at me, though," he said. "Yeah, I can see that. It would be natural for a guy like you to feel that. I can believe that you'd be so pissed off that you'd even . . ."

He twisted farther around so that he could look directly at Talley again. "All right, Tom, here it is: Murtaugh was not a mole when Czerny was arrested. He started working for the Czechs after that, after he was made a scapegoat and pushed out of his job. We knew that. We got on to him very early on. But we're trying to feed the Czechs some disinformation.

"You say you've got this thing figured out, you know the Czerny investigation was a fraud. So you must have worked it out that it was something like that.

"We're trying to make them believe that certain high-level strategic plans are true when, in fact, they're false. You really do not need to know what those plans are.

"If we can get the Czechs to accept the plans as true, then we will be in position to do a lot of good things for our side. You can appreciate that, without my telling you what—specifically—those things might be. And you can appreciate also that you *shouldn't* know—I'm not deceiving you—you just shouldn't know what those things are.

"But even without knowing any more than this, you can see that this operation is really important. Right?"

After a moment of silence, McCluskie asked again, "Right?"

"All right, Steve. I would agree that—if you are telling me the truth—that would be an important operation."

"Would you help with such an operation?"

"No!" Jane broke in.

"No? How about that, Tom? You wanted credit for helping. I give it to you. I apologize if I didn't before. How about it now? Now you're informed. You agree that it's important. Do you help, or do you just say, 'It's a job for the garbagemen'?"

"Tom—"

Talley stared at McCluskie. "I guess I would think it was my duty."

"I appreciate that, Tom. I appreciate I may have underestimated you. I'm sorry. I don't expect my apologizing will make you any less angry, but for what it's worth . . ." McCluskie shrugged.

"As a matter of fact, Tom," he continued, "I don't really want it to make you any less angry. I can see how having you so pissed off that you'd want 'to bring this whole thing crashing down' on my ears could make you try to do just that."

"What do you mean?"

"I mean that—not that you'd really be a traitor: got to work for the other side, take money, anything like that. You'd never do that. But I can imagine that—to get even, to spit out the bad taste you've got about this—you'd call up Suk and spill the whole thing: what you suspect, the impression you got from your debriefing. That you're sure the investigation *is* a fraud, and you believe the purpose was to make the Czechs believe something false is true."

"I wouldn't do that."

"Good!" Jane said, and glared at McCluskie.

"Suk would know I'd never do that."

"Tom . . . ?"

"Oh, he might. If he thought you were really angry enough. Why shouldn't you be angry, Tom? I really did treat you shitty. Led you along, cynically played on your thoroughness and your sense of responsibility. I did do that. It's the truth. I really did use you, and you know it, don't you?"

Talley met McCluskie's eyes levelly.

"Tom . . ." Jane twisted to look at Talley directly. "You wouldn't . . . you're not going to let him . . ."

"I used you. It's the truth, and you know it."

"Yes."

"I did put you in danger; and even if I didn't mean to, I didn't care. I really didn't care. You know it."

"Yes."

"And he'll do it again, Tom!"

"Oh, I will, Professor. I sure will. It's in a good cause. Tom can see that. He knows about this business. He understands the good a thing like this could do. He knows that's more important than what happens to him. I'm giving him credit for that."

McCluskie swung on Talley again. "And that's why I let you go into Czechoslovakia. And you know—when you were caught—I wouldn't have done a thing to get you out. I just snatched Czerny so I wouldn't have to go in myself. I couldn't have gone in. Never mind my neck, I couldn't have gone in because that would have blown the operation. And the operation is important. More important than my neck, more important than yours. I snatched Czerny to save the operation. You, you could have rotted in there for years until we had somebody of theirs, equally insignificant, to exchange for you."

"You son of a bitch," Talley said.

"Yeah," McCluskie agreed.

"Tom, don't let him . . . !"

"Don't let him?" McCluskie snapped. "Why not? Why shouldn't Tom do this? Come on, Professor: give me some more analysis of the American system. Tell me about how a democratic government is supposed to operate. What are the responsibilities and duties of the individual citizen? Are you going to tell me that everything should be left up to the professionals, and there's no time when an ordinary citizen has a duty to help?"

"No. I . . . there are *some* times, but—"

"But this isn't one of them? Tom can see it's one of them. Tom can understand what an operation like this could do to—"

"Stop it!" Talley shouted. "Goddamn you, McCluskie! Don't you try to put her and me against each other! We are *not* going to be at opposite sides on this!" He had taken Jane's hand again, and clutched it as he yelled at McCluskie.

Then he turned to her. "Steve McCluskie is a lying, hypocritical, manipulating bastard. I despise his guts. But in this case, what he's trying to do, this operation—even without him telling me, I can see some of the implications. This is an important thing. It's something I think I'd have a duty to help with. A duty, a responsibility, for myself. Not because of anything he— In spite of him.

"But you're out of luck, Steve," Talley said, looking up at McCluskie again. "I'd never get away with it. You know—and I know perfectly well—they'd never accept my just calling somebody on the phone and dropping this. They'd want to see me in person to get a reading on me, at least; and I'd never be able— Suk himself said—just this morning—that I haven't got the talent for lying. They'd see right through me."

"Oh, you do all right, Tom. You may not be a natural, but

. . . remember how you got Hovey away from us in Maryland? I remember. I never suspected you. And you got him all the way up to New Hampshire; sitting right there in the car with you: he never suspected. Don't sell yourself short. When you're motivated, Tom, you can lie with the best of them.''

CHAPTER 16

"The things I got from Suk,'' Talley said as he began talking about his interrogation, ''were, first, that he thought the Czerny reinvestigation was a fraud, and, second, that he wanted us to think Murtaugh had become his agent only recently. The first he hit very hard, the second he tried to slip in on me.

''Now, on the basis of everything, I'd think these were his objectives: one, to find out if the reinvestigation was for real; two, to tell us he thinks it's a fake because, three, Murtaugh became a Czech agent only recently, and we—you—know that. The first of those is a goal in itself. The second and third go together to make another goal of disinforming us—you. That is, if you don't already know *exactly* when Murtaugh went over, he'd like you to believe his version. You want me to start through it blow by blow?''

''No. Not now, not for me. But I want you to take a minute and run it in your head and tell me: what does Suk want to believe? I mean, you said he kept hitting that he thinks the investigation was a fraud. Is he really most inclined to believe that?''

After several moments Talley answered, ''Yeah. He wasn't sure, but I think that's what he believes to be most probable.''

McCluskie nodded appreciatively. ''He's a smart man. So he most likely figures this unbelievably valuable material Murtaugh gave him really is unbelievable.''

McCluskie turned to Jane. More than merely resigning

himself to the fact that she could not be kept in ignorance, he understood that gaining Talley's continued help required drawing her in. "What do you think about this international intrigue business, Professor?"

"I think it's absurd, and ridiculous, and childish."

McCluskie nodded in vigorous agreement. "Ain't it the truth. The only thing—now, I'm not the historian you are—but as far as I know, it's always been like this. You know of anybody in history has ever done it all just up and up?"

"Unfortunately not. That seems to be one of the reasons political history is a catalog of disasters."

"Yep. I wish there was another way. You work one out, Professor, or hear of one, please let me know. But anyway, what do you think about this particular operation?"

"I don't. I can't understand it. You told Tom your purpose is to make the Czechs believe that something false is true. Is that right? Do I have that right?"

"Correct."

"But you want Tom to pretend to be angry—no, to use his anger, he doesn't have to pretend. He's supposed to pretend to betray you by telling Colonel Suk the investigation was a fraud—which is the truth. He's supposed to say that you must be trying to make the Czechs accept something false as true—which is the truth. If he tells the Czechs that, he really is betraying you. If they believe it—and apparently they are already inclined to believe it—then they'll be believing the opposite of what you say you want. I don't understand it."

McCluskie nodded, but Jane still looked bewildered.

"That's the thing, Jane," Talley explained. "If I tell them that now, they won't believe me."

Talley and Jane didn't talk about it, all the way, walking from their hotel to the park at the Hofburg, arriving without having planned to go there. McCluskie had dropped them at their hotel, but they had been afraid to talk in their room. And they had to talk.

Afternoon had withdrawn from the city with the setting sun. Rush hour had passed, and those people who remained on the streets were strolling. Light still descended from a bright sky, but gently, without thrusting shadows ahead. Talley and

Jane settled on a bench facing the pond, where ducks floated on their reflections.

"It's the same thing again, Tom. Do you see?" she asked. "There's something you have to do. And it's important. You have to go off and do it by yourself. And when you're done, you'll come back. And I'm supposed to be waiting, but in suspended animation."

"Jane, that's not true. In the first place, you know what—"

"I do know, this time, what you would be doing. Or, at least, what you'd be trying to do. But I always know what you're doing, in that sense. You have some project, some problem, some worry; I know that. Sometimes I even know what it is. And you go off and work on it, and then you come back and—maybe—report the result you've arrived at. I just get to hear what you've decided.

"Let me help you. I don't like this, Tom. I don't like the idea. I don't like McCluskie, or the CIA, or this kind of business. I'm afraid for you. My first inclination is to try to persuade you to say no. But I don't think I could persuade you, and I don't want to lose—I don't want to have an argument about this. I would rather accept that you're going to do it—"

Talley leaned forward, starting to protest; but she went on.

"I know you haven't agreed. You're still making up your mind." She smiled at him. "I just know—when you've thought it over very, very carefully—what you'll decide. I accept that. So instead of fighting this and driving us further apart, I want to use it as a way of learning to work together."

"How could we work together?" Talley demanded.

Jane made herself smile again, ignoring the anger in Talley's astonishment, taking his question only in the immediate context.

"That man, their agent, Anton Korda: he gave me a number—a direct line to him at the Czech embassy—in case I wanted to reach him. I could call him and make the contact for you. He knows how angry I was at the CIA. I could go with you to meet him. My being there, my anger, would reinforce yours, give what you're doing more credibility."

"No! I won't have you . . ." Talley drew a breath, sat back against the bench again. He took Jane's hand. "I really understand what you're trying to do. Thank you. All right. Please help me with this. Call this guy and make the contact.

That would be better than me going to the embassy on my own, blind. You do that, and we'll set it up together, and we will be working together. But you can't come with me to meet him."

"Why not, Tom?"

"Because . . ."

"Not because of any danger. McCluskie said there wouldn't be any danger. He assured us, '*this* time . . .' If you don't believe him, Tom, then the deal is off. Then I won't help you, and I'll do everything I can to stop you—including calling Anton Korda and telling him what's going on."

"Jane," Talley said sharply.

"I mean it, Tom. If that ends it between us, so be it. Two years ago you were willing to do *anything* to save my life. I will . . ."—her voice broke, but she went on—"do anything to save yours."

"There won't be any danger," Talley assured her. "We'll set it up in a safe place. McCluskie will have me covered. The Czechs will hear what I have to say, and they'll go away, and they'll think about it and believe me, or they won't. But they won't try to do anything to me.

"But . . . but, sure, there could be some danger. There's always that one in a million . . ." Talley heard himself, and stopped, and was silent.

Jane folded her hands. "You decide, Tom. You know more about this kind of thing than I do. If the chance is one in a million, all right. That's not much of a risk for us to take. Together. But if it's too dangerous for me, then it's too dangerous for you. I hope you'll agree to that; that we'll see it that way and agree together that you aren't going to do it in that case."

"I . . ." Talley put his hand over hers. "Okay. We'll talk to McCluskie."

"This is Jane Boudreau, Mr. Korda. You remember?

"Yes. Fine, thank you.

"Mr. Korda, the reason I'm calling you is . . . Tom and I have been talking. We're both pretty upset— We're both really angry about the way Tom has been treated by the CIA and we . . . Here, let me put Tom on the line."

Talley took the phone from Jane. He was standing. He was

too tense to sit. McCluskie seemed perfectly relaxed in a swivel chair across the desk. He held a receiver to one ear.

"Now," McCluskie had said, "the way we've got to do this is: you're acting on impulse. You're so damned teed off you just want to swing out and smash somebody—me—right in the nose. Keep that as your image."

Talley had nodded to show he could.

"On the other hand, you—and the professor here—you're not flakes. You don't ever—no matter how emotional you get—you don't fly off and do something wild without thinking at least a little bit about how you're going to do it. Am I right?

"So you want to dump on me by blowing my operation. Not changing sides, you don't really want to help them; it's 'a plague on both your houses.' You want to do it, and get done with it, and go home. You're not concerned about setting up a big, complex procedure.

"But you know this is a bad business. You don't want to take any chance that I might be still watching you. Likewise, you don't want to put yourself in a position that the Czechs could pull something on you. You can't even imagine what they might pull, but you distrust everybody.

"Actually I can't see why this would put you in any jeopardy. I think they're going to listen to you, and nod their heads, and say thanks, and go home, and think about whether what you told them is worth anything. But I am playing it safe. When you meet this guy, I promise you we are going to be all around you like a great, woolly blanket.

"Now, you're not going to do it tonight—you're not about to meet anybody in the dark. Tomorrow. What you would want to ask Anton for is also what I need: a meeting place that you can get to on your own, innocently—you're just tourists—that lets you talk without being overheard, but that's fairly public so nobody can pull any hanky-panky. I'd suggest the zoo, or the Prater amusement park, or the botanical garden. Someplace like that. It doesn't matter exactly, and, like I said, this is supposed to be enough of an impulse that you're not going to quibble. If he wants to name the place, okay. As long as it meets the criteria."

In addition to Talley, Jane, and McCluskie there were two other men in McCluskie's office: Paul Deming, whom McCluskie had introduced as his assistant, and "the guy who got you out of the pokey—Jake Kacmarczyk, we call him Jake Kaz. He's the guy who snatched Janos Czerny!'' Jake and Deming also were using earpieces to listen to the call.

''Hello, Mr. Korda? This is Thomas Talley. As Jane said, I am very angry about the CIA. Your Colonel Suk was right; I was used, and it's clear to me now that they put me in danger, and they didn't care what happened to me. Now, I'm not very happy about how Colonel Suk acted toward me, either. My feeling is, 'a plague on both your houses.' '' Talley glanced at McCluskie, who nodded back.

''I have been debriefed here. I've told Steve McCluskie everything I know and everything I think about your operation; and now I'd like to tell you what I know about McCluskie's. And I hope the whole thing comes crashing down on both of you.

''That's right.

''Why do we have to meet? Why can't I just tell you over the phone?''

McCluskie nodded. Talley listened. ''Okay. I can see that,'' he said resignedly, as though he had needed to be persuaded.

''No, I don't want you to call my hotel. I wouldn't put it past McCluskie to have tapped the line. I'm calling from a public phone. I'll call you.

''Okay, in an hour.''

''You got Janos Czerny out?'' Talley asked Jake. They were all sitting in McCluskie's office, waiting for the hour to pass.

Jake shrugged. ''Yeah. Me and some friends.''

''How?''

Jake told the story.

''Wow!'' Talley said at the end. He asked McCluskie, ''Where's Czerny now?''

''In the embassy's best guest suite. I haven't seen him—don't expect to; but I hear he's beside himself—and two of him is about one and a half more than anybody wants to take. He's really happy and grateful that we sprung him, but absolutely pissed off that we did it right in the middle of his movie. We're offering him asylum in the States if he wants it. Or to negotiate for him to go to France, or wherever. I guess he hasn't sorted out how he feels enough to decide yet.''

Talley turned to Jake again. "You must be the guy who got Larry Hovey out two years ago."

"Yeah. I was part of it."

"Jake was our man in Czechoslovakia for—what was it? —nearly sixteen years."

"You were under cover that long?"

"Not really. They knew about me. I was sort of, I guess, what you might call an institution."

Talley heard the mixed chord of pride, modesty, and regret in Jake's voice.

McCluskie explained about BigOx. "But Jake's out of that line now. The Czerny snatch was his last inside operation. He's going to be an outside man now. Our expert. He'll be with us on this, when you meet Anton. He'll be translating."

"Translating?"

"Well, you and Anton will be speaking English, of course. But he'll have somebody with him. Close, I mean. And—no question—he'll have other people all around. He's going to be as edgy about this as you are. They'll be in contact—radio contact—and we'll listen."

"Are you going to have me and Jane wired?"

"No. My guess is they'll have a sweep: pick up the signal if you had a mike on you. What we'll do, we'll have long-range mikes. Pick you up from a distance. I've got a team flying in. As soon as you and Anton agree on a meeting site, we'll start finding our places."

Talley was silent for a moment. "You know what I'd do if I were him? I'd name a meeting place tonight, and then I'd call tomorrow and switch to another place at the last minute."

McCluskie regarded him, then said, "You know, Tom, it really is a shame you quit the agency. However, I don't think he'll pull that one. If he tries it, you just refuse—you can get all indignant, and suspicious. But I don't think he'll try. I think he'd rather set it up now, and not change, and then just see if we show up, too."

Jane spoke up, "So he'll expect this may be a trick. He'll be watching for you. He'll be exercising more than whatever normal caution you people would use in such a situation. He'll really be expecting you'll be there. Then how can you possibly think you can avoid being detected?"

"By being really very careful, Professor."

"But all he would have to do—even supposing he doesn't detect your presence—all he would have to do is make some threatening gesture toward us. You'd have to reveal yourselves then."

"That's right. The game would be up."

"But it would be so easy for him to do that and expose you. This whole thing doesn't seem to me worth the effort."

"It's not a lot of effort, Professor. It's a gamble, maybe a long shot; but I think it's worth trying."

Jane stared at him levelly. "Would you really reveal yourselves?"

"Of course, Professor." After another moment McCluskie said, "Of course," again. But Talley could see he hadn't convinced her.

"Good, Mr. Korda." Talley was standing, as before, to make his call. "Now, for a meeting place, I had thought of someplace outside, public, so we can both—

"Yes. Right. Glad we agree. I was thinking of the zoo, or—

"Where?

"I had thought of someplace here in Vienna. Why do you want to go—

"I see. Where is it, exactly? No, I don't have a map with me."

McCluskie pulled a map from the drawer of his desk, quickly opened it. Jake and Deming came to look over his shoulder. As Anton located the place for Talley, Jake found it with his finger for the other men.

"I'd have to rent a car . . ." Talley stalled. McCluskie shrugged an unwillingness to decide yet. He wheeled his hand, motioning for Talley to get more information.

"What's this place like?" Talley listened. McCluskie put a forefinger along his nose and squinted.

"It is in a town? There will be other people around?"

McCluskie nodded assent.

"Okay, I accept that you want to be able to see who's around us; but I want to make sure *somebody* is. If this turns out to be a crossroads with nobody but you and a bunch of your heavies, I'm going to do a one-eighty and flush the whole thing.

"Of course I'm suspicious. You're being suspicious, too. This whole spy business is nothing but stabbing other people in the back. I've got enough daggers in mine to know.

"Oh, I *would* put one in yours, Mr. Korda. I'm not kidding you for a minute. But the one that I want to deliver most immediately is the one with Steve McCluskie's name on it. So what time tomorrow?"

"Thirteen hundred. Okay. See you then."

As soon as Talley had hung up, McCluskie congratulated him. "Terrific, Tom. You were just terrific. Just the right tone. When you said that about putting a dagger in my back, I could feel the pain."

"Good. You're right, Steve: it's easy to act when you really believe in what you're saying."

Two weeks before, Talley hadn't known Austria at all. Now he felt he was beginning to know the route north from Vienna like a commuter.

The weather continued fine, high and sunny. It would have been a lovely day, he thought, for visiting the countryside, finding their way to the top of a hill, and lolling away the afternoon with a bottle of wine.

They went through Poysdorf and then left at the very crossroad where Jake and Czerny and the others had waited for their bus. Talley could still see the highway in his rearview mirror when a gray car turned in after them and began following.

"The Czechs have picked us up," he said.

Jane looked around, then met his eyes. They each smiled, trying to reassure the other.

Talley pulled into the parking lot across from the *Gasthof*. The car that had tailed them had halted at one side of the road half a mile away from the edge of the village, and let them go on in alone. Eight or ten cars were parked in the lot. Talley and Jane got out. They didn't lock their doors. They crossed the road.

A hundred feet farther into the village a man stood with his back to the window of a shop. Another loitered just beyond him, on the other side of the street. They didn't look like either natives or tourists. Talley and Jane turned away from them and went along the front of the *Gasthof*.

The building must have been centuries old. Its peach-colored stucco was chipped in places, revealing dark brown stonework underneath. Windows and the arched door were deeply set. Following Anton's directions, Talley and Jane went past the doorway to the garden at one side. It was separated from the narrow sidewalk and the road by a line of wooden planters from which shrubs grew nearly to shoulder height. Although the barrier would give diners in the garden a sense of privacy, they actually could be seen over it. Talley restrained himself from looking back across the road to try to find McCluskie's men.

Jane squeezed his arm. "There he is." She indicated a man sitting alone at one of the small tables. Talley forced himself not to focus on that man at once, but to scan the entire garden.

The hedge continued around the side and rear, lower than at the front, so that diners might enjoy a view over it to the hills beyond. The nearest place that Talley could see where any protecting army of McCluskie's men might hide was a vineyard at least half a mile away. The field behind the garden was planted in potatoes. A few trees stood at one of its distant corners, but they offered no cover at ground level. The hay field beyond the parking lot across the road had been mowed. About a mile before they reached the town, Talley had seen a narrow dirt road leading off to the right down between two hills, following the course of a little stream that led it around out of sight. Unless a company of cavalry had been hidden there ready to come thundering up over the crest of the hill, he didn't see how anyone could reach the garden quickly if there should be trouble.

Except for Talley's particular fears, though, the garden seemed a pleasant place, a lovely place for an alfresco luncheon or a quiet afternoon with a glass of wine and a book. Old trees shaded it. They were like the sycamores he knew in America: their bark flaking off in patches so that their trunks were mottled gray-brown, pale green, and cream. Sunlight through their foliage dappled the blue-and-white-checked cloths on the tables and the flagstones between which tufts of grass grew.

Two men sat at a table closer to the hedge than Anton's, and two more at one farther to the rear. Every one of them had a half-liter glass of beer before him; none of the glasses had been sipped. The nearer pair had a black box like a portable radio or cassette player lying on the table in front of them.

There were other, more innocent-looking guests as well. A middle-aged couple, both red-faced and very stout, stared dully past each other across plates from which every trace of food had been wiped clean. An elderly man wearing a collarless loden jacket and green felt Tyrolean hat sat in the far corner, with his back to the road, reading a newspaper. A young couple, close to the corner of a square table, leaned together, speaking quietly. The girl's head was propped on one hand. Her other arm lay on the table in front of the man, and he moved one finger up and down it as though picking out a little tune.

Since Anton Korda's men were taking no trouble to conceal themselves, the other people were probably genuine civilians. Talley took Jane's hand. "Okay, love, let's go." He smiled encouragingly, and she smiled back, and matched the tightness of his grip on her hand. At a break in the hedge an arched trellis of vines made the entrance to the garden. They went through it.

Anton rose as they came toward him. "Ah, Professor Boudreau. How delightful to see you again. What a lovely dress." He extended his hand, and before Jane could check herself she had given him her own. He didn't actually kiss it, but turned it as though he might. "Such a pleasure." Only then did he release her hand and turn to Talley. "And Mr. Talley, of course."

Talley didn't want to shake hands with the man, and he wanted to project anger at everyone; but Anton's charm and confidence couldn't be combated without starting the meeting at too high a level of intensity. He countered with a quick grip of the hand and a curt nod. He felt that to be crudely rude would make him seem oafish, thereby giving Anton a kind of superior position, a control.

To assert his own control he said, "I can't honestly say it's nice to meet you. Shall we get to business?"

"By all means," Anton said. "Please." He indicated chairs, and reaffirmed his own authority by waiting until Talley and Jane obeyed before seating himself again.

His chair had its back to the building. Jane sat on his right, her back to the road, Talley across the table from him.

Before Talley could speak again Anton said, "The waitress

will have seen you come in, and will be here in a moment. Please, may I offer you a glass of wine?''

''Thank you, how kind of you,'' Jane said with a tone and smile of well-mannered marble.

''Have you visited this part of Austria previously?'' Anton asked.

The waitress appeared. Jane ordered a glass of white wine. Talley asked for beer, just to be perverse.

''She'll be back in a moment,'' Anton said. ''I was asking . . .''

Clearly they could not begin their serious conversation until their drinks had come, but Talley let Jane handle the niceties.

''No,'' she said. ''Except for the drive to Czechoslovakia and back the other day.''

''Yes. It's very pleasant here, isn't it? Everyone who visits Austria goes to the Alps, of course, and never sees this; which is too bad. Don't you think?''

Jane replied, and she and Anton went on talking.

The middle-aged couple suddenly—by some signal that required no words—simultaneously heaved themselves up and lumbered out to the road.

Talley looked first to one side, then to the other—casually, he hoped: just checking, not worried. The men at the other tables were keeping up the same kind of surveillance of him, of the garden, the road, the countryside, and, it seemed, of any suspicious movements made by the ants going up and down the tree trunks.

''. . . Don't you think so, Mr. Talley?''

''What?''

''I was saying that when one travels to a country where one has been before, one should always make a point of going to at least one new area. Don't you agree?''

''Yeah.''

''Ah, here are your drinks.''

The waitress set Jane's wine in front of her, then moved around Talley to put down his beer. She went back to place the check on the table next to Anton, but he had a bill ready. ''*Ist gut*,'' he said.

She said, ''*Danke vielmals*,'' pocketing the change and going back into the building.

Talley had been watching the transaction, vaguely aware that the old man at the back of the garden had risen, folded his newspaper, and started toward the archway onto the road.

"Okay, can we get down to business now, Mr. Korda?" he asked.

"Certainly," Anton said, "I think getting down to business would please us all." It seemed he was going to let Talley speak his piece before asking anything. Talley drew a breath, thought about acting, thought about how really enraged he was at the way McCluskie had treated him.

"Well, to begin with . . ." he said.

A gnarled-knuckled hand appeared and set down a glass of red wine on the table to his right. "Before you begin, may I join you?"

Talley looked up in shock at the man standing there. "Colonel Suk!" he said.

CHAPTER 17

"Holy shit!" said McCluskie.

"Suk? Himself? Here!" For over sixteen years Jake had known of Suk, and feared him. Never had he been so close to the man. Even hidden in a van down by the stream a mile distant from Suk, Jake felt chills go up his back from awe and dread.

"Could we get him?" Deming asked. "Is there any, any way?"

"No," McCluskie answered at once. "Don't even think about it. *That* explains why they've got half of CIS security down here." He held up one hand for silence while he pressed the earpiece closer with the other. Then he spoke again, quickly. "If I'd had any idea he'd come himself . . . But no. It'd be a shoot-out at the O.K. Corral." He listened again. "No, we couldn't do it. Not in Austria."

After another moment he said, "Well, at least we'll get a little idea firsthand how Suk takes Talley's bullshit."

"All right," Talley said after Suk sat down. "This was meant for you, anyway." He looked the colonel directly in the eye and began.

On the drive north from Vienna he had tried once more to explain the trick to Jane. "Start with one basic fact: McCluskie wants Suk to believe something that's false. To try to achieve that he pretends to be reinvestigating the Czerny business. Call that Plan A.

"It failed. We gave it a good try—God knows, I did, since I thought it was for real. But Suk isn't buying. He doesn't *know* it was a fake, but he sure thinks so.

"So, we could just say, 'Win some, lose some,' and go home. But McCluskie is trying a last-minute save by playing the whole thing over upside down and backward. I give the son of a bitch credit, he's clever.

"So, Plan B: I come up here and give Colonel Suk the word, through this Anton Korda, that 'yes, the investigation was a fake, and that means the material you were given is false.'

"However, I am not a good liar. It is not in my character to betray McCluskie, or the CIA, or my country this way, no matter how angry I am. So Suk says to himself, 'Why is true-blue Thomas Talley doing this terrible thing?' The answer has got to be that it's a ploy. I did not come just because I'm angry. I must have been sent by the CIA.

"It follows that everything I say must be considered disinformation. If I am lying about wanting to betray McCluskie, then I must be lying in what I say about the material. Therefore, Suk realizes, he nearly made a terrible mistake, and the material that he was about to discard is true.

"*My* problem is this: I have got to do a really good job about *trying* to lie. If I get into that meeting, and they can say, 'Oh, come on, Tom old buddy, anybody can see you're kidding us. Even you, yourself, don't expect us to take this effort seriously,' then they won't take it seriously. They won't be faked into making the reversal. In fact, it'll confirm what we *don't* want them to believe.

"The one thing I've got going for me is that everything I have to say—the real facts, at least—*is* true."

Suk had taken the pose that Talley knew well, sitting at ease in the wooden chair, one hand laid on the other on his knee. To all appearances, he was a genial old man who had eaten a good lunch, and now expected to spend an indolent afternoon exchanging anecdotes with friends.

Talley's voice was low but firm. "At my debriefing—after Steve McCluskie picked me up at the border yesterday—it became clear to me that the thing that interested him was whether you believed the reinvestigation of the Czerny-Hovey affair was for real. The fact that Czerny had been snatched, that McCluskie supposedly now knew what he had sent me in to find out, didn't matter. He kept going over and over your reaction.

"That made it all very plain to me."

Talley had dropped his own hands to his lap when he began speaking. He brought them up to the table again. His fingertips were quivering, but he thought revealing that was better than suggesting he had something to hide.

"You were right: you said yesterday morning—in your office, before I left—that I was beginning to have my doubts. I didn't anymore. I put it straight to McCluskie. I said, 'You sent me into Czechoslovakia on a wild-goose chase. I could have been put in prison—I could have been killed—and it was all part of a trick that you were playing as much on me as on the Czechs.'

"The son of a bitch just looked at me, and finally he said, 'Yeah. Too bad it didn't work.' "

Although slightly altered, that dialogue was for Talley a dramatization of reality. He was grateful to McCluskie for having goaded him, for giving him the material with which to play this scene. His fingers trembled more noticeably, and he clenched his fists with true anger.

"I don't know what you'll make of this. The analysis I made when you were holding me, that we talked about when I was trying to talk you into letting me go . . . I imagine what I'm telling you now has a bearing on the reliability of whatever material that man Murtaugh gave you. I've given up trying to figure for myself what's true and what's false in this. I can only tell you that I know the reinvestigation was a fraud; that the CIA knows Murtaugh wasn't your agent two years ago; that they probably know when he did go over to you; at least, they know it wasn't recently. You draw your own conclusions."

Suk continued to look at Talley. Talley shifted his own eyes long enough to take a sip of his beer, then made himself meet the old man's again.

"One can understand your anger, Mr. Talley," Suk said at

last. "The CIA did use you very badly. However, I am surprised that you regard us so favorably as to bring us this information."

"I don't. I told Korda yesterday—and McCluskie, too—that I don't see much difference between you and him. I'd do anything I could to get you both. Right now, I have this way of getting McCluskie."

Suk suddenly shifted to Jane. "And how do you feel about this, Professor Boudreau?"

"I suggested to Tom that we come here together," she said. "I think my own outrage over this matter may have influenced him to do so."

"Indeed? I am surprised. Not at your feeling toward the CIA, but that it would lead you to help us. You did seem quite angry at our having detained Mr. Talley."

"I haven't forgotten that, Colonel Suk. Nor am I likely to."

"But yet you encourage Mr. Talley to help us."

"I don't think of it as helping you. I think of it as hurting the CIA." She leaned across toward Suk with a thin smile. "I assure you, Colonel, if I had a pair of pliers that would reach you, I would clamp your balls and twist them right off."

For an instant even Suk lost his composure. Then he exclaimed, "Wonderful, wonderful!" throwing his hands all the way up beside his head and sweeping them together in a single clap. "What a wonderful couple you two are. Such directness. Such unanimity of outlook. You really must be together, always!"

"God, they're great!" McCluskie smacked his thigh. "What a team! And I thought *I* could act!"

"Do you think Suk'll buy them?" Deming asked.

"How could he not? When I get 'em home, I'm going to put 'em on Broadway."

"What'll he do to tip them?"

"Probably just bore in. They can't keep it up for—" McCluskie's hand shot up again.

Suk raised his glass and took a sip of wine in toast to Jane and Talley. Anton followed his example. Replacing the glass on the table, Suk said, "Mr. Talley, Professor, it is impossible to doubt your sincerity. Almost impossible. Unfortunately those of us in my profession develop a thoroughly reprehensible, but inescapable, skepticism."

Talley shrugged.

"However, your story is so interesting to me that I would like to put all my doubts to rest."

Talley opened his hands. "If there are things you want to ask me, ask. I'll try to answer them. If that doesn't convince you, I'm sorry." Talley paused, shook his head. "No, I won't be sorry. I don't really care whether you believe me or not."

"Yes," Suk said. "But this really is not a good place to carry on an extensive discussion. I wonder, Mr. Talley, would you consider returning to Prague with me?"

"You're kidding."

"No. Quite serious. I did say I hoped you would return some day—for a holiday. Please come today. Be my guests. Let me show you the beauties of Prague."

"Another time."

"Have no fears. Let me make plain what I have in mind: I would like to hear your story again, ask you questions, form my opinion of its credibility with the assistance of a polygraph."

"No."

But Suk went on as though Talley hadn't spoken. "That machine is not universally reliable, of course. But when used by someone who knows how to ask the right sort of questions, and upon someone not trained to evade them . . . And I assure you, the polygraph alone—it is entirely painless—would tell me all I wish to know."

"No."

Again Suk took no notice. "And no matter what the result, you and Professor Boudreau would be free to leave whenever you felt you had seen enough of our beautiful capital. True or false, I would know what I wished and would have no reason to detain you."

"No."

"Why not, Mr. Talley?" For the first time, Suk paused. "This test would prove the veracity of your story. In fact, one might even regard your response to my request as a test, in itself. If you refuse, I fear your credibility suffers."

"As I told you, Colonel, I really don't care whether you

believe me. I think it would be pretty ironic if you refused to believe me, now that you are being told the absolute truth. But that's your problem.

"Now, unless that waitress, and the lovers over there, and everybody in this whole town is really part of your organization, Jane and I are going to get up and drive back to Vienna. Okay?"

Talley and Suk stared at each other for a moment. "Okay, Mr. Talley," Suk said quietly. "If you insist." Then he shifted position and smiled. "Although I do regret your decision. I have come to quite like you. And your charming lady."

Suk and Anton rose as Talley and Jane did. Both men bowed.

Despite himself, Talley couldn't be so impolite as to keep himself from nodding in return. He and Jane went out of the garden, got into their car, and drove down the road. They passed the car with the Czech agents, who watched without starting their own engine.

Then Talley let out his breath in a rush. "Wow, oh wow, oh wow! We did it!" he shouted. Jane squealed and threw herself across the seat and hugged him and kissed his face, making him swerve back and forth across the road.

"We did it!" Talley shouted again. "We gave him the story, and then— We did it! By refusing to go to Prague, that tipped it! That proved we were lying. We told him the truth, and then we proved we were lying. We did it! We did it! We did it!" he sang over and over, and Jane joined him in chorus, and then they both began giggling wildly.

"Jesus Christ, Steve!" Jake shouted. "Anton's calling all his units. Suk's ordering them to grab Talley and the woman!"

As the narrow road led them up a rise, Talley felt that he might almost be able to pull back on the steering wheel and soar into the clear blue sky, lifting the car by the power of his exhilaration. In the fields on either side, sunlight struck the rows of grapevines trellised on staked wires, making the leaves glow as though the light were within them; and pink, yellow, and purple wildflowers along the road's shoulders were jewels scattered by a prodigal hand.

They went straight along the broad crest of the hill feeling that they were at the top of the world. No other cars were in sight ahead; they were deep in the backcountry; Talley wasn't paying close attention. Suddenly—without his having been aware of its approach from behind—a car darted around and shot roaring past him. Shocked, he swerved. Jane gasped.

"My God! Where did he come from?"

"I didn't see him! He was just there!"

Racing on ahead, the other car flashed to the left around a wide curve and disappeared down over the hill.

"My God, he's in a hurry."

Instinctively, as the car had passed, Talley lifted his foot from the accelerator. He had started to press down to resume his previous speed. Then he let up again, continuing on, but more slowly.

"Yeah?"

"What's the matter?"

"That was that gray car we passed a few minutes ago. The one with the guys who followed us in here."

One hand on the dashboard, Jane leaned forward stiffly. All she could see of the road ahead, as they approached the long, descending curve, was empty. She swiveled and looked behind.

"There's another car way back there, behind us. There's two of them."

"Yeah," Talley said. He had seen them in his mirror.

"What do you think . . . ?"

"I don't know. But I don't like it." Talley decreased his speed further.

They started down the hill. The road bore around, then—at the bottom—curved right again. Always the ground sloped up on the left; after that curve to the right a hill began on the right side, too, so that when the road bent left once more it disappeared into what would be a passage between two steep upward slopes.

"They're gaining on us," Jane said.

"Yeah."

"Do you think . . . ?"

"I don't know."

"McCluskie is supposed to be protecting us."

"Yeah. Well, I'm sure he will." Talley spoke slowly and calmly, but his eyes darted back and forth between the road ahead and his mirror. "Assuming he knows something's wrong." If he continued to go slowly, the two cars behind could overtake him, and one might pass, and he'd be boxed. "Assuming he can get to us." If he speeded up, he could take the center of the road, run ahead until he reached the main highway. Except for the car that had already passed him, which he imagined ready to pull across the road to block the defile as he came into it.

He scanned, trying to see an alternative.

"Hang on!" he said.

Talley floored the gas pedal, shooting the car down the road. As he approached the right-hand curve at the bottom, he hit the brake, went into third gear, powered around. Then suddenly he braked again. Dropping to second, tromping the gas and spewing a plume of dust, he swerved left and right, hurtling up the dirt track that rose above the road and along the side of the vineyard.

Ruts and humps jolted them violently. Talley gripped the steering wheel, trying to hold himself in place as much as to drive. Jane clutched the back of her seat with one hand and pushed the other with all her strength against the dashboard. Stones thrown up struck the wheel wells like a drumfire of cannon shells, terrifyingly, as though each impact must tear through the metal and into their flesh.

On the right a steep grassy bank dropped down to the road. The track provided access to the rows of grapes that ran straight to the left, up the rounding slope.

Talley's instinct had been to take any course that seemed to lead out of the trap. As he went up the track, he hoped—he imagined—that it might come down again somewhere beyond the car that had gone ahead to block the road. Bearing left, the track rose, crested, started down again, and—suddenly Talley could see all the way along it—rejoined the road twenty yards or so before the place where the gray car was waiting.

Standing on the brake, he brought the car to a sliding stop. Dust billowed up all around.

"Come on!" Talley shouted, pulling the handle and flinging his door open. He held his breath and squinted against the yellow dust. He could see Jane's head come up on her side of the car, but the view behind was obscured for another instant. He didn't want to wait until he could see. "Come on!" he shouted again.

Grabbing her hand as she came around the front of the car, Talley led them off, running, up one of the wide aisles of vines. Moving away from the thinning cloud of dust, they could see the two cars starting up the track.

Running straight along between two rows of trellises seemed to offer the best escape. Each row was about four feet high; the foliage wasn't dense; so there was no real possibility of hiding behind one. And—at least until Talley and Jane had reached and gone over the crest of the hill—anyone moving along the track could look up each aisle and see which one they were in.

"Wait!" Jane pulled back against his grip. She paused, slipped off her sling-back low-heeled shoes. "Okay!"

They ran on up the hill. Talley began panting. Getting his hand free, but not halting, he pulled off his jacket and flung it away.

They heard the clattering cars coming up the track back behind them.

The ground between the rows had been cultivated. It was soft, tiring to run on, much more so than the hill up to the church. He'd known he should exercise more.

Abruptly the sound from the cars stopped. There were shouts. Still running, Talley half turned to look back. Two men were already starting to sprint up the row behind him and Jane. Two more were coming around from the off sides of their cars. He tried to make his legs go faster. Lifting each—drawing up each thigh, driving it down again—seemed to require conscious direction. Like blocks of stone, so heavy, without strength in them, they had to be moved by mental energy, by repeated acts of will.

Jane had drawn a pace ahead. Realizing he was lagging, she reached back and grabbed his hand to pull him along.

"Go on!" he gasped.

"Come on!"

"Go on!" He tried to shake her off.

"No!" She pulled, almost making him stumble, but giving him an impetus to stagger up to the top of the slope.

For a moment, the almost level ground there seemed so easy by comparison with the slope that he thought the great lungfuls of air he dragged into himself would be enough, that he could keep going forever. He darted a glance behind.

The first two men were barely a dozen yards away, gaining quickly. Compared with them, he was loping. He tried to find more strength, more speed. He had none.

Ahead, the rows of trellises ran straight, as though they'd been ruled, as though some giant comb had been drawn with great care over and down the hill. The trellises, their wires, were fences. He doubted they could be run through. He and Jane were penned. Even starting downhill, they couldn't run fast enough to get away. Over his own wheezing gasps, over the pounding of his blood in his ears, he could hear the breathing and the footfalls of the men coming up behind.

No escape. He and Jane would be run down. Better—while he still had any strength at all—to whirl and stand and fight. He could do that: stop them, delay them, at least, while she went on.

If he only had something to fight with! A stone?

Frantically, as he ran, he scanned the ground from side to side. Lying along the row to his left, three yards ahead, he saw a stake, five or six feet long. He realized he had passed others. They must have been left here and there as spares, in case one of those that held the wires had to be replaced.

Stumbling, almost falling, he lurched for the stake, grabbed it up, wheeled, staggering, to face the pursuers. Held across his body with both hands, at chest level, the stake was almost as long as the aisle was wide. Although his desperately heavy breathing rocked his whole torso, although his ears rang and his vision was blurred, he set his feet apart, bent his legs, and, hunching his shoulders, prepared himself for impact.

"Tom!" Jane had run four strides farther before realizing he wasn't with her.

"Run!" he gasped. "Go on!"

Side by side, the two men came up on Talley. They didn't stop so much as coast for the merest instant, shifting gears. The one who faced him directly came on as though in low, leaning forward, hands outstretched, to close the two steps' distance between them. His partner, to his right, went past him in second, reaching to grab the portion of the stake that barred his way.

Talley swung as though to hit that man, then reversed and

drove the heel of the pole at the one directly in front of him. His feint failed with both. Each recoiled and lunged again. Talley swung the long end once more, this time meaning truly to hit. But the man caught hold of the stake. The other hurled himself onto Talley, grabbing the stake between Talley's hands and smashing the heel of his palm into the center of Talley's chest.

Jane had spun around, the movement bringing her almost to one knee. She sprang upward again, sweeping up a handful of soil as she did.

Talley felt as though a bomb had exploded in his chest. His breath knocked out of him, everything before his eyes going black, he doubled half over. But that his hands had spasmodically clenched the stake, which his assailant gripped as tightly, he would have fallen backward.

The other man, raising the end of the stake that he had grabbed with his left hand, was half ducking to get under it when Jane flung the clod of soil into his face from two steps away. Although some of the dirt went into his eyes, and his eyelids clamped down involuntarily, he completed the movement and, arms outstretched, lunged at her.

She hadn't halted, had meant to throw herself against him. They crashed into one another. He seized her in a bear hug, burying his forehead into her shoulder, the back of his head against her neck and jaw, so that she couldn't get at his eyes or throat. He twisted, trying to throw her off-balance, and his right hand swept up her back, reaching for her hair so that he could jerk her head back and force her to the ground.

The man who had hit Talley had raised his hand, palm flattened, to strike again. But the jerking of the end of the stake by his partner had toppled Talley's precarious balance. He collapsed. The man released his own grip on the stake and watched him fall.

Legs buckling, Talley dropped backward in a sitting position. His rump struck the soft earth, and he rolled onto his back with his legs coming up as though he were intending to somersault. His feet fell again, and he stared past his knees at the half-blurred figure looming beyond them.

Jane got one foot back to brace herself and keep her balance. Then—as she'd learned to do at the Woman's Center classes—she drove her other knee up into the man's crotch. He gasped, a great moan beside her ear; and his grip loosened.

Instantly, while the first pain and shock still flashed, she kneed him again and shoved against his chest, breaking his grip and throwing him backward to the ground. She whirled to hurl herself at the other man.

Although focused on Talley, he had caught the other struggle from the corner of his eye. He pivoted to face her, hands on guard. Not blinded as his partner had been, he would have caught her and knocked her senseless with one blow.

But Talley hit him.

Even when falling, lying flat, he had continued to hold on to the stake. Sliding his hands together as though gripping a baseball bat, lifting the pole above his head and swinging it vertically as he sat up, he struck. The blow caught the man's shoulder beside his neck, staggering him. Talley flung his arms up, the stake angled back far beyond his head, and smashed down again, hitting the man full on the crown. The man dropped at Talley's feet as though driven into the ground.

For an instant Talley stared at him, and then at the other man, who lay on his side, legs drawn up, groaning. Talley got his feet under himself and, using the stake as a prop, stood up. He looked at Jane and grinned. Although his head was clearing, he was still a little dizzy. Perhaps that's why for a moment he thought they had triumphed.

Then he realized that there were two other men, one on the other side of each trellis that bordered their row. Each of the men had a pistol gripped in his hands. Both of them were pointing at Talley.

Talley's head cleared at once. He shifted the stake to his left hand, reached toward Jane with the other. "It's all right, Jane," he said. "They won't shoot. If they shoot me, they can't get any information out of me. We'll just keep walking, and if they start to try to come over into this row, I'll clobber them."

One of the Czechs said two words. Perhaps he understood English. Perhaps he had merely understood the situation as Talley had. In any case, both men swung their hands and pointed their pistols directly at Jane.

Colonel Suk had carefully minimized the risk to himself when he decided to come into Austria. At the moment Anton Korda had hung up after agreeing to the meeting place, he spoke on another already open line, and the first CIS team waiting at the border went in. They were at the town within thirty minutes—long before any American agents could have reached it. Others followed, taking outlying positions on the few roads that led into the area. While those watchers could not vouch for the authenticity of every farmer or tourist who used the roads between their arrival and Talley's the next day, they could assure that no CIA ambush had been set.

When Suk himself came in, just before noon, he rode in his dark and armor-plated car. Four other cars accompanied him: one a kilometer ahead, one immediately in front and one in back of his own, and the last a kilometer behind. One guard rode in his car in addition to the driver. There were four men in each of the others. All of the cars were in radio contact.

The men in the three cars that had been sent to capture Talley and Jane were from the original teams of watchers. Suk did not break his own guard for that purpose. The most distant of the watchers remained where they had been since the night before, still assuring that no force could sweep in and take Suk by surprise.

He and Anton remained at their table finishing their wine until the message came that Talley and Jane had left their car, were being pursued on foot, and might be expected to be taken within a few moments. Then they and the guards who were with them in the restaurant garden walked leisurely to its entrance and waited for a moment while the cars were brought up.

They got in, the vanguard took its lead, and they all proceeded at a stately pace.

Talley's legs trembled from the exertion of running up the hill. Only from that exertion, he told himself. He had nothing, really, to fear. McCluskie would save them. He tried not to think about how impossible that might be. Most of all, he tried not to think that McCluskie would decide that letting Suk take Jane and him away would be the perfect way to complete the plot.

Although McCluskie had been surprised at the extensiveness of Suk's precautions, and astounded when he learned the true reason for them, they were essentially what he had expected. He had, therefore, not planned to bring any large force into the area. And he took his own precautions to disguise the few men he did bring. The three who handled the long-range microphones (one crouching behind a grape trellis, one in a tree, and one sweating and itching in a haystack) had made their way to their places on foot, their equipment on their backs, in the middle of the night from points as much as five kilometers away.

Two young men had come into the little town just after noon, arriving from the west. They had stopped to have lunch at a café at the other end of the street from the one where Talley was to meet Korda. Their car was a Saab with German plates; they spoke German, they wore the kind of clothes that smart young German men wear. They ate quickly, but lingered over further half-liter glasses of beer.

A little earlier that morning, two older men had pulled up in an old orange BMW 2002 to a stream beyond the other side of the town. The car had Lower Austria plates, and the men had looked Austrian—one of them even wore knee breeches. They had picnicked and fished.

Three other teams lay back, outside the perimeter the Czechs had set; but those four men were the only actives McCluskie had inside.

Right after Jake called out that Talley and Jane were to be snatched, McCluskie had alerted them to get to their cars and be ready. When Jake translated the report of the imminent capture, he got them moving and had Deming start the van. As they jounced and rattled along toward the road, he tried to think what he'd have them do.

The four men, and Deming, Jake, and himself. Seven. When Suk reached the place where Talley and Jane had been caught, eight cars full of Czechs would be gathered there.

"Hold it here," he said when they reached the apex of the final turn before their dirt track approached the road. They would be able to glimpse cars going by, while barely being seen themselves.

"We can call one of the perimeter teams," Deming offered. "Get them up to the border, throw in our hand, get the Austrians to stop Suk."

"Yeah. Maybe," McCluskie said as though really thinking

of something else. He was opening the large-scale contour map of the district across his lap.

"I wouldn't count on it," Jake said. "Suk probably had this in mind all along as a possibility. You wouldn't want to put it past him to do a shell game: shuffle them off to some safe house near the border and go through clean himself. You'd end up with egg on your face; the Austrians'd be pissed off at you, and then they might not check so carefully. And then he'd just slip them through inside a crate whenever he felt like it."

"There!" Deming said as a car flashed across their view. "That was his front-runner." He tried another thought. "If we could just get close enough to see what car they're put in, then maybe there'd be a way to cut it out."

Again, McCluskie disagreed. "Not unless we could materialize above them and snatch them up to heaven. We're never going to break up that armada."

"We won't do it going for *them*," Jake said. "We'd have to get *him*."

After a second, McCluskie said, "Right."

Deming said, "When we see him, I'll floor it, and we'll just knock him off the road!"

Without looking up, McCluskie shook his head. "We'd bounce right off him, Paul."

"There they are!" Jake called out as the car in front of Suk's appeared. McCluskie glanced up just in time to see the colonel's black one pass, and was looking down again even as the one behind followed it into sight.

"When the rear guard goes by, pull out; but hang back. We'll just see what's going on."

"Right." Deming tried to think of another plan. "We've got enough cars, we could get them together by the time he gets to the main road."

"And then it would be blood and guts all over the highway. Jake, where did the guy who reported say they were when they started chasing Talley on foot? Where did they leave the cars?" McCluskie held up the map, his finger on a point. "Could this be it?"

Jake looked over McCluskie's shoulder. "Yeah."

"Well, we've got to do something, Steve!" Deming exploded. "We can't trust that Suk'll let them go after he wrings them out. He might hold them until we've got somebody he wants to exchange for. Goddammit, he might even kill them to get us back for pulling this on him! We've got to make a strike!"

"Yeah?" McCluskie said.

The tiny dot of the vanguard car, a space, three more spots—black one in the middle—space, the rear guard, a larger space, the beige speck of the van, closing up the distance; behind it a maroon speck—the Saab: the cars speeding along the spine of the hill gave scale, emphasizing the immensity of the rolling landscape. In the hot, straight-down sunlight of early afternoon the countryside seemed profoundly still, no more affected by the speeding vehicles than a great boulder would be by the scurrying of half a dozen ants.

In the vineyard Talley and Jane trudged on, hand in hand, back down the aisle between the trellises. They didn't try to go especially slowly, and the men lagging just behind, one in the row on either side, didn't hurry them.

"Where's McCluskie!" Jane hissed.

"I don't know," Talley whispered back.

"Do you suppose he even knows?"

"I don't know."

One of the Czechs called out an order. They turned to look at him, and he waved a finger in front of his lips.

When they came to where Talley had dropped his jacket, Talley pointed and said firmly, "My jacket." He didn't know if they understood the words, but they let him pick it up. A little farther on Jane said, "My shoes," and they let her stop and put them on.

The first car of Suk's train swept down around the hillside. It paused where the dirt track forked off and up until the following three were in view. Since there were other men—the ones in the car that had passed Talley—out on the road ahead, this one led the way up the track. It halted in back of the two that were stopped behind Talley's car. In a moment the three came up, too. The rear guard waited down by the side of the road just before the place where the track began.

Although thinning, the dust cloud that the four cars had raised still hung in the air when Talley and Jane came out of the vineyard. Talley halted, trying to see into it, trying to assess the situation. The dust drifted farther, and then the window of the black car, down the track to Talley's right, lowered. Suk's voice called out, in Czech. The window went up again. One of the men behind Talley said something, also in Czech. Talley and Jane didn't have to understand the words. Still holding hands, they walked to the car.

Suk lowered the window again to speak to them. Either he didn't want to step out into the dusty air, or he didn't care about appearing gracious anymore. "So, Mr. Talley," he said. "It seems you will be my guest, after all. Had you accepted my invitation previously, I would have felt honor-bound to observe the conditions that I stated. But now, under the present circumstances . . . now that I have gone to so much trouble . . . it occurs to me that taking you into Czechoslovakia in order to obtain information is very parallel to the recent abduction of Janos Czerny *from* Czechoslovakia. I think we might complete the symmetry with a re-exchange."

Talley stood stunned, trying to think what to say. Without waiting to hear what he might come up with, Suk raised his window, turned and spoke to Anton.

Anton stepped out of the car on the far side, spoke over the roof. "Come around to this side, please. You may ride in the rear with Colonel Suk. I shall take the front seat."

Frightened and angry as Talley and Jane were, neither resisted or protested when the men who had brought them out of the vineyard gestured. They went around behind the car and stepped inside the door that Anton was holding open for them.

Anton spoke to the two guards. They must have explained about their colleagues. He gave them an order. They turned to go back into the vineyard. He spoke to the bodyguard sitting in the front seat. The man came out and started after the others. Anton slipped into his place next to the driver. He lifted a microphone from the dashboard, spoke, looking into the outside rearview mirror, obviously giving the order for the car behind to back down the track to the road.

The driver behind had just shifted into reverse when the rapidly approaching VW van swung wide of the rearguard car and came speeding, roaring, bouncing, and shaking up the track. The Saab had closed in and was tight behind.

At almost the same instant, the voice of the vanguard driver crashed over the radio as another car—the orange BMW—

swerving from the road, raced up the track from the other direction, skidding to a stop against the bumper of Talley's car at the head of the line.

Anton shouted into the microphone, at the same time striking a button on the dash. A panel dropped open, and he snatched out an automatic pistol. The driver jerked one of his own from a shoulder holster. Talley imagined other weapons flashing out in all of the cars.

Suk snapped a command. Anton repeated it into the microphone. Everyone sat still.

For nearly a minute nothing happened. Looking through the windshield, Talley could see the four men in the car ahead: two turned in his direction, their guns showing above the rear seat back, the other two looking forward, also with pistols in their hands—one resting his on the steering wheel, the other on the dashboard. Craning around to peer through the small rear window, he saw that the men in the car behind were armed and watching, too.

Everyone waited. No one seemed to want to expose himself by opening a side window and leaning out to look. None of Suk's men, it appeared, would make a movement without his order. Talley could only pray that he did not want to initiate a battle by giving one.

Talley decided he would push Jane to the floor and throw himself over her if gunfire began.

Again, the dust blew and dissipated. Then a voice spoke from the radio. Anton and Suk started. It was Jake, using the Czech's channel. Suk paused for a moment, considering. He nodded. Anton replied.

Another moment passed. A car door slammed somewhere down the row. Talley looked.

It had been the door of the van. Very slowly, keeping his empty hands in plain view, McCluskie went between the front of the van and the car ahead, coming up slowly along the line. Jake was following him. All of the Czechs in the cars watched them, turning as they passed, tracking them with pistol muzzles.

McCluskie halted beside Suk's window. Suk lowered it.

"Colonel Suk? I'm Steve McCluskie. Pleased to meet you." McCluskie leaned down, looked into the car. He moved smoothly and cautiously, but otherwise showed no apprehension at all.

"Hi, Tom, Professor. Everything okay? Hi, Anton. How's tricks?"

"So," Suk said. "Mr. Steve McCluskie. Indeed."

"In deed, in the flesh. Sorry I couldn't take you up on your invitation to visit you in Czecho. Great experience for me to meet you now, though. Oh, this is Jake Kaczmarczyk. You know who he is."

"Most certainly." Suk spoke to Jake in Czech. Jake replied, almost stuttering.

"So," Suk said again, returning his attention to McCluskie. "What is your view of our situation here?"

"Well, we seem to have you boxed. You'd have to move two of our cars—counting the one Tom was driving—to go either forward or back. We're all closed up so tight together here, I doubt that you could maneuver to get out to the side, but if you could . . . it's about twenty feet—six or seven meters—straight down on that side over there; and you'd have to plow through a whole lot of trellises to try to get around the other. I don't know if you could do it, especially if we were trying to stop you."

Suk nodded. "We do, I believe, outnumber you several times."

"Oh, yeah. Not even counting your two carfuls down there on the road. I can see your guys there now. They're leaning across their car roofs covering us with submachine guns. What that means to me is that when the police get here—my guys outside your perimeter are going to call them if they don't hear from the man in my van every three minutes—you'll be the ones left to explain what was going on. Whichever ones of you *are* left, that is.

"So, Colonel, my view is that you ought to give me Talley and the professor, and we ought to all of us just back off and go home."

McCluskie stepped away from the car so that he could straighten while still looking directly at Suk.

Suk stared back, his head tipped slightly to one side. Talley and Jane stared at him, holding their breath.

Finally Suk nodded. "Yes, Mr. McCluskie, I agree that that is what we should do." He smiled. "And I seem to have learned what I wished to know without the necessity of taking Mr. Talley back to Prague with me."

McCluskie looked embarrassed. ''I don't suppose you'd believe it if I told you Tom didn't know we were here, that we'd followed him because we thought he might be going to sell us out?''

Suk's smile broadened. ''No, I wouldn't believe that.''

McCluskie sighed. ''I didn't think you would.'' He shrugged.

''Nice try, Steve,'' Anton called from the front seat.

McCluskie leaned forward again. ''Thanks, Anton. See you around.'' He waved.

Anton waved back.

''So long, Colonel. Real pleasure to have met you.''

''The same, Mr. McCluskie.'' Suk turned to Jane and Talley. ''Professor Boudreau, Mr. Talley: good-bye, and my compliments and my very best wishes.'' He was giving them his most genial smile. Jane refused to acknowledge it or his words. Talley merely nodded and opened the door. They both slid over and stepped out.

Suk refused to be offended by their manner. He leaned to look after them. His eyes had their customary sparkle.

No, Talley thought as they caught his, the light in them was the gleam of triumph. ''And my thanks to you, Mr. Talley,'' Suk continued, ''for making it possible for me, at last, to know the truth.''

AFTERWORD

The director's ad hoc committee considered all available evidence about the NATO battle plan provided by George Murtaugh. There was the program of surveying undertaken by the Bavarian state government in preparation for strengthening and widening bridges that seemed to require no improvement at current traffic levels. There was the attempt by the CIA, acting through their agent Milos Nagy, to acquire military information about the Bohemian forest area. There were a variety of other hints.

Colonel Suk presented his view that while no single item could be considered definitive, the elaborate and determined attempt by the CIA, using Thomas Talley, to make him believe the plan was false—that, taken with all the rest—convinced him it was true. His analysis was accepted.

Although the director, in private, informed Suk again of widespread and severe disapproval on the part of upper-level officials concerning some of the risks Suk had taken, the methods he had used, and about the entire Czerny incident, nevertheless, "success justified the measures taken." In that private meeting as in public, Suk was congratulated effusively.

The Metropolitan Opera informed M. D'Avignon that a change in plans made impossible further discussions about his coming to New York. He was not surprised. He did receive offers to work with opera companies and state theaters in Prague, Budapest, and Moscow. He accepted them, but insisted on scheduling that would allow him to work mostly in France, Austria, and Italy, where the pay was better.

Talley and Jane returned to New Hampshire and buried themselves in their work to make up for lost time, in finding their garden among the weeds and trying to salvage it. They enjoyed the simple sense of being together, being safe. They hugged often, and made love, and didn't really talk much. They didn't quarrel, but decided after two weeks to have a short vacation from one another. Jane went back to her house in Massachusetts.

Because the Czech government continued to refer to Janos Czerny as a wanted criminal, he decided to accept asylum in the United States. He had no difficulty finding work.

About a year later, the film *In the Year 1805* was premiered in Prague. Credit for direction was given to a group—the people who had been Czerny's unit directors. His name did not appear anywhere. The picture was acclaimed in Prague, and in all the Eastern capitals. Western critics were less enthusiastic. Many acknowledged "moments of penetrating sensitivity" and "painterly scenes of fluidly choreographed spectacle," but they also used adjectives like "chaotic," "undigested," and even "gargantuan" and "elephantine." Most attributed the failure of the work to the fact that Czerny hadn't completed it himself. Czerny, with his customary grand humility, refused to accept this means of disassociating himself from the fiasco. He simply refused to talk about it at all. He did announce that he had signed a contract to direct a film adapted from a Strindberg play that would have essentially a single setting and only four characters. He said that such material, dealing with intimate human reality, was what most interested him, being the true test of artistic skill.

The CIA offered Jake Kaczmarczyk a place either in Bonn or back at Langley. Before deciding, he took six weeks of accrued leave and went to visit his relatives and old friends in Iowa. Hardly any of his grandparents' generation were still around; few of his parents'. Still, there were some old-timers with whom he could speak Czech. When his six weeks was up, he asked for a leave of absence. Before that was officially over he sent in his resignation and took a job as a Toro salesman. BigOx had offered him a desk job in St. Louis, because they already had an Iowa rep they were pleased with. Jake decided he'd rather stay in the field, even if it meant going with the competition and having to learn all their machines. The BigOx guy was due to retire in two years. Jake and BigOx reached an understanding.

People often asked him if he missed the excitement of working in a foreign country. He'd smile and shrug and say, yes, he did, sometimes, about the way he missed being sixteen and just starting to go with girls.

Talley occasionally talked with Walter Simson, but heard nothing from or about Steve McCluskie. He assumed McCluskie had simply disappeared back into the agency and was doing whatever he always did, with his usual sincerity.

Then in November of the year after Talley last saw Colonel Suk several things occurred to close the entire affair.

A reporter for the *Washington Post* who happened to be vacationing on an off-island of Hawaii happened to see someone he had known back in D.C. He called one of his contacts in the CIA, but the man happened to be out of town. The person who took the call blundered. Instead of taking the reporter into some degree of confidence in order to assure his cooperation on a matter of national security, he denied and stonewalled in a way that left the reporter free to publish. The Sunday edition carried a story in the upper left block of the front page that featured a photograph of George Murtaugh sitting on white sand under a palm tree drinking a piña colada.

McCluskie called Talley on Tuesday. Then Talley called Jane.

"Steve McCluskie just called."

"About the Murtaugh business? What did he tell you?"

"The truth, at last. I think. What we figured when we talked Sunday night: it was a setup from the beginning—Murtaugh never did go over. Everything he gave the Czechs, his trying to 'escape,' shooting him in the airport—it was all a fake. It was all just to make the Czechs—Colonel Suk—believe the NATO plan was true."

"Just a trick, a game, from the beginning. Everything we did—you did: all the danger . . ." She was silent for a moment. "So now that Murtaugh has been discovered, it's over. It's all lost."

"It's over. But not lost. You see, the point was . . . Steve's told me all kinds of things. Not having any of it be secret now is part of it. Steve told me the Czechs and the

Russians have been reacting to the phony plan all year. Shifting army units, putting in tank traps, lots of things. They really bought it. Of course, they'd probably have discovered the truth eventually, but it's cost them a lot. Wasted. And now they know they were taken, made fools of. That's the real killer. I mean that literally. Steve tells me that according to the Prague papers, Colonel Suk suffered a brain hemorrhage in his office yesterday and died."

"Oh!"

"Yeah."

"You mean they shot him?"

"Or he shot himself. Or maybe he just had a brain hemorrhage when he found out. Anyway, that's what this whole thing was—McCluskie, the CIA, all along—they were getting Suk."

"So what we were really doing—you and I—we were killing that old man."

"Yeah. That kindly, sweet old man who played all those tricks on all of us, and killed Alexandrovitch, and nearly killed us, too—me three times. Him."

"Oh, Tom. I feel terrible."

"Yeah. Me, too."

"Oh, I want to be with you."

"Yeah. Well, tomorrow . . ."

"Yes. I'll try to get up there early. Until tomorrow."

Talley hung up the phone. He felt both triumph and disgust. Jane must, too. He was glad she was coming.

It would be her Thanksgiving vacation. They would have five days at his house. They had developed a pattern of a week or so together, one apart. The arrangement wasn't one either of them considered perfect; but, thought Talley, neither were they.